97

J

99

I

DI

THE GOOD SPY

Also by John Griffiths

A LOYAL AND DEDICATED SERVANT
THE MEMORY MAN
SNAKE CHARMER

THE
GOOD
SPY

JOHN GRIFFITHS

F-GR
1990

Carroll & Graf Publishers, Inc.
New York

For Christopher and Kevin

Copyright © 1990 by John Griffiths
All rights reserved
Second printing 1990
First Carroll & Graf edition 1990

Carroll & Graf Publishers, Inc.
260 Fifth Avenue
New York, NY 10001

Library of Congress Cataloging-in-Publication Data

Griffiths, John, 1940–
    The good spy / John Griffiths. — 1st ed.
      p.   cm.
    ISBN: 0-88184-516-7 : $17.95
    I. Title.
  PR6057.R513G6   1989
  823'.914—dc20   89-27674
                                          CIP

Manufactured in the United States of America

PROLOGUE

IT WAS ALWAYS LIKE THIS, THE SPECIALIST THOUGHT; ALWAYS THIS silence afterwards when the only sound in the room, the only sound in the *universe* it sometimes seemed, was the ticking of somebody's watch.

"So . . ." It seemed to cost de Freitas an effort to speak. "This is it. Sentence of death, no appeal. . . . Is that what you're telling me?"

Eye contact was the important thing, assurance of an empathy which, since one wasn't imminently terminal oneself, it was impossible really to feel. But words in this situation were useless, so the specialist, who wasn't good with them anyway, maintained eye contact. . . . Richard de Freitas, the record asserted. Age: fifty-two. Marital status: divorced. Residence: Silver Spring, Maryland. Occupation: government. De Freitas was a tall, heavyset man, greying slightly, with a gaze that took everything in and let little back out, and, wrapped around him like a cloak, an aura . . . of power, the specialist thought, or not so much power, perhaps, as influence. He had the air, at any rate, of someone whose memos got read. Occupation: government. One suspected one knew what *that* meant.

"How long?" de Freitas asked.

The specialist paused, affected to consider, delivered the formula he'd devised, over the years, for dealing with this question.

"It's hard to be precise. The dynamics vary so. . . . We're talking months, I'm afraid, rather than years."

1

De Freitas inspected him in silence. His gaze had a force to it, a weight, which the specialist found himself wanting to avoid.

"You don't have to look like a sick cow," de Freitas said. "I happen to harbor an insurrection of cells, unfortunately not nipped in the bud, now out of control. A kind of biological Vietnam." His smile was a mask with empty eyes. "It's not your fault. You don't need to feel sorry. I've never believed in shooting the messenger boy." He paused. Belying his words, his stare was a pistol, aimed at the specialist's head. "What I want from you are answers. . . . *I want to know how long.*"

The specialist hesitated. "Three or four months . . . six at most."

"And there'll be pain." It was not a question. "Incapacitating pain."

"Towards the end." The specialist nodded. "'But we have drugs, of course, to handle that."

"Drugs . . ." De Freitas made a face. "Checking out in a fog of controlled substances. A final treat to look forward to."

For a moment, face bleak, he looked forward to it. Then, collecting himself, he looked up. "Well . . . No point in taking up more of your time. Thank you for being . . . candid."

He stood up and extended his hand.

"Wait . . ." The specialist felt cheated. This was not how these conversations normally went. He had a role to play here, an important role. This de Freitas was making him *feel* like a messenger boy. He attempted to reassert himself. "About treatment . . ."

"So my hair can fall out?" De Freitas eyed him with incredulous contempt. "Unless I've misunderstood, you just got through telling me I haven't a chance. I'm paying you the compliment of taking you seriously."

"You haven't misunderstood. Only . . ." The specialist hesitated, called upon dwindling reserves of authority. "Professionally speaking, I've always found the willingness not to dismiss the possibility of miracles . . . how shall I put this? . . . salutary."

"Have you?" De Freitas smiled faintly. "Professionally speaking, I've always found just the reverse."

The specialist shrugged. "As you wish. . . . But when the time comes, you'll need care. At least let me make the arrangements."

De Freitas shook his head. "You mean a helping hand with the needle? Thank you. But when the time comes, I shall be making my own arrangements.''

He paused then and smiled. It was almost a grin, a flicker of mockery and wry amusement, as if at the memory of some private joke. But there was something else, something secret and inward, something almost pleased and not altogether pleasant. A snide satisfaction—the specialist surprised himself with the thought—a kind of bitter triumph.

"I'll tell you what," de Freitas said. "There's this consolation. I'm going, as they say, to be widely missed. . . . In fact"—he grinned again—"if everyone's there who ought to be there, it should make for an interesting funeral."

PART I

"Chief of Staff Ts'ao once pardoned a condemned man whom he then disguised as a monk and caused to swallow a ball of wax and enter Tangut. When the false monk arrived he was imprisoned. The monk told his captors about the ball of wax and soon discharged it in stool. When the ball was opened the Tanguts read a letter transmitted by Chief of Staff Ts'ao to their Director of Strategic Planning. The chieftain of the barbarians was enraged, put his minister to death, and executed the spy monk."

Sun Tzu—*The Art of War*

CHAPTER ONE

WHEN HIS ANSWERS TO THEIR QUESTIONS PROVED UNSATISFACTORY, they took the prisoner, whose name was Conlan—but to whom, in the necessarily much-censored records of their proceedings, they would refer invariably as "the subject"—to a room in the basement. It was the kind of room that is always in the basement, the kind always used in such proceedings: a concrete box with no windows, the only light coming from a single bulb strung from the ceiling. Its atmosphere was pervaded by creeping damp and an odor that smelled like despair, but which was, in fact, urine and vomit. The furniture consisted of four chairs, three in a half circle facing the fourth. This last was directly under the light; straight-backed, wooden, very sturdy; in design much like the others, but distinguished from them by the leather straps attached to its arms and front legs, and by the opening, roughly circular and some fifteen inches in diameter, cut into its seat. Under it, someone had placed, with perhaps deliberate suggestiveness, a bucket. Otherwise the room was empty. But an observant person—and people brought here tended by this time to be very observant—might have noticed, given the seeming absence of any need for them, a surprising number of electrical outlets.

There were three debriefers, this being the number, experience had shown, most likely to induce in the subject a proper sense of isolation without provoking irrational displays of defiance. The debriefers carried spotlights, two portable tape recorders, and a stubby, rodlike, instrument,

7

which anyone raised on a farm would instantly have recognized, but which became for Conlan an object of anxious, if short-lived, speculation. It was cold in the basement. The debriefers were warmly clothed. Conlan, on the other hand, was naked.

Without speaking, as if following a routine in which the moves had long since become automatic, two of the debriefers marched Conlan to the center chair and strapped him in. The third plugged the tape recorders and spotlights into the wall outlets, shining the spotlights into Conlan's face. The senior debriefer, whose name, Cartwright, was also omitted from the record, took the rodlike instrument and held it in front of Conlan's face.

"In case you don't know what this is—" He placed the tip against Conlan's throat and drew it gently down his chest towards the belly. "—it's a cattle prod. It gives electric shocks. Not lethal, but they hurt like a bitch. Cattle hate it. And what I want you think about"—pause— "carefully, is how *you're* going to like it when we shove it up your ass."

On this note, he and his assistants left.

They returned half an hour later. Cartwright, approaching Conlan, grabbed a handful of his hair and, yanking his head back, scrutinized his face. Conlan was weeping, the tears streaming silently down his cheeks and neck, leaking steadily into the dark mat of hair on his chest.

"It seems the subject has decided to cooperate." Cartwright looked disappointed. "He is going to cooperate because he is chickenshit. Greedy, treacherous, venal, and chickenshit."

He paused for a moment, then slapped Conlan, a heavy open-handed blow across the face.

"Now read me and read me good. . . . We've no time for your self-pity or for any more of your lies. We want the truth, the whole truth, nothing but. We're going to ask, and you're going to answer. As candidly and as fully as you can. And if we ever feel you're not being totally candid, we're going to hurt you and go on hurting you until you convince us you *are* being totally candid. And in that case, believe me, we won't be easy to convince." He paused. "Do you read me?"

There was a pause. Conlan nodded, a barely perceptible twitch of his head. Cartwright hit him again. Blood began to trickle from the corner of Conlan's mouth.

"I asked you a question." Cartwright's voice remained level, almost detached, as if there were no connection between it and the violence, as if the violence, indeed, were Conlan's responsibility, somehow mechanically linked to his behavior. "When I ask you a question, I expect an answer. . . . Do you read me?"

"Yes." The answer was barely audible, a strangulated sob.

"Good." Cartwright motioned to one of the others to start the tape recorders. "OK . . . When, and under what circumstances, did you first meet the Russian who called himself Alex Andreiev?"

CHAPTER TWO

HOLLISTER WAS READING WHEN SHERWOOD ANSWERED HIS SUMMONS. At Sherwood's entrance, he looked up, smiled, gestured to Sherwood to take a seat, and went back to his reading. Sherwood sat down in one of the two armchairs that faced Hollister's desk. From experience, he knew he might have to wait five or ten minutes, perhaps longer, for Hollister to finish, but he didn't mind. He was new here, for one thing, and his job, when you cut through the thicket of obfuscation with which the Agency had characteristically seen fit to surround it, was to serve as Hollister's gofer. If Hollister's notion of that service was to have him sit and wait, he was perfectly happy to do it. He liked Hollister, admired him, was flattered by the degree of trust that being Hollister's gofer conferred on him. And any offense that might have been given by Hollister's indifference to the value of his time had been removed, long since, by Hollister's smile— more a grin than a smile, really, at once boyish and slightly conspiratorial—and by the explanation, sometimes offered by way of apology, that standing and waiting was at times unavoidable because Hollister had the kind of mind that could keep track of only one train of thought at a time. Sherwood found this apology, the characteristic self-deprecation, charming but unconvincing. It was flattering that Hollister should bother to offer it, but he didn't believe a word. He believed that Hollister's mind was a perfectly organized subway system, a labyrinth where the trains of Hollister's thought ran swiftly and precisely, silently as ghosts.

From the corner of his eye, he watched Hollister reading. He had a patrician assurance about him, Sherwood thought, an authority seldom asserted but nonetheless always there, that sorted well with the kinds of orders he sometimes gave and Sherwood, on occasion, found himself taking. Not everyone could give those kinds of orders. Not everyone could be trusted to. But someone had to be, Sherwood thought; *someone* had to be willing to do the dirty work, to take the kinds of tough decisions that would have had Congress and the nation howling in outrage (had any of these decisions ever come to their attention) but which were necessary, nonetheless, to preserve the very system in which Congress, all sound and fury, asserted its right to howl. And Hollister was just that kind of someone; had the brains, the balls, the *moral fiber* to weigh the national interest and take those decisions. He belonged, indeed, by breeding and ability, to that group of men to whom weighing the national interest came as naturally as breathing. And you could see this, Sherwood thought; you could sense Hollister's real as opposed to his nominal power (which itself was not inconsiderable) by the absence, here in his office, of the normal touches of bureaucratic vanity. Where others might cover their walls with diplomas, cum laude, from Harvard or Princeton, photos of themselves with record-breaking black marlin, letters of gratitude from foreign heads of state, or official White House portraits inscribed "To Randy from Jack," Hollister's panelling was unadorned except by a poster from some chamber music festival and a studio portrait of Hollister and his family. But the portrait, of course, said it all: the little girls, enchanting in their Liberty print frocks; Hollister's wife, serenely elegant, radiating the practiced graciousness she had radiated on occasion from the pages of *Town and Country*; and Hollister himself, tall and boyish, looking as if he could still, at a pinch, climb into football gear and take the field for Yale. As a family they looked the embodiment of everything that was right with America. They looked, Sherwood thought, like Kennedys, only more so.

"So . . ." Hollister laid down the report, favored Sherwood with another of his smiles. "It seems that our friend, in more conducive surroundings, became confiding."

"Practically shat himself." Sherwood nodded. "Fell over himself in his effort to be helpful."

"So I see." Hollister tapped the report. It was more than two inches thick and had taken three typists from the Special Clearances Pool most of the night to transcribe. Only one copy had been made, and it would be kept in Hollister's personal safe. Later, when the contents had been thoroughly scanned, it would be shredded. There would be no record that it had ever existed. "Question is, what did he tell us?"

Sherwood shrugged. "We lost ourselves a whole slew of secrets."

"That, certainly . . ." Hollister didn't actually sigh, but his tone suggested he'd have liked to. He reminded Sherwood of a professor at law school, whose mere presence in a room, people said, was enough to make everyone else feel stupid. "Anything strike you about that slew of secrets?"

Sherwood thought hard. While he had every confidence in Hollister's trains of thought, he was not always sure where they were going. He shook his head.

"How about the appendix?" Hollister prompted. "The survey you very thoughtfully compiled of all the stuff that little shithead passed them."

Again Sherwood considered. The appendix listed the intelligence by subject, probable source, country of origin, approximate date, and security classification. None of these groupings, to his admittedly untutored eye, had seemed revealing.

"Very high-grade stuff." He took a despairing flyer. "Only about twenty percent chicken feed. Usually, I understand, it goes the other way."

"Correct," Hollister nodded. "And what does *that* tell you?"

"He knew what he was looking for." Sherwood had never claimed to be brilliant, but he could add two and two. The result, however, struck him as disappointing. "But it *says* that in the report. First they told him what they wanted, then he went to work with the Minox."

"They told him what they wanted." Hollister's face was expressionless. "Stuff about rifts in NATO, for instance. Then he went to work with the Minox and in almost every instance managed to hit upon the really crucial files. But he was a *filing clerk*, for Christ's sake, not a bloody analyst."

Silence.

"What you're asking, in other words," Sherlock plunged in again, "is how did he hit upon the really crucial files?"

"How indeed." Hollister nodded.

"Oh . . ." A great light dawned upon Sherwood. "You mean you hink there was somebody else, somebody here who was helping Conlan."

"Not was." Hollister shook his head. "I think there *is*."

CHAPTER THREE

IT WAS IN THE RESTAURANT, OVER A LAST CUP OF COFFEE AND AT some stage of his daily wrestling match with the airmail edition of *The New York Times*, that Becker first focussed on the woman. Or, to put things accurately, though this didn't strike him until later, it was she who focussed on him. He became aware of her, at any rate, when a generalized suspicion that his efforts to subdue the newspaper might render him ridiculous to anyone watching, gave way to the conviction that he was, in fact, being watched. Looking up, he saw her at the table by the window, watching and smiling.

She didn't immediately look away. Instead, she met his glance and still half smiling, held it for a moment with a gaze that was friendly but kept its distance. It seemed to convey that, while his struggles with the paper were a legitimate object of curiosity and amusement, this didn't, in itself, constitute grounds for acquaintance. Becker, receiving this message, found himself prey to vague regret. Though not quite beautiful— her jaw was too strong perhaps, her nose a shade aquiline—she had the kind of looks that, because they hinted at character, might tend to linger in memory. His impression was of candor and liveliness, spiced with a hint of mockery, but it was only an impression; by the time he started to form it, she had looked away. For a while he tried willing her to meet his eye again, but she didn't. Presently, losing interest, he paid for his breakfast and left, filing her mentally under "Opportunities, Lost."

Fifteen minutes later he had almost forgotten her. He didn't notice when she entered the bookstore, nor yet when she showed up in the section in which he was browsing and started to drift up the stacks towards him. He was aware, just an instant before she spoke, of someone at his elbow, but till then he'd been deep in a poem about vampires, off guard and relaxed in the comfortable conviction that if there were anywhere he could afford to relax it was in the poetry section of a bookstore in Georgetown.

"Is that Richard Wilbur you have there?"

Her question took him off guard. It was a moment before he could place her. The same, her look conveyed, was true of her; when their eyes met, hers betrayed no recognition. He noticed, however, that she colored a little.

"I've been hunting for a copy of his poems in the shelves. Did you happen to notice if they had another?"

He shook his head. "I didn't see one."

"Oh . . ." She hesitated. "'Were you planning to buy that, or just browsing?"

"Actually, I was planning to buy." Actually, he hadn't made up his mind. He was convinced now that she had recognized him, that this meeting in the poetry section was not altogether chance. Her question was therefore some kind of gambit. It seemed only proper to accept.

"Pity." She hesitated again, then gave a half smile and shrugged. "Well, first come first served, I guess."

Pause . . . Her gaze, if not quite expectant, conveyed that the exchange was incomplete. My move, Becker thought.

"I guess they could order one up."

"Wouldn't help." She shook her head. "I need it for a paper due Monday. The library copies are all AWOL, of course."

Further pause. Presumably this tidbit of biographical information was an invitation to take matters further. She was a student, then. In her twenties, to judge from her looks, and not, to judge from her chocolate-colored suede trench coat and matching kneelength boots, on a very tight budget. He noticed—it was a kind of reflex with him—that she wore no wedding ring. A graduate student, he guessed, killing time before marriage with a leisurely Ph.D., at Daddy's, or someone's, expense.

"What I meant," he smiled, "is I guess they could order another one up for *me*."

He offered her the book.

"Are you sure?" She hesitated, seeming suddenly quite genuinely awkward. "I feel I'm being terribly pushy. I've more or less marched up and snatched the thing out of your hands."

"You didn't snatch, I offered. Besides," he said gravely, "*my* paper's not due till next week."

"Your paper? . . . But *you're* not in Modern American Poetry." For a moment she looked blank, then she registered his smile. "Oh . . . You don't have a paper, do you?"

He shook his head. "Do *you*?"

She paused, startled. What he most enjoyed, he thought, was the way her features mirrored her emotions like weather on the surface of a lake: first, storm clouds of resentment, then a drifting cirrus of indecision, which, clearing, gave way to a delicate blush, like a sunrise.

"Actually . . ." She lifted her chin a little, looked him square in the eye. "In point of fact, no, I don't."

"We should start by getting things right," Arlen said. "I'm a nice girl. Normally I don't pick people up."

She paused, inviting a response. Becker took a pull at his beer. She was Arlen Singer, he'd learned on their way to the bar, a Ph.D. candidate in literature at Georgetown. She didn't have a paper on Wilbur due Monday, but the part about Modern American Poetry had been true.

"But you made an exception for me." He spoke without irony; she *looked* like someone who didn't pick people up. "I think I'm flattered."

She ignored this, thought for a moment.

"Have you ever dreamed of being totally honest? Cutting out all the bullshit, the hinting and inferring and reading between the lines? Have you ever wished, just once, that you could say what you mean, be who you are, and be taken at face value, not misunderstood? Have you had that fantasy, ever?"

The fantasy of total honesty . . . The question startled him. He wondered if she could possibly have any idea what she was asking, or of whom she was asking it. Total honesty? Even partial honesty would be something.

"I've had it." He nodded. "Why do you ask?"

"To explain why I made an exception. I saw you in the coffee shop with your newspaper. You looked"—she caught his eye and laughed— "you looked so . . . *funny*. Kind of calmly desperate, sitting there struggling with armfuls of newsprint, doing your best to look unruffled, and all the time with this odd little smile on your face, as if you knew how silly you must look. You saw me laughing, but you didn't mind. And you thought of trying to pick me up, but you didn't." She paused. "I just knew you were someone I would like."

He studied her. She seemed young to have achieved this impressive feat of mind reading, *was* younger, he guessed, than he'd at first thought. *Early* twenties, probably, though she dressed a little older. But he'd been right about her looks; they were the kind that grew on you, especially the eyes.

"So you saw me go into the bookstore and decided to follow?"

She shrugged. "It wasn't that premeditated. I saw you go into the bookstore and it seemed like a good idea. The bookstore, that is. I wasn't planning to pick you up. I wasn't planning, period. But then I found you reading that poem—it happened to be one we'd discussed in class—and that seemed to resolve things."

"Resolve things how?"

"Significant coincidence." She smiled. "It reassured me. Confirmed my first impression. I was writing a check in a bookstore once—it was an out of state check to a clerk who didn't know me from Adam—but when I offered him ID, he wouldn't take it. He said that, in his experience, people who bought books didn't write bad checks. I felt the same way about the poem."

"People who read poems must be OK?"

She nodded.

"Nero was a great lover of literature," Becker said. "And the commandant of Auschwitz played Mozart like an angel."

Pause. For a moment she studied him. Her eyes had a marvelous candor, he noted, seemed to belong to someone with nothing to hide. He had a fantasy of changing places with her, of being able to see himself as she saw him. He wondered what someone who had nothing to hide would *see* in his eyes, and whether there *was* anyone who had nothing to hide.

"That's true, of course. For all I know you could be Jack the Ripper. But I went with my hunch. I saw you reading and I acted on impulse. What I wanted to say was: 'I like the look of you; I'd like to know more.' I had that dream of acting on what I felt. But then it came to the crunch and of course"—she smiled ruefully—"I chickened out. I found myself giving you some bullshit about term papers, and it was only because you made it clear you knew it was bullshit that I managed, in the end, to be honest."

She paused.

"Which brings us back to the subject of misunderstanding. I'm saying I like the look of you; I'd like to know more. That's all I'm saying. Is that OK with you?"

He nodded. "Why not?"

"Well, that's a relief. This honesty can be a strain, I find." Her smile was dangerous, he thought, the sort that might be hard to resist. "Now it's your turn. Are you Jack the Ripper?"

CHAPTER FOUR

THERE WAS TOO MUCH LIGHT.

Conlan checked his watch again. Five after five. If that was right, they were twenty minutes early. Yet from the look of the sky, there was still a good hour of daylight left. This time last week—give or take a bit—it had been nearly dusk. And this was October. The days were getting shorter, not longer.

So there was far too much light.

Then maybe the watch was wrong. That was certainly possible. He'd reset it, he recalled, when they'd given it back, when they'd let him out of the cell and handed back his valuables and clothes. The watch had run down, so he'd asked them the time and they'd told him three-thirty. He must have set it wrong. Under the circumstances, a pardonable error. You could do it by mistake—people did all the time—you didn't need the excuse of what he had been through, those days of naked, unrelenting terror. But though on the surface this explanation seemed plausible, it suffered the drawback of not really explaining. For however his watch had come to be wrong—and it was also possible they'd deliberately misled him—the fact remained that they were here too early.

The Volvo was into the trees now, forest gloom and underbrush on either side, the sky obscured by a lattice of pine branches. For a moment he could almost convince himself he was wrong, that his visual memory was playing him tricks. But then they came to the first clearing, and he knew it wasn't.

19

He turned to Cartwright.

"What time is it?"

"What's the problem?" Evidently Cartwright had been watching him. "That solid gold Rolex quit on you?"

"I must've set it wrong. I've got five after five."

Cartwright shrugged. "It's ten after four."

"But when I asked, they told me three-thirty." His auditory memory was excellent, and he distinctly remembered now hearing them say it. He stared at Cartwright accusingly. "They gave me the wrong time."

"Did they?" Cartwright didn't pretend to be interested. "Why would they do that?"

Good question. Conlan felt a prickle of anxiety.

"But aren't we way too early?"

He addressed his questions to Cartwright because the other one, the one they called Bird, scared him. Not that Cartwright didn't, of course. At the start, when he'd still been trying to hold out, it had been Cartwright, mostly, who had hit him, stinging open-handed slaps that had bruised his face and brought tears to his eyes. But at least Cartwright was familiar, offering, in the midst of new uncertainty, the comfort of the known. Bird, on the other hand, had ice in his look. Not anger or contempt. Not menace. Bird's eyes were colder than a January sky. Bird looked at him as if he weren't there.

"*Aren't* we too early?" he repeated.

"No," Cartwright said.

"But they won't be here for more than an hour. What are we going to do all that time?"

"Wait," Cartwright said.

It made sense, he supposed. In the past he'd made a point of being first, but it was always possible *they'd* decide to come early. Cartwright was preempting that, presumably. All the same, he thought, an hour and a quarter was overdoing things, wasn't it?

The hut was in sight now. Bird had the Volvo in second gear, creeping over the carpet of pine needles at little more than walking pace and almost silently, except for an occasional protest from the motor. Conlan itched to tell him to change gear, that the revs were too low and he was straining the engine. It annoyed him, suddenly, that they hadn't let him drive. The Volvo was his, after all. His property, bought and paid for.

But paid for how? From the proceeds—he could almost hear their flat response—of his treason. The car, the condo, the solid gold Rolex, the twenty-one-inch state-of-the-art color TV, the VCR, the holiday in Hawaii—all courtesy of that fat little creep of a cultural attaché, whom Sue Ann had met at an embassy party and invited home because, she said, he was so much fun and charming, so unlike a Russian. . . .

And so he had been, at first. So much fun and so generous. So free with tickets to the Kennedy Center and the Redskins. So insistent on taking them out and always picking up the tab, because it was so nice, he said, to make friends with a real American family. And besides, he said, it was government money, and if he didn't spend it, someone else would. So tactful, above all, about their relative poverty, their efforts to reciprocate, their constant struggle to keep up. And then, of course, he had offered the loan. To help out, he'd said, with the expenses of the baby. Interest free, of course—because only Jews or uncultured people looked to make money from their friends—and totally without strings.

Without strings. The irony prompted a wave of bitterness. The strings on that loan had been a net to snare him. The strings on that loan had made him their puppet. The strings on that loan had bound him hand and foot. And he'd been caught, of course, as he'd always known he would. They'd grabbed him three days ago on his way to Langley and had taken him somewhere. The Farm, he guessed, but he'd been in the back of a van and hadn't known for certain. Then the questions had started.

He'd held out at first. Even faced with their photographs and careless brutality, he'd lied and prevaricated, faked memory lapses, used every ploy of the reluctant witness. He'd even hoped, after a day of stonewalling, that he might bluff his way clear, that, lacking his confession, the case against him would collapse for lack of proof. But the next day Bird had been there. And after listening for five minutes, he'd shrugged and said, "Why don't we stop horsing around?" And they had taken him to the basement.

They had shown him the instruments of torture. He remembered the phrase from a play he'd seen somewhere. They had stripped him and sat him in a cell and left that cattle prod on a chair where he could see it.

They had let him imagine his agony and shame, and his blood still froze and his bowels still loosened at the memory.

They had shown him the instruments, and that had been enough.

But it was over now, wasn't it? He'd told them everything, signed the confession. And afterwards they'd said if he helped them now—if he showed them the place and made this one last run—they would make things easier for him at the trial, perhaps even drop the charges altogether. It was a case, they hinted, which for reasons of national security they might prefer not to pursue. So it was almost over, and he should be feeling better. If he did go to prison, he'd at least be spared Sue Ann's nagging, the Russian's constantly escalating demands, the anxiety and terror.

He should be feeling a *lot* better. Then how come, he wondered, what he actually felt was a mounting sense of dread?

Because none of this quite made sense. He'd been tired before, too wrung out emotionally to see things clearly, but he was thinking now, and none of it made sense. Because Alex Grigorievitch, or Andreiev, or whatever his real name was, never did come to the drop in person. Conlan was never sure exactly who would, but as he'd told them in the interrogation, it was only bagmen. And if all they wanted was to nab a couple of bagmen, why were they making him carry the film? And why, above all, were they here so early?

They were at the hut now. Bird put the Volvo into neutral.

"Where do you generally park?" His voice had a slight Midwestern twang, would even have been pleasant, Conlan thought, but for the lack of variety in its tone. When Bird asked questions, it was without apparent interest in the answers.

"No place in particular," Conlan told him. "Here is fine."

Bird cut the motor, took the keys from the ignition, got out. He walked over to the hut and looked in the door. Then, without glancing back at the others, he started down the jeep track on the far side of the hut. He was wearing a beige trench coat with the collar turned up, and he kept his hands in his pockets, his shoulders hunched up as if against the cold. He walked deliberately, without hurry, as if for a purpose specific but not urgent. Presently he turned a bend in the jeep track and was lost to view.

"What's he doing?" Conlan said. He and Cartwright had stayed in the car.

"Checking," Cartwright said.

Checking for what, for Christ's sake? No point in checking for bagmen. If there were bagmen here, they wouldn't stay long once they spotted Bird. And Bird, it seemed, didn't care much whether he was spotted. Besides, Conlan thought, the bagmen weren't here. At least, their car wasn't; and they'd never have walked. It was half a mile at least to the highway, and if there was one thing he'd learned about the Russians, it was this: They never walked.

"Look," he said, "I don't quite get it. I mean, what the hell is all this in aid of?"

"In aid of?" Cartwright looked blank.

"Yes," Conlan said. "Why am I carrying the film? Why are we here so goddamn early?"

"The film's evidence," Cartwright said patiently. "Just meeting you in a wood doesn't constitute espionage, though it probably should. We need to catch them with their hands in the till."

"OK . . ." Conlan was slightly mollified. "But then why so early?"

For a second Cartwright studied him. His look had lost its hostility and struck Conlan now as being merely professional, the eyes neither friendly nor otherwise but just appraising, as if—and this thought, too, made Conlan uncomfortable—as if they were measuring him for something.

"Why so early?" Conlan repeated.

Cartwright shrugged. "It seemed wise."

For some minutes they sat in silence. Then Bird came back into view, emerging like a ghost from the gloom on their left. He was moving more briskly now, hands still in his pockets, shoulders still hunched. He made for the side of the car on which Cartwright was sitting. Cartwright rolled down the window.

"All clear?" Cartwright asked.

Bird nodded. Cartwright turned to Conlan.

"Get out of the car."

"Why?"

"Just do it." Cartwright was starting to sound angry. As Conlan obeyed, he saw Cartwright's eyes flick to Bird. It was just a glance, but it seemed to confirm the worst of his fears. What he saw was complicity, suppressed excitement, and hidden malice—the snide, unspoken message exchanged by practical jokers when the laugh is on somebody else.

And he understood. They were going to kill him—kill him, plant the film, then frame the bagmen for murder, to put the squeeze on the bagmen and get them to finger the principals. And that, of course, was why Bird had gone checking. For witnesses, Conlan thought, the panic rising in his throat like vomit. To make sure there were no witnesses.

"You can't do this!" His voice rode a wave of hysteria and terror. "You can't kill me and hope to get away with it. There were witnesses. People saw me get into the van that morning. People who'll come forward and testify . . ."

Cartwright slapped him in the face. Twice. Hard.

"What the fuck are you talking about?" Cartwright, though angry, seemed also genuinely astonished, and it was this, more than the blows, that quieted Conlan. "We just want you to wait in the hut, same as you always do. Bird and I will be back in the trees, so that when they show up we can grab them." He paused, stared at Conlan in contempt. "So what's all this shit about killing people? I mean where the fuck do you think you are? . . . Mother Russia?"

Conlan said nothing. His lip was bleeding where Cartwright had hit him. His face was scalding with hurt and shame. Tears had started in his eyes again, and he turned away so Cartwright wouldn't see them.

"Go wait in the hut, for Christ's sake," Cartwright said.

Conlan stumbled towards the hut. He felt defeated, shamed in some deep, irrevocable way by everything that had happened since the day of his arrest, and most of all by this last abject capitulation to panic. They had broken him. Sue Ann, the Russians, and now these soft-voiced bullies. Between them they'd made him so he'd never quite look anyone straight in the eye again. And what was worse, he thought, was it hadn't taken much.

Then Bird, sounding vaguely irritated, said, "Why don't we stop horsing around?"

Conlan turned.

Bird had a gun in his hand. A nickel-plated revolver, Conlan had time to notice, with a tube attached to the barrel. And he had just time to

notice, too, that while Cartwright was wearing a look of queasy fascination, Bird's look, as he brought the gun up, was as clear and empty as
ever.

Bird unscrewed the silencer, put it and the gun in his pocket. He
glanced over at Cartwright. Cartwright stood rigid, staring down at the
body. He seemed to be holding his breath.

"What are you waiting for?" Bird jerked his head in the direction of
the body. "Get on with it."

Cartwright let his breath out in a long sigh. He hesitated and looked
back at Bird, a kind of appeal in his eye.

"Jesus . . ." he said shakily. "Half his head's blown away."

"That's what happens," Bird said. "Now do it. We don't have all
day."

Cartwright knelt down beside the body, avoided looking at Conlan's
face. Gingerly, as if death were some catching disease, he felt inside
Conlan's coat and withdrew his wallet. He removed the cash and credit
cards then dropped the wallet beside the body.

"The watch too," Bird said. "Then the wedding band and pinky
ring."

Again Cartwright hesitated. "That wedding band's inscribed on the
inside," he objected. "I noticed when we gave him his stuff back. And
the watch has initials on the back of the movement. Nobody'd be dumb
enough to steal those."

"Wanna bet?" Bird said. "There are people who'll kill for the price
of a couple of lines. People with IQs in low single figures. Look, this is
an *unpremeditated* crime, muggers surprising a target of opportunity,
acting on impulse, improvising. Their first instinct is to grab everything
in sight, then later they start thinking." He paused. "When we dump
the car, we'll leave his stuff inside. For the cops to find when they get
around to it."

"Or for someone else to steal . . ." Cartwright thought for a moment, then grinned. ". . . who could end up talking awful fast to the
cops."

Bird shrugged. "Then maybe we better ditch the plastic here. Don't
want all our eggs in one basket."

Cartwright removed the watch and rings. The rings he had to wrestle off. He was looking sick when he handed them to Bird. He walked a few steps up the jeep track and pitched the credit cards in a clump of bushes.

"And the cash?" he asked. "There's over two hundred dollars."

"You want it, keep it," Bird said. "He won't miss it."

"I dunno . . ." Cartwright looked doubtful. "It's dumb, I guess, but somehow that doesn't seem to sit so well with me."

"Then don't keep it." Bird shrugged. "Christ, I don't know. Give it to someone. Make a donation to the United Way. . . . Better yet," he said, "turn it in to accounting with a detailed report on how you got it. Maybe they'll give you the Boy Scout medal."

CHAPTER FIVE

MAJOR PAVEL IVANOVITCH VOLKHOV, ASSISTANT CULTURAL ATTACHÉ to the Soviet Embassy in Washington, stared down at the words that were scrawled on the paper in front of him. Then, with a brisk stroke, he put his pen through them. That was the problem with Russian, he thought: It was too rich, it offered too many choices. As you followed your meaning along its chosen highroad, words beckoned seductively from too many byways. You turned off, and before you knew it, you were lost.

"Swift-footed servants of bleak dawn . . ." he wrote, then scratched out "bleak." Perhaps, after all, "pale" was better. "Pale" continued the feeling of "watery" from the previous image. "Bleak-*faced*," on the other hand . . .

The intercom buzzer sounded.

Damn.

Since the new Resident's arrival, Volkhov had come to detest the buzzer. It was uncivilized, altogether too curt, too sharp a reminder of military degree, of the gulf that separated major from colonel. As a means of communicating, it displayed, in his opinion, no proper regard for the human niceties. And the noise itself was offensive, like a prolonged and deliberate breaking of wind.

But there it went again. Three buzzes in quick succession. Flat. Uncompromising. Peremptory.

Sighing, he hit the speaker button.

27

"Yes, Colonel?"

"Meet me at the Vault in five minutes please, Major." Electronics exaggerated a tinny quality in the voice. "Bring the file with you."

"Yes, Colonel."

No mention of which file, he noticed. No recognition that he might, since their conversation of yesterday, have had other things on his mind. Just the careless assumption—in this case infuriatingly correct, since the file in question was underneath his poem—that the preoccupations of his superior would naturally be his also. How different, he thought wistfully, from Stein's regime. The same machinery, of course, and driven by the same compulsions; but lubricated, then, by a courtesy that had made it bearable. When Stein had wanted to talk, he'd come to *you* . . . discreet knock . . . polite pause for your answer. Then the head craning round the side of the door, the quick, diffident smile, the soft voice that was almost a whisper: "A word in your ear, Pavel Ivanovitch, if you can spare a moment." But Stein was gone, recalled to Moscow and an uncertain future, and with him had gone all regard for the human niceties. In their place was this infernal contraption, this buzzer.

He stuffed the poem in his pocket, gathered up the file, closed and locked his safe, reset the alarm system, and let himself out of the office, closing the door behind him and testing it once to make sure the lock had caught. Since the new Resident's arrival, also, security had gotten tighter. There were people out prowling the corridors, these days, looking for doors unlocked or files left out on desks. And for Major Volkhov, hostage of fortune, leftover from a Resident who was clearly out of favor, a security breach, even minor, was not a thing he needed on his record.

The Vault was in the Registry, the heart of that storehouse of secrets, the massively fortified sanctum of a place already, in Volkhov's opinion, sufficiently protected. Had the Vault contained files or gold bars, then the efforts to guard its integrity—the walls of reinforced concrete, two feet thick and lined with cork; the ponderous armored door; the series of combination locks—might not have seemed so excessive. But the Vault, like the last but one in a nest of Chinese boxes, was merely the housing for another container: a soundproof cubicle, not much larger than a telephone kiosk, which enclosed, in turn, nothing but seats that faced each other across a small table. This final box, attached by electric hoist to the ceiling, was thought, when raised, to offer the ultimate in protection against listening devices. It was known, almost inevitably, as "the coffin."

All this had existed in Stein's day, of course, but Stein had seldom used it. "The occupational disease of security services," he'd been fond of saying, "is paranoia. We imagine the other side as God, always there, always watching. But according to their newspapers, which tell the truth quite surprisingly often, they're even more incompetent than we are. Besides,"—quick smile—"whenever I climb into that thing, I forget what it was I had wanted to say." Stein had liked to hold confidential discussions outdoors, preferably on visits to Washington's tourist attractions. His favorite had been the National Cemetery in Arlington. He said it reminded him of what they were there for.

When Volkhov arrived, the door to the Vault was open. Kasparov, the duty clerk, was standing beside it looking bored.

"Am I late?" Volkhov asked.

Kasparov shrugged, rolled his eyes. Since the new Resident's arrival, he'd once confided to Volkhov, he'd come to feel like an elevator attendant.

The door of the cubicle was also open. Volkhov entered, shut the door and sat down facing the Resident. There was a pause, a brief electrical hum as the hoist went into action, then silence. Words from a poem floated through Volkhov's head . . . "Nor in thy marble vault shall sound my echoing song" . . . Marvell, he seemed to recall reading somewhere, had also worked for his country's secret service. So had Marlowe. It was—the thought had struck him more than once—an odd occupation for a poet.

"You've read the file?"

Volkhov nodded. His eyes met the Resident's in a moment of mutual appraisal. She wasn't bad looking, this new colonel with the bad manners and whizz-kid reputation. Good bones. And she'd taken some care of herself. Comfortably fleshed, of course, and in the proper places, but no sign in her yet of the dumpiness that overtook so many Slav women in their forties. She was well dressed, too, the skirt elegant, if a little conservative, the rollneck and cardigan cashmere by the look of them. And someone competent had done her hair. A typical

Andropov appointee, he thought: a technocrat in a sweater set and costume jewelry, a Russian steamroller with coachwork by Pininfarina, a worthy representative of the new socialist chic.

"So . . . What is your opinion?"

Volkhov shrugged. "We're talking about a very valuable asset."

"*Potentially* valuable," she corrected. "So far he's done nothing. Value—doesn't it?—implies use."

That was open to question, he thought. Value, to him, implied *potential* use. But whatever it was they were here to discuss, it wasn't philosophy. He shrugged again. "Use, certainly. But what we spoke of before, I'm afraid, strikes me as waste."

She stared at him coldly, her eyes weighing him, not with hostility but rather a kind of impersonal scepticism, as if he were merely the embodiment of some discredited line of thought. He'd heard nothing from Stein since his recall, nothing *of* him. The reason, he thought, was becoming clear.

"You don't think that the target is worth it?"

He shrugged. "It is if there *is* a target. I just don't happen to believe there is."

"Because of what happened to Daisy."

Volkhov nodded. It was typical, he thought, that even down here, in this claustrophobic box, she insisted on using the code name. Hearing it, he felt a twinge something like guilt. How mortified the little man would have been had he ever found out what they'd called him. Not, of course, that there were any real grounds for resentment. At least the flower was adaptable and hardy. The man, on the other hand, had been weak; too tender for the climate he'd found himself in; too fragile to survive the exposure to those brutal elements, fear and greed. Poor Daisy, Volkhov thought. Poor dead Daisy.

"You're convinced, then, that he wasn't mugged?"

He pursed his lips. "I'm not convinced that he was. Look, Colonel. Consider the situation objectively. Walk around it a little. *Smell* it. An agent making a drop is shot and killed. Circumstances seem to suggest a mugging; his money, watch, and rings are taken, his credit cards tossed in the bushes as if the mugger had thought of using them and realized, later, the risk. The microfilm in his wallet, on the other hand, is undisturbed, and the wallet itself is discarded casually by the body, where our people, when they arrive, cannot fail to spot it." Volkhov paused. "What I ask myself is this: Is the film a remarkable piece of luck? Or were we meant to find it?"

For a while, she inspected him without speaking. He was sleek, well fed, with a feline grace and an almost palpable aura of sex about him, like a tomcat. Volkhov the ladies' man. Volkhov the charmer. Volkhov the celebrated recruiter of agents. Volkhov the corrupter. But talented to this limited extent, at least, that he instinctively sensed in others a taint he couldn't quite hide in himself. Corruption, she thought, invariably attracted corruption; filth, inevitably, was drawn to filth.

"So you think the microfilm is bait? Daisy, you're saying, was killed by his own people?"

He nodded.

"What makes you think so? Just the coincidence?"

"The several coincidences. The muggers could just as easily have taken the wallet with them, discarded it later with the watch and the rings, but conveniently for us, or for someone, they didn't. And then they had the extraordinary luck, assuming Daisy was his usual half hour early, to be in the right place at exactly the right time. Fifteen minutes earlier and they'd probably have missed him; fifteen minutes later and our people might not have missed *them*." Volkhov paused. "I'm suspicious, too, at how soon the police got called in. That place is really lonely. I can imagine him lying there for weeks without being discovered. But the next day, or so I read in this morning's paper, the police received an anonymous phone call, and by ten o'clock that night they'd found the car in the parking lot of a suburban shopping mall. The radio was gone, but the watch and rings were in the glove compartment." He paused. "A half empty phial of cocaine was found under one of the seats."

She continued to look sceptical. "And therefore you conclude that, after killing him, his own people called the police? But why not the simpler and more obvious hypothesis: He was robbed and killed by muggers, and later someone just happened to find the body but didn't wish to get involved with the police?"

He said nothing, merely pursed his lips and shook his head gravely.

"Why not?" she demanded. "If his own people did it, why on earth would they *want* to involve the police?"

"The police were bound to be more involved. Sooner or later *someone* was going to report finding that body. Why not involve the police from the start, to lend some color to this little piece of fiction? After all"—he shrugged—"what's a murder mystery without the police?"

"I wouldn't know. I don't have your knowledge of bourgeois pulp fiction. I also wish you would make your point more clearly."

"What I meant," he said, "is they needed the police to bring the details—those little compelling touches of color—to our attention. They want us to believe he was mugged, let's say, so they take his cash to suggest that was the motive. But since only addicts, usually, will murder for as little as the average man carries in his wallet, cocaine is left in the car to suggest that the killers were addicts. But unless they know about the killing, the police won't be looking for the car, won't find the cocaine, and hence won't be able to tell us about it. Therefore the anonymous phone call."

She considered for a moment. "That all strikes me as rather elaborate."

"Very elaborate." He nodded. "Not very subtle. Typically American."
She thought for a moment.

"If the microfilm is bait in a trap, who is this trap set for?"

"It's obvious, isn't it?" He paused and leaned forward, keeping his voice level, trying not to lecture her, but speaking more urgently now because he sensed he was losing, knew from her set face and her tone that her mind was all but made up, the discussion all but over. "Look, Colonel. It's a matter of logic. If Daisy was killed by his people, Daisy was questioned. If Daisy was questioned, Daisy talked. They'll have a complete list, therefore, of every paper he passed us. It will have occurred to them to wonder—don't you think?—how Daisy, a mere clerk, always knew exactly which files to copy, which to ignore. They're bound to have concluded—since, though they're not subtle, they're also not usually stupid—that Daisy was getting inside assistance, that within their organization there is someone else working for us. Someone, moreover, very highly placed." He paused. "The trap is for Marigold. They offer a target for us to aim him at. They hope that in moving towards it he will give himself away."

"And they had to kill Daisy to keep us from knowing it's a trap. That makes a certain sense." She nodded. "*If* we grant your premise. But should we grant it, necessarily? You have much field experience, of course, a highly developed nose for bad smells. And I agree, of course, that, because this may be a trap, it's out of the question for us to risk Marigold. But what if Daisy was *not* killed by his people? What if the microfilm was *not* planted? Can't you see what possibilities that opens up?"

He almost sighed. Possibilities? The only possibilities he could see were gloomy. This *was* a trap. Instinct told him so, and instinct, that sixth sense, born of experience, whose promptings only those who had shared the experience could properly value and respect, almost never let him down. If they took this bait they would pay for it: casualties, loss of assets it had taken them years to build up. The Americans, he thought bitterly, had had lots of luck with their timing: Stein, who would never for a minute have been taken in by this, was gone, and in his place was this woman, presumably skilled in office politics but pitifully short on field experience, the intelligence bureaucrat—a breed he had learned to despise—eager to win victories for herself and for her sex. They were going to lose one here. Or rather, the sleeper was. This woman too, probably. In other circumstances, perhaps, *that* prospect would have been appealing. But not here. He had never been able to tolerate waste.

"I should like to state for the record, Colonel, that in my opinion the film is bait and therefore garbage. Our priority here must be protecting assets. We'd be fools to risk someone as valuable as the sleeper on a target that may not even exist."

She thought for a moment, eyes narrowed. His mention of the record, he saw, had been heard and noted.

"Protecting assets. But isn't that always your priority, Major? You and your friend Stein? You treat them like buried treasure. Because they're so precious, you're terrified to use them. But as I've said, nothing has value unless it's used." She paused. "What we just may have here, Major, is the chance for a major victory for world socialism. It may be small, but you have to admit it exists."

Silence. She eyed him enquiringly. *A major victory for world socialism*? But no one took these slogans seriously. No one used them, except in speeches. Evidently she, too, had her eye on the record. Could it be—the question was accompanied by a sudden stab of anxiety—that she was having the conversation taped?

"You do have to admit it, don't you, Major? Your nose is excellent; everyone says so, but isn't there a chance that for once it could be wrong?"

More silence. Reluctantly, he nodded.

"And if it's wrong . . ." She paused. "Think about it, Major. A chance to change history, to tip the scales of battle in our favor, perhaps permanently. Wouldn't this be worth more than Marigold or Daisy, or the sleeper? Or all three? Wouldn't it, indeed, be worth all Colonel Stein's little garden of flowers?"

Stein's little garden of flowers. The contemptuous phrase revealed more than vindictiveness, or the new broom's need to sweep clean. In the end, he thought, it was a matter of outlook: the bureaucrat's preference for systems over people, the theorist's hostility to the messiness of life. The victory she was after here, the real pot of gold at the end of this rainbow, was ousting people like Stein and him, replacing them with clerks and computers.

"Before we commit to this, Colonel,"—he decided to give it one last try—"before we embark on a course of action I believe we may come to regret, could we take another look at what we are risking? A researcher into the weapons applications of artificial intelligence, a field, I need hardly remind you, which our latest directive designates a primary target. An illegal, moreover, with perfect credentials, with a legend detailed and perfect enough to stand up to the closest scrutiny. An American citizen, polygraph resistant, to whose penetration to the highest levels of the U.S. defense industry there exists no apparent obstacle. I can see no limits to how far he can go, no end to his potential as an asset." He reached for the file and began to read. ". . . fled Czechoslovakia in the uprising of 1968. Granted political asylum in Britain. Attended London University on a government scholarship to study computers . . ."

She cut him off.

"I'm familiar with the file. More so than you, it seems, since you fail to mention the most crucial of the facts. We have many sources—do we not?—in the U.S. computer industry. But only *one*, so far as I know, who happens to work for the company which has just won the contract to write new software for the CIA's computer system.''

She paused. ''This is really very straightforward, Major. A matter of simple economics, of weighing risk against probable return. We have here a chance to win a decisive advantage. To penetrate the CIA's computer. To enter its memory and empty out the secrets. To cripple our enemy for the foreseeable future. And against such a chance''—she drew the conclusion gently, without triumph, a parent patiently instructing a child—''what weight can we give to the life of a single agent, a sleeper?''

After Volkhov had left, the Resident sat for a moment, reminded, by a sideways skip of thought that was unexpected but by no means inexplicable, of her father. Of the day, more than twenty years before, when, if any precise starting point could be assigned to anything, her career had really begun. She'd received, in the same post, letters of acceptance to the Advanced Degree Program at the University and to the Special Services Training Program, and she had gone to the kitchen to give him the news. He'd been about to leave, standing beside the ancient and lumbering bicycle on which, for as long as she could remember, he would pedal to work, his flat wool cap pulled down over one eye, the collar of his jacket turned up against the chill, his trousers tucked into the tops of his patched rubber boots. When she'd handed him the letters, he had gazed for a moment with a grave but otherwise inscrutable expression at her flushed face and shining eyes. Without speaking, he had read the letters through. Then he'd folded them up and handed them back.

''The Special Services? . . . Advanced studies in languages? . . . You need advanced studies in languages now to wear a uniform?''

''I won't be wearing a uniform.'' The Special Services had many branches, not all of which, as they both knew, wore uniforms. She made an effort at self-deprecation. ''Most probably I'll end up commanding a desk.''

''Commanding a desk . . . Your mother would have been proud.'' It had been hard to know at the time whether the comment was ironic, but she'd come to feel, later, that if it was, the irony hadn't been entirely for her. Her mother had been the brainy one, the one whose frustrated ambition for herself had transferred itself to her daughter. "Komsomol leader . . . Party member . . . University Honors program." Tonelessly he recited the litany of her achievements. "Advanced Degree Program . . . Special Services Training Program"—pause—"whatever *that* means. . . . And so it goes. Onwards and upwards. Where to, who can say? But out of *here*, at any rate."

She'd followed his glance round the dingy kitchen: the chipped sink with its pile of unwashed dishes, the peeling walls adorned by last year's calendar, the single threadbare armchair, the deal table, the food cupboard, its shelves, mostly empty, lined with an oilcloth that no amount of scrubbing could get clean. He'd felt reproached by her ambition, her achievements. She'd understood that, of course. He always had. But she'd been hurt once again by his failure to feel ambition for her, and scornful, as ever, of his failure to understand.

"It's not for that. Not for money or privileges. I want to do something with my life. Something important. I don't want just to have babies and grow old."

It was a tactless thing to say—even at the time she'd known that; especially when he was about to set out for the factory where, in twenty years, he'd risen no higher than foreman—a tactless comment, but even so, she hadn't been ready for the bitter scorn of his response.

"Important? . . . If you get to be a general, commanding an army of desks, you'll never do anything as important as having a baby."

The attitude haunted her, had done so all her career, making her work twice as hard to achieve twice as much as the males she'd competed against. And always she met with this patronizing assumption, because she was halfway decent-looking, that what she *should* be doing was getting married. Or that somehow her rise had been unmerited, that probably she had slept her way to the top. Or, whatever else, that she was disqualified, by some weakness inherent in her sex, from developing fully that mix of sensitivity and ruthlessness needed for success in her field. . . . It continued, she thought. And now this Volkhov, with his irritating assumption of superior knowledge, this Volkhov, who reminded her constantly of what she'd had to fight and whose continued presence in her post could therefore not be tolerated, this Volkhov would be only the latest in a long line of men who'd underrated her and lived to regret it. . . . Of course there was risk here. There was always risk.

But risk had to be set against reward. And the question of who *incurred* the risk and who would *reap* the reward had also to be thought of. Which was why, since she'd known in advance what he'd say, she'd even bothered to have the conversation with Volkhov, and why she'd had it taped. The rewards, if any, would accrue to her; the risks, if any, would be borne by Volkhov. And by Igor too, of course, Volkhov's so precious sleeper. She'd show them what it was to be ruthless.

Her thoughts returned to that conversation of twenty years ago and to how she'd answered her father:

"I want to *do* something with my life. Any mongoloid can have a baby."

CHAPTER SIX

AFTER RETURNING TO HIS OFFICE FROM HIS MEETING WITH THE RESIDENT, Volkhov devoted what was left of the morning to a careful review of his situation. He'd not been surprised by the outcome of the meeting, nor dismayed, unduly, by its tone. When colonels called for discussions with majors, their object, he'd learned, was not so much to exchange views as impose them, and a certain amount of gratuitous muscle flexing could be expected along with the imposing. Witness, for instance, the deliberate ambiguity of the Resident's parting remark: ("We are all dispensable, Major. Some of us, of course, more so than others.") What *had* disturbed him—and a second look at things did nothing to dispel his unease—was the Resident's announcement that he, Volkhov, would be Igor's control.

He was boxed. Office politics were her specialty, and she'd outplayed him. By making him control, committing him to a scheme he'd made more than clear he considered ill-advised, she'd left him no choice but to give it his best efforts. And, by taping the meeting at which he'd voiced his objections, she'd ensured, if her scheme succeeded, that he wouldn't get much of the credit, and if it failed, that he'd end up with the lion's share of the blame. She'd undoubtedly claim that the cause of any failure was not her planning but his halfhearted support. And the record would bear her out, he reflected sourly, at least as regards the halfhearted support. But that was far from the only danger. If things did go wrong—and given his conviction that Daisy was bait, it was hard to see how they couldn't—it was likely that Igor, the sleeper whose future she was recklessly hazarding here, would end his career in a safe house in Virginia and on the receiving end of what, in the jargon of the trade, was delicately called "a debriefing." And when that happened to an agent, as Volkhov well knew, the control was apt to find himself, cover in shreds, squirming in the spotlight of an unwelcome publicity.

Volkhov, of course, had no illusions about cover. Undoubtedly he'd been noticed, most recently perhaps for having, among other sins, recruited Conlan. But diplomatic cover was a relative sort of thing. One could afford to be noticed; what one couldn't afford was to be noticed too often. If one's name appeared too frequently in FBI reports, if one's picture got taken in too many restaurants *a deux* with employees of State and Defense, a consensus was apt to develop that one was getting blatant, that the benefits of knowing *what* one was and, most of the time, *where* one was were outweighed by the mischief one was probably up to. The result could be a note from the Secretary of State informing the Soviet Ambassador that his Assistant Cultural Attaché had twenty-four hours to pack and leave the country. And that, Volkhov thought, was serious . . . not quite as serious as displeasing Moscow perhaps, but almost. It would mean, at any rate, no more quiet lunches and dinners, no more tickets to the Redskins, no more outings to the Kennedy Center. It would mean, since those expelled from one western capital were seldom welcome in others, that one's chances for further diplomatic postings, or at least one's chances for *civilized* diplomatic postings, were seriously impaired.

Volkhov, the Resident's suspicions notwithstanding, was not more than normally corrupt. His conviction that his proper place was here, in the midst of this misguided but thoroughly enjoyable people, was based on an objective assessment of his talents and his government's best interests. That the latter happened to coincide with his own preferences in the matter was, he felt, merely fortunate. He knew these people. He liked them. He understood—it was his greatest talent—how to lead them astray. His return to Moscow, therefore, either by request of the Resident or the U.S. Department of State, was at all costs to be avoided. He would have to play his cards skillfully here. Very skillfully. And the key to that, obviously, would be the proper management of this sleeper, Igor.

But sleepers, unfortunately, were sometimes hard to manage. When you took a man (in this case hardly more than a boy), grafted him like a cancer cell on the body politic of another nation, then left him dormant for years, even decades, the effect on his personality was unpredictable. Some sleepers, perhaps the majority, were sociopaths, isolates who took pleasure in secrecy and betrayal, to whom their cover was an end in itself, a drama played out before an audience of one, a kind of psychic masturbation. Controlling such people was seldom much of a problem, since it called for no disturbance of their fantasy lives, no drastic realignment of perception. For others, however, the invented self could achieve, in the years of dormancy, real depth and substance, could come to seem—and therefore, since reality here was mostly in the eye of the beholder, could come to be—more real than the purpose that lay beneath it. For such sleepers the awakening—the abrupt collision with the fact that what had come to seem real (work, friends, home, family) had never been more than a prop, that their lives were fictions in the service of some distant abstraction called "Soviet Policy"— could often be utterly traumatic.

Which kind of sleeper was Igor? How hard would he be to control? And what was the best way? It was necessary, before one did anything else, to find answers to these questions. And the place to start looking was the file. Not the summary version kept in the Registry here, but the full record from the Archive in Moscow.

Meanwhile, of course, he would need to warn Marigold about Daisy.

CHAPTER SEVEN

IT WAS ONE OF THE RULES BY WHICH BECKER GOVERNED HIS LIFE THAT by the end of the third date the issues be mostly settled. Defined as issues were questions concerned principally with what, if the relationship were to continue, could be expected of him. Expectations could include sex, friendship, some degree of fidelity, and a reasonable, but not unlimited, amount of his time. Excluded were promises of undying devotion, invitations to move in and take over his life, and marriage. The rule was not utterly inflexible—rules, he believed, should be servants, not masters—but experience had shown it to be generally sound. Three dates were plenty for intentions to be mutually made clear; and things not settled early, he'd found, had a tendency not to get settled. Nor had he ever been tempted to compromise much on the issues. If it suited his temperament to stay clear of involvement, to stake out an area at the center of his life and make it off limits to others, it was also dictated by circumstances. To love was, in his situation, to offer gratuitous hostages to fortune. He'd long ago taught himself to settle for less.

How *much* less was the question occupying his mind as he neared the end of his third date with Arlen.

Truth was, she'd unsettled him slightly, had gotten just a little bit under his guard. In the restaurant, he'd found himself pondering the ten-year difference in their ages, wondering if her appeal for him wasn't, perhaps, mostly her youth, if he might not be seeking from her reassurance against the intimations of age which, at thirty-six, were starting to disturb him. And what troubled him now about this line of thought was not the possible answer to his question—reassurance, after all, was a reasonable thing for a person to seek from another—so much at that the question had arisen. It was not one that had ever much bothered him before. So why now? . . . And was it really her youth that most appealed to him, or was it something else? On seeing her again, he'd felt instantly compelled to reopen the question of who she was and whether she'd been sent. And this in turn raised, in a different form, the question of what he was really seeking from her. Why did it matter so much, this issue of her genuineness? What did it have to do—for it certainly seemed connected—with what it was he wanted from her? Was what he wanted from her reassurance, or was it absolution?

Whatever it was, he was going to get it resolved.

And he was going to have to be careful.

He stole a look at her profile, silhouetted in the darkness beside him and illuminated, every so often, by oncoming headlights. She was driving fast, about thirty miles over the limit, but with a relaxed, unhurried confidence that had long since put to rest his fears about her skill. He'd been right about her looks, he thought. They did reflect character. The more he knew her, the more they grew on him. There was a clarity to them and, in the straight nose and the strong clean line of the jaw, a forthrightness. Yet the strength, the hint in her gaze of what might have come across as intransigence, was softened by the fullness of her mouth, its tolerant, ironic curve. He'd thought of her, since their first meeting, as decidedly good looking; but the better word, it now came to him, the *right* word, was beautiful. He studied her more openly. Her eyes were on the road, but she must have felt his scrutiny, for presently, when the traffic permitted, she glanced over.

"What are you thinking about, right at this moment?"

"There was this meat-packing firm, somewhere in the Midwest. Catered exclusively to the kosher market, which involved, among other things, blessing the meat."

"'So?" She sounded, perhaps, a shade disappointed. "Be a job for a rabbi, I'd imagine."

"It was. . . . But it was full-time employment, you understand. Eight hours a day, five days a week, forty-nine weeks a year, this guy did nothing but talk to meat. Raises some interesting questions, don't you think?''

"It does? What sort of questions?''

"Well, technical, for a start . . . about the logistics of working on that scale. Do you bless by the pound or by the carcass? Can you freeze it before you bless it? And how long do the benefits of blessing last? Is it like baptism, a one-shot deal? Or does it wear off, like vaccination?''

"Search me. I guess you could ask someone." She paused. "If you really wanted to know.''

He shrugged. "What interests me are the larger issues. Psychology, for instance. What kind of man takes a job like that? What does it do to his spiritual outlook? Think what clouds of existential despair must gather round a life spent blessing meat.''

She considered this.

"I think you're asking the wrong questions. What would interest me is what happened to the rabbi.''

"I know what happened. He got arrested for shoplifting. Apprehended in Safeway with the goods about his person—a copy of *Hustler* and a three-pound can of ham.''

They had reached his driveway. She slowed for the turn, swung in, and pulled up in front of the house. Cutting the ignition, she reached up and turned on the interior light.

"Ham?" She was laughing now. "The ham in this story is you. You made this up, didn't you? It's pure fabrication.''

"Not fabrication," Becker said. "Perhaps displacement activity.''

"Displacement activity? You mean when you're asked what's on your mind, you come up with some tale about a meat-blessing rabbi?''

"It's not a tale," Becker said. "A tale would be fabrication.''

"But it's not what you were thinking about either, is it?''

"No," Becker said. "I was thinking about whether we're going to go to bed.''

Silence.

"That's an interesting tactic." She seemed less shocked than amused. "Reminds me of my fencing instructor—some moments of indirection, then the sudden thrust to the heart." She paused. "But in answer to your question, I don't know. It's not, shall we say, ultimately out of the question. But I'm an old-fashioned girl, I need to be properly wooed.

Tell you what, though. Promise not to jump me, I'll come in for a nightcap.''

"How many languages *do* you speak?"

Arlen, a cognac in hand, was studying the bookshelves. In spite of the ease with which she'd fended off his pass she was, he sensed, still slightly rattled and taking refuge, therefore, in small talk. He regretted the pass. But for her deftness, it could have spoiled things. But it wasn't something he had planned, rather an impulse indulged without thought; a reflex attempt to settle the issues. He was getting shallow. Apart from his work, his life was habit, a routine of itches, routinely scratched. Suddenly he felt depressed.

"Come clean," she demanded. "How many?"

"Six. But not all of them well."

"Which six?"

"Well English, of course. Then Russian, Czech, and German. Hungarian I can get around in, just. And Spanish,"—he smiled—"for the cleaning lady."

"German?" She appeared to find the list mind boggling. "Russian I can see. And Czech, since it's your native tongue. But why German?"

"Geography." He shrugged. "And history. In Czechoslovakia, since we expect to be overrun about every twenty years by either or both of our principal neighbors, we find it convenient to speak their languages."

This answer struck him as wistful, even bitter. It was the note of exile, he reflected wryly, the voice of displaced Central Europe, of those who, lacking the other freedoms, found consolation in irony.

She took a book from the shelf nearest her, opened it to a page at random. She studied it for a moment, then showed it to him.

"It's Russian, isn't it? A poem . . . what is it?"

"*Evgenyi Onegin* . . . Pushkin."

"I've never really understood about him." She frowned at the Cyrillic script as if the effort of concentration alone could force it to give up its secrets. "I don't see why Russians consider him so great. He strikes me as minor compared to, say, Dostoevski."

"He doesn't translate," Becker said. "You prefer Dostoevski because in English his vision survives. With Pushkin, perhaps even more than most poets, the vision depends on the language. Without the Russian, it dies.''

"Read some, will you?"

Reading aloud, as he did alone sometimes, he could feel himself almost change character. It was not just a matter of the language—the swish of sibilants, the twisting diphthongs, the liquid quality of vowels and labials—but of something his voice itself took on, the faint plaintive note of his feeling for home; the echo, he thought, of deep woods and long winters.

"It's beautiful," she said. "Beautiful and sad."

"Actually not sad." He shut the book with a smile. "Not that passage anyway. I just read it that way. It reminds me of childhood, you see. It's my mother tongue, and it reminds me."

The moment the words were out, he could have kicked himself. . . . Fool, he thought. *Idiot*. A beautiful woman, a bottle of wine, a few lines of Pushkin, and your heart's on your sleeve, your brain's running out of your mouth.

"Childhood?" She looked puzzled. "But I thought you said you grew up in Prague. . . . Your mother tongue, surely, isn't Russian, it's Czech?"

"It's true . . . about Prague, I mean." His mind, racing, came up with something. "But my mother was Russian. It was my *father* who was Czech. And Russian was what we spoke at home. So Czechoslovakia is my homeland, but Russian is literally my mother tongue."

"Then how do you think of yourself basically?" To him his explanation had sounded labored, but if she'd noticed she didn't let on. "Russian or Czech?"

He shrugged. "Actually, I think of myself as American. It's the nationality I *chose*. This song of exile is for late at night, when we Slavs yield to the temptations of melancholy." He cocked his head and looked at her sideways. "When the bottle is empty and there are women's hearts to be wrung."

"Women's hearts?" For a moment she studied him, not quite smiling, then she started to drift towards him, an approach that appeared both casual and deliberate and that ended by bringing her closer than mere conversation required. "Does this mean you're still hatching plans?"

He didn't answer. The impulse to lean forward and kiss her was almost overwhelming, but he'd made his move earlier. It was up to her.

"You know . . ." She tilted her face up to his. "What we talked about earlier, about not jumping me, you didn't have to take it literally."

He continued to resist. "If not literally, how?"

"Well kissing's not jumping," she said. "Not really jumping, that is."

"But risky," he said. "It's death on promises."

"Promises . . ." Her tone dismissed them. She reached up and brushed her lips against his. " 'Oaths. Straws to the fire in the blood.' "

"Straws?"

"Shakespeare." She kissed him again. "Referring to hay . . . Lights easily, burns like a son of a bitch."

But it settled nothing, he thought later. Not one of the issues had been resolved. Except, maybe, that she hadn't been sent.

She simply *couldn't* have been sent.

CHAPTER EIGHT

THE ORDER CAME IN, BY PHONE AS USUAL, ON TUESDAY, ABOUT HALF
an hour before closing. Eakins took it himself.

"Roses this week? . . . The usual half dozen? . . . Price is up a bit,
sorry to say. Early frost or something . . . Yeah, ain't that the truth? It's
always *something*. . . . Of course. I'll see they're delivered first thing
in the morning . . . Bye then, Mr. Miller. And thanks."

Six roses at six fifty. Including delivery, forty-four dollars. . . . But
Mr. Miller never quibbled about price. He wanted roses, he ordered
roses, regardless. It wasn't always roses, of course; some weeks it was
lilies or carnations, but the tab was always up around fifty. And always
paid promptly, too, fifteenth of the month, by a check drawn on the
Riggs National Bank, the Acme Enterprises, Inc., client-entertainment
account, signed by a Mr. Signature Illegible, Comptroller. Mr. Miller
worked out of Kentucky, of course, which explained why he couldn't
take the blooms in person, but he always phoned in the order himself.
Eakins had once suggested that having a standing order, week in week
out, would save a lot in phone calls, but Mr. Miller had said no, that
would take away the point. If you wanted to honor someone's memory,
he said, you had to take the trouble to actually remember.

Nice man, Mr. Miller. At least nice to talk to on the phone. (Eakins
had actually only seen him once, and that so long ago he wouldn't
recognize him now.) Rich too, presumably, and like most rich people,

careful. He'd seen to it—and how could you blame him?—that his memorial flowers were tax deductible. And he checked up on them, too, every so often. Sent someone from his company to see if the flowers were on the grave. They hadn't been, once—a delivery boy cutting corners, for which he'd promptly been fired—and since then Eakins had made the delivery himself. It wasn't really much extra trouble, since the cemetery was right on his way home. And a customer like Mr. Miller, worth a steady average of twenty-five hundred a year for the last four years, was a customer worth keeping. Besides, Eakins thought, it was a pleasure these days to find someone who loved his mother.

The roses were in place at six-thirty P.M. Tuesday. Ten hours later, an envelope was hand delivered to an address in the poorer section of Silver Spring, Maryland. It contained thirty dollars—a twenty and two fives—and a slip of paper on which someone had typed a date, October 9, a time, four-thirty P.M., and a sequence of lower case letters: grqurt-sthoehvst. The addressee, a certain Aurindo Gomez, a Cuban, was a part-time employee of the Laurel Race Track who supplemented his meager official earnings by doing what he called "small favors for people." These consisted mostly of fetching and carrying for people whose need for anonymity precluded their fetching and carrying for themselves. Aurindo Gomez seldom knew exactly what he was dealing with, and never whom he was dealing for. A naturally curious man, he was also intelligent enough to realize that in his chosen sideline curiosity might prove hazardous to his health. He was content to carry out simple instructions to the letter.

His instructions with regard to envelopes of the kind he had just received were simplicity itself: The slip of paper was to be placed, surreptitiously, and exactly twenty-four hours *before* the date and time specified on the slip, between the pages of a certain book in the reading room of the Silver Spring Library. The thirty dollars were to be placed in his pocket.

Aurindo Gomez was professionally incurious. But this didn't prevent him from pursuing, on occasion, his own speculations as to the real nature of the errands he was running, and in these speculations he was aided by being an avid reader of a certain kind of mystery novel. He believed he had figured out, at least in its general outlines, this business with the envelopes. The sequence of letters, obviously, was some kind of code. The reading room of the Silver Spring Library was being used as what was known in the mysteries he favored as a "dead drop." And since the acquaintance who'd originally put him in the way of this little piece of fetching and carrying was heavily involved in the local traffic in controlled substances, the conclusion to be drawn was elementary: The boys in the drug business were taking lessons from the spooks.

This, though reasonable, was in error. Something closer to the reverse was actually the truth.

Aurindo Gomez made his trip to the library on Thursday. At four twenty-five P.M. on the following day a member of the Soviet Embassy staff entered a public phone booth in Bethesda. His instructions were also simple: to take a call from someone who'd identify himself as Ross, to give the caller a phone number, and then to hang up and go home. He waited until four thirty-five. No call came through. In accordance with his instructions for this contingency, he got in his car, a beige Nissan Sentra with D.C. plates, and drove by a roundabout route to a phone booth on Wisconsin Avenue. It was busy when he arrived, but by 5:15 P.M., which was when he needed it, it was free. He entered and went through the motions of searching the phone book for a number. Since nobody else seemed to need the phone booth, he was able to prolong this activity until five twenty-five. At five twenty-seven no call having come through, he returned to the Embassy and went looking for Volkhov.

"Somebody screwed up," Volkhov said.

Kasparov shook his head. "I don't think so. The roses were placed—I checked on that. The Cuban did his bit. And both of the phone lines were in order."

"Then there must have been an error in the coding."

"The *decoding*, possibly. There was no error on our side. I coded it myself and had Samsonov check me. In any case," Kasparov added, "even an error in decoding is unlikely. If he screwed up the first time and got a wrong number, he'd have been extra careful—wouldn't he?—next time round." He paused. "It's not what you'd call a complicated code."

Volkhov frowned. "What you're saying, then, is that for some reason he couldn't respond?"

"Couldn't"—Kasparov shrugged—"or wouldn't. He's made no effort, since, to contact us. Maybe he's feeling the heat, keeping his head down to avoid any fall-out from Daisy."

Volkhov considered . . . It was possible, he supposed, but unlikely. For one thing, the contact mechanism was virtually foolproof. Three cut-offs, fail-safe at each stage, the whole thing built, moreover, around normal living patterns: habits—like the weekly trips to the library and the orders for flowers to be put on his mother's grave—that Marigold had established long ago, years before he'd been recruited. He could take every step but the last with an FBI agent right at his elbow and raise not a flicker of suspicion. And if he was feeling so much heat that he couldn't risk calling from a phone booth chosen at random from the hundreds available in the D.C. area, then he must be feeling the heat indeed. He must have surveillance crawling all over him.

All of which was highly unlikely, Volkhov thought, because apart from anything else, it was also unlikely that there *was* any heat or indeed any fall-out from Daisy. If Daisy had been executed by his own people, those responsible would hardly advertise the fact, even to members of their own organization, and far less to someone who had, as a consequence of Daisy, become an object of suspicion. In a mole hunt, after all, the last thing you did was alert the quarry.

And that was reassuring in one way, but not in another. For if, as common sense suggested, Marigold was feeling no heat, why had he suddenly gone silent? And why especially—Volkhov asked the question with some exasperation—at this precise moment? If Marigold didn't know about Daisy—and he almost certainly didn't—then he had to be warned. And not just for his own sake. Marigold was not only a KGB asset; he was *Volkhov's* asset. He was Volkhov's insurance, his prestige in Dzerzinskii Square, his passport, perhaps, to several more years of *la dolce vita*, and at this point the only thing standing between him and the Resident's evident determination to have his head. If Marigold were now to go absent without leave, the effect on the career of Major Volkhov might be nothing short of disastrous.

"What do you want us to do?" Kasparov asked.

Volkhov regarded him bleakly.

"I want you to try again. I want you to keep trying. And in the meantime . . ." Volkhov jerked his head upwards in the general direction of the Resident's office, two floors above, and laid a finger to his lips.

CHAPTER NINE

WHEN SHERWOOD SAW WHAT WAS ON THE SCREEN, HE FELT LET DOWN. It was too much, he thought, thus not quite enough. Four days spent surrounded by files and circulation lists, four days of analyzing, extracting, double-checking, coding and entering, had been reduced at the touch of a key to this column of numbers, which the computer had produced instantly, without hesitation, without even pausing for thought. Somehow it seemed a mockery of his efforts.

He wrote the numbers on a scratch pad, then hit a key, blanking the screen. He removed the disk and inserted another, waited for the program to boot. "Don't use the mainframe," Hollister had told him. "Don't use anything tied into a network. Don't put everything onto one program. And remember,"—this without any hint of humor—"if anyone gets wind of this, your days with us are numbered."

Your days with us are numbered. It hadn't at first struck Sherwood how grave this thing was. It had been like hearing a description of nuclear winter: You took in the words, and you thought you knew what they meant, but the import got lost in some realm of the abstract; your skin never crawled, the fear never slithered in your gut. When he'd realized what Hollister was driving at, he'd been shocked, of course, horrified, but it hadn't seemed anything that touched him personally. It hadn't, that is, until Hollister sent him to be fluttered.

Sherwood hated being fluttered. The Agency jargon, though suggestive of the physical effect, conveyed less than nothing of the trauma. It made no difference that you had nothing to hide, or nothing of interest to the Agency, because everything, once you were hooked up to the polygraph, was of interest to the Agency. No corner of your life was too private to be probed—whether you picked your nose, whether you'd shoplifted, how and how often you jerked off. Nothing was off limits, they said, because they needed to know where you were vulnerable, what made you nervous, what happened to your heartbeat when you lied. And you always did lie, because sooner or later they'd hit a nerve, ask something so intimate your whole being rebelled against telling. Then the needles would go haywire, and the examiner would say, in the bored, clinical voice that only made it all worse: "We just recorded some kind of earthquake. Maybe we should run that one again." By the end, when they told you you were "clean," you felt anything but. You felt soiled. Invaded. Emotionally cornholed.

So when Hollister had sent him to be fluttered again, he'd come very close to baulking.

"Should I take it,"—his voice had been stiff with resentment—"that I'm personally under suspicion?"

"Of being Conlan's big brother? How could you be?" Hollister's surprise had been almost insulting. "Conlan's big brother is very high level. You're not even cleared for most of that stuff."

"Then why the flutter?"

"I need to know that this vessel,"—the nod in Sherwood's direction was accompanied by a disarming smile—"is watertight."

"I've said nothing to anyone. You told me not to; I didn't." He hesitated, then added because he was still angry, "I'd hoped that by this time my word would be enough."

"Your word? . . ." Hollister's eyes rested on him briefly, half amused, half incredulous. "Do grow up," they seemed to implore him. "Do, for Christ's sake, grow up." Hollister said, "I'd hoped that by this time you'd have understood: We don't rely on anyone's word."

"I see."

"I'm not sure you do." Hollister leaned forward, his voice suddenly chilly. "Look . . . one of our top people is a KGB agent. Instead of getting all bent out of shape, perhaps you could think about what that means."

Silence.

"We're at war," Hollister said, "though sometimes we forget it. While you and I sit here in comfort, grooving towards our pensions, there are people out there in the trenches, taking risks. And the risks they take are already plenty, without the added prospect of being shot in the back. And I do mean shot," he emphasized. "I want you to understand that. Until we find this guy and stop him, our people in the field are going to die. They'll be pulled in, questioned, tortured till they're broken. The bullet that ends it will seem like a gift of peace." He paused. "You'll forgive me, perhaps, when I think of what *they* have at stake, if I can't get too excited about your privacy."

Silence. His stare seemed as sharp as an ice pick. Sherwood lowered his gaze. He felt his face begin to burn.

"I need to know who I can trust," Hollister said. "I need to know everyone who knows about this. I need to plug all the possible leaks. If our man finds out, he'll go to ground; flushing him out will be almost impossible. . . . Now do you understand?"

"Yes."

"Good." Hollister looked at his watch. "Then get yourself fluttered. And when you're done, come back. I've a job I need you to do."

A job . . . in theory it was simple. You worked backwards from the transcript. From the list of the intelligence Conlan had passed, you tried to infer which files he must have copied. Since most of these were "Restricted Access," circulated only on a need-to-know basis, there were logs kept by Registry of everyone who had seen them. A computer analysis would tell you who, if anyone, appeared in all the logs. With luck, you would have yourself a suspect.

In theory it was simple. In practice it was more or less a bitch. The transcript was seldom detailed enough to let you draw confident conclusions, and the need for discretion kept getting in the way. You couldn't just descend on Registry and ransack the files because, though Registry wasn't staffed by mental giants, there were people there who could add two and two. In the end, by routing requests for information through various "research projects" Hollister had set up as cover, it had been possible to isolate some forty or fifty files that Conlan had *probably*— in most cases it was no more than that—photographed. The names on the circulation list for each of these files (in some cases more than thirty) had then been number coded—an additional security measure—

and fed into the computer. That process alone had taken almost a day. Then a burp from the computer and the problem had been reduced to manageable proportions—to the column of numbers that had shown on the screen.

When the program had booted, Sherwood entered the numbers from the scratch pad and punched in another code. Now for the bottom line.

He hit a key. Names appeared on the screen.

Sherwood read down the list, let out his breath in an astonished sigh.

They had themselves a suspect. In fact, they had themselves six.

"Polygraph?" Hollister looked amused. "You want me to polygraph six of the most senior officers in the Agency?"

Why not? Sherwood thought. We're at war, aren't we? While we sit here in comfort et cetera, people are out there in the trenches, taking risks . . . Aloud, he said, "Well I know how you feel about taking anyone's word."

Silence . . . For a moment Hollister seemed unsure how to react to this; his gaze mingled incredulity and a certain reluctant respect, as if he had just been savaged by a mouse. Finally he smiled.

"You think suspicion should be democratic, is that it? If you can be polygraphed, why not deputy directors?"

Sherwood nodded. "Something like that."

"So do I," Hollister said. "But I also believe in not going berserk. If you'd come up with one name, or two, I'd be willing to push it. But six?" He gazed at Sherwood and shook his head. "No way."

Sherwood said nothing.

"I believe in not going berserk." Hollister repeated. "Which in your vocabulary is another term for 'chickenshit.' Am I right?"

"I didn't say so." Sherwood shrugged.

"You didn't have to." Hollister leaned back in his chair, considering. His eyes, resting on Sherwood, were friendly, but at the same time detached. He reminded Sherwood of his housemaster at Exeter: civilized, courteous, willing to tolerate discussion, but only—and this had always been clearly understood—only up to a point. "Your moral courage is admirable, of course, but there's also such a thing as a sense of proportion. Have you ever heard the name Spearman?"

Sherwood thought. "It sounds familiar . . ."

"Thomas Osgood Spearman. My predecessor but three. Probably the most brilliant man ever to occupy my position, and plentifully endowed with moral courage. He found himself in much the same position as I do. Thought the Agency was harboring a mole. Had himself a shortlist of suspects. Went berserk. Turned the whole place upside down. Came up with nothing." Hollister paused. "Ended up taking early retirement."

"Early retirement . . . he was forced out, you mean?"

"Too many enemies." Hollister nodded. "Counterintelligence is never popular. Our job requires us to suspect the worst; that always makes people uncomfortable. But Spearman created a reign of terror. Polygraphed people in droves, reviewed their fitness reports and vetting records, re-opened closed security investigations. His hope was to panic the mole—if there was a mole—into giving himself away. Instead he may have driven him deeper underground, and in the process he almost destroyed the Agency. In the end, there were people willing to say that Spearman himself was the mole. Or at least that he couldn't have hurt the Agency more if he had been." Hollister paused. "We're not going to do that. We're not going to turn the place upside down. We're not going to start fluttering deputy directors on what they will certainly feel is less than adequate evidence. We're not going to warn the mole we're on his track and give him the time to dig himself in."

Sherwood considered this.

"What *are* we going to do?"

"We're going to wait," Hollister said. "We've set our trap, baited it; now we have to be patient. We're going to sit tight and keep quiet, watch what comes out of the woodwork."

CHAPTER TEN

VOLKHOV HAD ALWAYS BEEN FASCINATED BY HISTORY. AS A BOY, he'd read avidly the popular accounts of his country's past, stories of Peter, and Catharine, and the War of 1812, told with a wealth of colorful, if sometimes implausible, detail and therefore combining with the edification of fact something akin to the appeal of fiction. In college, his interest in mere narrative had given way to a Marxist concern for analysis, the mapping of trends and factors, the stern compulsions of the dialectic. More recently his focus had been on method: the problems inherent in proceeding, from evidence that was always incomplete and not always perfectly factual, to an accurate reconstruction of events. They were problems, he'd sometimes thought, like the one he faced often in his chosen line of work: to gauge from a fragmentary record of behavior the personality that lay behind it.

This was the problem he faced with Igor.

To anyone shut up, as he'd been for most of the day, in a cubbyhole in Registry with the microfilmed files provided by the Moscow Archive, the analogy with history seemed especially compelling. Facts were important, of course, but what most struck Volkhov, as he sought to form a coherent picture from the profusion of fact available to him, was just how much of Igor, in spite of that profusion, had escaped. . . . Recruited, 1967. Kiev Training School, February to July 1967. University of Prague, September 1967 to August 1968. "Defected" to the West, September 1968, following the collapse of the Dubcek regime. Granted political asylum in London, October 1968. London University, 1969. Graduated, first class honors in math and physics, June 1972.

Scholarship to Cal Tech, 1973. Masters in computer science, 1975. Scholarship to Stanford, 1975. Ph.D. in computer engineering, 1978 . . . What did all this—this impressive chronicle of achievement—really tell you about the man behind it? In a sense, Volkhov thought, one got more from pictures. Yet, even here, his strongest impression was of how much was missing.

This latest snapshot, for instance: Igor, emerging from a restaurant in Georgetown. A black-and-white exposure, taken from a car across the street at a moment when the subject, since he had no idea it was being taken, might have been expected to be off his guard. But he *hadn't* been off his guard—at least that was Volkhov's impression—or perhaps it was just that his face was of the kind that, in repose, gave very little away. It was a strong face, self-possessed and even (Volkhov, with his habit of regarding all other men as potential sexual competitors, was prepared to concede this) good-looking. The features were regular and pleasant, and the thick mop of hair fell attractively into the eyes. At the same time, it was oddly anonymous. If one covered it up, one could remember liking it but find oneself hazy as to detail. Except in the case of the eyes. These were notable for their wiped-clean look, a look found most often in soldiers on parade and mistaken so easily, in soldiers not on parade, for stupidity. But Igor was not stupid. Academically, at least, he was brilliant. Not that that meant much, of course. Volkhov had known several distinguished academics who, for most practical purposes, were imbeciles. But in Igor's case the record of *un*academic ability was also impressive.

Prague, for instance . . . In his mind's eye, Volkhov could see the nineteen-year-old Igor, less than a year after finishing training, taking to the streets of Prague in that turbulent summer of '68, a KGB *provocateur* posing as an anti-Soviet militant. He had fooled the Czech authorities, fooled his fellow students. He had even, when the Soviet tanks rolled into the city, fooled the British Embassy, no less, into helping him out of the country and onto the first stage of a larger career in deception. But his very success made one wonder, Volkhov thought. It made one wonder, just a little, who else he might have been fooling. . . .

And especially in view of certain facts.

Fact: Igor was not absolutely Russian. His father had been, but his mother had been Czech. He'd therefore received a major infusion of the culture whose patron saints included both Kafka and Good Soldier Schweik. Volkhov was not happy about this. In his vocabulary, after due allowance was made for national prejudice, "Czech" was still a close synonym for "unreliable."

Fact: Both of Igor's parents were dead. With no close living relatives, either in Czechoslovakia or the Soviet Union, his attachment to the cause of world socialism consisted at this point of such intangible ties as loyalty and affection. Volkhov was not happy about this either. In his experience, intangible lies, especially after sixteen years exposure to the West and its seductions, could be less than binding. He far preferred reins he could twitch.

Fact: Igor has been startlingly successful. He'd assembled, since that day in the fall of 1968 when, still less than twenty years old, he'd crossed into Austria and walked briskly away from his past, most components of the American Dream: prestige, a well-paid job, a house in a fashionable Washington surburb, a fat portfolio of investments, a Porsche. And he'd achieved them entirely through his own abilities and efforts. How willing would he be to risk giving them up?

Fact: Igor was "polygraph resistant." It was this, culled from the original vetting report, which, for Volkhov, really sounded the alarm. It set off, in facts that by themselves might not have seemed significant, disquieting vibrations. Why, for instance, the periodic trips to Geneva? He was squirrelling away cash, presumably, since he seemed not to spend more than a fraction of his income. But squirrelling it away why? With no motive more sinister, perhaps, than reluctance to pay U.S. taxes? But there were other possibilities, and some of them brought one back to that disturbing phrase, "polygraph resistant." Volkhov had little faith in machines, especially those which claimed to be able to tell from blood pressure and the like when a given individual was lying, but in his experience it was a very rare bird indeed who, when faced with the polygraph, displayed, as Igor had in three separate encounters, a total control of his physical responses. It was very rare, Volkhov thought, and rather dangerous. For a person like that could be, in the most literal sense, self-possessed, belonging to no one, to no state, no ideology. Such a person could lie without anxiety, perhaps, because he made his own rules and chose his own loyalties, because he practiced, on his own behalf, that *realpolitik* applauded in governments but condemned in individuals. For an agent, of course, such moral independence offered practical advantages. It could render him, if he were otherwise careful, virtually detection proof. For his control, on the other hand, it could spell trouble.

It boiled down to this, Volkhov thought: This sleeper's loyalties might or might not be stable, but he'd been left undisturbed now for sixteen years, and in circumstances that might make for volatility. So it behooved him, Volkhov, to handle this sleeper as gingerly as he would dynamite.

CHAPTER ELEVEN

IT HAD NEVER CEASED TO AMAZE BECKER THAT THERE WERE PEOPLE willing to pay him, handsomely, for what, to him, was essentially playing. His father, condemned to a lifetime's unwilling service in his country's Ministry of Labor, had often claimed that his dearest ambition was to become "profitably unemployed," and it seemed to Becker that this was roughly what he himself had succeeded in doing. Not only were people willing to pay him for playing, they were also willing to provide the toys—a terminal and its peripheral gadgetry had been installed in his house at company expense. And he was allowed, within limits, to pick his own hours. All of which was why he was about to begin work, at midnight, in the comfort and convenience of his basement. Only in America, he thought; only in the Land of the Free.

His company, of course, took a somewhat different view. They called his work "research into the defense applications of artificial intelligence" and anticipated a payoff, or so they assured stockholders, at some point in the not so distant future. Becker's alternative description of what he was doing was "teaching computers to think like people." He usually added, though not when people from his company were listening, that he wasn't optimistic about the outcome. Teaching computers to think like people, he said, would be doing no favor to either.

But tonight, though he would use their equipment, he wasn't planning to work for the Company. Tonight, and for as long as it took, he'd be writing the program for a game of global strategy to be called "Geopolitics." He had worked out the details with a friend, a professor in the international relations program at Georgetown, and sold the concept to a software firm in California. All that remained was the hacking. The game was complex and realistic—nearly all avenues led to disaster— and the publisher was demanding spectacular graphics in addition to user friendliness. The nuclear holocaust that constituted the normal outcome should, he'd told Becker, "Sear the eyeballs." The problem was doing all this for the 64K machines that made up the bulk of the game market. But Becker wasn't worried. With his talent for shortcuts, he was sure he could do it. His last game, after all, had been nearly as demanding, and the programming had taken him less than two days. It had also earned him ninety thousand dollars. Only in America, he thought, only in the Land of the Free.

Seating himself at the terminal, arranging pencils and his folder of notes on the space to the left of the work station, he felt, as always, a lifting of the spirit, a thrill like that of beginning a journey. Yesterday, with the same pleasant anticipation he might have felt provisioning a ship, he had restocked the refrigerator—beer and mineral water, chicken chow mein and Poptarts, yoghurt and several varieties of dried fruit— and had checked that there were shorts and T-shirts in the cupboard, towels and soap in the bathroom, sharpened pencils on the desk. Younger, he would have scorned such preparations. In those days he'd just plopped down at the terminal and started in, careless of everything but the work, the fusion of fantasy and logic it demanded. Once he had hacked for forty-nine hours straight, halting only to pee, until, pausing to assess a possible need for coffee, he'd been sandbagged by sleep and fallen off his chair. These last years, however, he'd begun to pace himself. He found you programmed better if you sometimes ate and slept. And serious hacks were now planned like expeditions. His friends, however, were not far wrong in claiming that he hadn't really changed, that this workspace in his basement was where he really lived. He'd bought the house, in fact, mostly; for this basement, and the young architect he'd hired to plan the conversion had spent several days following him around to observe his work habits before setting out to create down here "the perfect environment for the serious hacker."

The result, though it reminded some of a fallout shelter, struck Becker as perfect. A self-contained, soundproof, underground cocoon, with the life support systems needed for an extended hack, it was virtually intrusion and distraction proof. There was no direct access from the rest of the house. The inside staircase had been torn out and sealed off, so one entered through a trapdoor in the floor of the garage. There were no windows—he was thus free from such irrelevances as night and day—and no communication with the outside except by one-way systems: an intercom to the house and an unlisted phone line whose number he'd not given to anyone and, in fact, had forgotten himself. He could lose himself down here, immerse himself in an imaginary universe where logic ruled and the real world entered by invitation only.

When he was comfortable at the terminal, he phone-patched into the Company computer, punched in the entry codes, and waited. When the screen was clear, he typed in: "GOOD EVENING, THIS IS BECKER."

This was not strictly necessary. But it had seemed to him that if he were going to teach this computer to think like a person, he might as well teach it to think like a reasonably polite person. What he expected to read on the screen was: "GOOD EVENING, DOCTOR BECKER. HOW ARE YOU TONIGHT?"

What appeared, however, was: "WELCOME BACK, IGOR."

Later, recalling the moment, it surprised him that he'd been at all shocked; he'd always known this summons would one day come. But at the instant he read them, the words on the screen seemed to turn his world to stone. The timing was so perfect. It was almost as if they'd been reading his mind, as if they'd informed themselves somehow of his heart's incipient revolt and had acted to nip it in the bud. He'd been on the point of committing the cardinal sin for a sleeper, of allowing himself to believe in his dream—so they'd jerked him awake, had reminded him, before he could forget, who he was, to whom he belonged.

They hadn't forgotten. By breaking into his program, by their brutal invasion of the very core of his life, they had demonstrated, in fact, how far they were from forgetting. And they would never let him go. He had sold himself to them, seventeen years ago. He had sold all of himself— for you couldn't, as his father had said, sell only a part of your soul to the devil—and the bargain had been properly sealed with blood. Since then he had merely been holding his life on loan. Now they were calling in the debt. The words on the screen were a statement of that fact. "Good job, Kolya," they seemed to be saying. "You've done well, thanks to the state's investment in you. Now the state reclaims its property." And as if to confirm this thought, the greeting on screen was replaced by a command: "BEGIN TREASUREHUNT."

This was a safety loop. Respond incorrectly, as anyone but he inevitably would, and the rest of the sequence would abort. But *he* had been trained to recognize, in this conjunction of "Igor" and "Treasure-hunt," a call sign—his activating call sign—and the response was burned into his memory. He typed it in: "METAMORPHOSIS."

The message that followed was precise and peremptory. It consisted of a set of instructions and the statement that he had thirty seconds to commit them to memory. He did so. After thirty seconds, the screen went blank. Then: "ENTER PROGRAM CODES."

He did this, too, using his normal salutation. As he had expected, there was now no sign of the Igor message. Evidently the sequence self-erased when completed. In its place was the usual query: "GOOD EVENING, DOCTOR BECKER. HOW ARE YOU TONIGHT?"

He was about to type in the response when the thought was derailed by a memory of Arlen, of their third date. They'd made love on the rug in front of the fire, and afterwards she'd sat gazing into the hearth, the flames' reflection dancing in her eyes. He'd been studying her feet, long and slender, with curled, delicate toes, the skin almost translucent, marbled with small blue veins, and it had struck him suddenly how vulnerable she was. He'd had to resist the urge to cover her feet with kisses, to atone in advance for the hurt he might bring. And as if sensing something of this, she'd turned to him with her gaze, which always seemed to be searching out the thoughts behind his thoughts.

"Becker," she'd asked, "can bodies lie?"

For a moment he'd been tempted to answer. "Anything can lie. Everything, sooner or later, *does*." But that would have been both more honesty than the moment could tolerate and less than it required. So instead he'd leaned over and kissed her. They'd made love again, so tenderly it seemed their bodies had not so much joined as melted together. It was just chemistry, he tried to tell himself. Just bodies lying. But the question—it posed itself now with even greater force—was exactly who had been lying to whom?

Or rather, who had been lying *more*?

He glanced back at the screen. The programmed civility was still there: "GOOD EVENING, DOCTOR BECKER. HOW ARE YOU TONIGHT?"

"GO FUCK YOURSELF," he typed in.

The computer's response was unhesitating: "SYNTAX ERROR."

Which only went to show, he thought, how far it still was from thinking like a person.

CHAPTER TWELVE

IT WAS JUST AFTER FIVE WHEN HOLLISTER SWUNG THE MERCEDES OUT
through the main gates and west towards the junction with the Beltway.
When he made the turn onto 173 there was plenty of daylight left, and
since it was there, if anywhere, that they'd pick him up, he checked in
the mirror for signs of a tail. As expected, there were none, but he
checked at intervals anyway, more from habit than from real anxiety.
He wasn't expecting surveillance, and surveillance of the type he had to
fear, detected or no, would certainly lose him before he got where he
was going. If there *were* someone following, on the other hand, he
wanted to know. It would dictate caution. And next time, possibly, a
change in procedure.

He was glad he'd brought the Mercedes today, instead of the Lotus
his wife had bought him for Christmas. Even under normal conditions
he preferred the Mercedes, for the quality masked by its respectably dull
exterior, but even more for the anonymity—even office boys like
Sherwood, he'd noticed, were driving Mercedeses these days. His wife
pouted sometimes, accused him, because he so seldom drove it to the
office, of not really liking the Lotus. But the Lotus looked even more
expensive than the fifty or so thousand dollars he knew she'd paid for it,
and in his profession, as he'd often pointed out, conspicuous display—
especially of one's wife's money—was not a good idea. Besides, when
a man his age drove a flame-red sports car shaped like a missile, it was
apt to raise questions about what he was trying to prove. And though

66

that might well have had something to do, he reflected wryly, with why his wife had chosen it in the first place, he didn't feel he needed to prove anything. Not to her.

At the Beltway he turned left and drove a few miles, exiting onto Leesburg Pike. He was happy to note that the white Fairlane, which had been behind him since Tyson's Corner, kept on down the Beltway towards Annandale. Just in case, however, he pulled into a rest area just beyond the junction with the turnpike and waited there for five minutes. Nothing followed him in; nothing followed when he left.

In Alexandria he drove to a medical office building whose garage, he'd discovered, had a separate entrance and exit. It was dark when he got there. He parked on the third level down and took the elevator up to the first. At this time of night—the doctors had long since gone home—there was no one around to observe him, or to wonder why, when he reached the first level, he at once took the elevator back to the second. When, presently, he emerged, he was driving an ancient Plymouth Fury.

On the Plymouth's dashboard was the parking ticket. On its back, faintly pencilled, was a message: "DIA 126." At the exit, Hollister paid the attendant (the Plymouth, he noticed, had been parked for less than an hour) and got rid of the ticket. He then drove to the Days Inn in Annandale—not Alexandria, that would have been "DIAX"—and parked outside room 126. The trip, he noted, had covered some thirty miles and had taken him more than an hour and a half.

Nevertheless the precautions were worth it. Though the tradecraft had been crude, crude was, in this case, more than enough. The switch of vehicles, at any rate, was guaranteed to foil any but professional surveillance, and professional surveillance—at least in his understanding of the term—was not to be expected here. Anyone halfway competent, of course, would know that he'd taken some pains *not* to be followed, but that didn't much matter. It wasn't something he couldn't talk his way out of. Indeed, under the circumstances, not wanting to be followed could be almost perfect cover. The great thing about working for the Agency was that people expected you to be a little furtive at times.

Besides, he needed the action. It was something he'd always found stimulating. The thought that there *might* be someone behind him, even when he was fairly sure there wasn't, always set his adrenalin flowing, wound him up tight like a spring. To someone who really knew what it meant, secrecy was the ultimate turn-on.

The woman waiting in 126 was in her thirties, handsome in a severe way—like Betteridge, only younger, Hollister thought, which meant he'd been very lucky to find her. Her features were regular, though slightly fleshy, her hair, in which there were already hints of grey, was pulled back from her face and twisted into a bun. As Hollister entered, she stood up and frowned at her watch, revealing a heavy but not undisciplined figure and muscular legs tapering to the slender ankles he particularly liked in women. She wore a tight-fitting white nylon dress, pulled in at the waist by a black leather belt, with buttons down the front all the way to the hem. The suggestion of a uniform was emphasized by sheer black nylon stockings but undermined by improbably high-heeled shoes in black patent leather and, above all, by the fact that the top four buttons of the dress were open, revealing the cleft of shadow between large, assertive breasts.

"You're late." Her tone was peremptory. "I've warned you about being late."

This was the moment that always made him nervous. The tone was crucial. Get it wrong and everything was wrecked. But a vision of Betteridge swam before his eyes and he knew it would be all right. He was swept by the same excitement he'd felt in the schoolroom that first evening with Betteridge, the feeling he was never, except sometimes like this, able to recapture. She was standing before him, swinging a strap in her hand, and her gown had fallen open a little. He'd realized, with a sudden almost unbearable rush of pleasure, that she'd meant it to fall open and that underneath she was naked.

"I'm sorry," he muttered.

"No use being sorry. . . . It doesn't do me any good." She paused, unbuckled the belt. "Nor you either, for that matter."

"I know." She even sounded like Betteridge. Under the smug self-righteousness of her tone, he could sense the same excitement, the same wicked note of anticipation.

"That's no use either. Words don't count for anything. All that count are actions. I'm afraid you leave me no alternative. You're going to have to be punished."

CHAPTER THIRTEEN

"HERE'S THAT DAMNED MUTT AGAIN," VLADEK SAID, "RIGHT ON TIME as usual."

Becker looked at the dog and back again at his plate. There was still a mouthful of food on the plate—cube of sirloin, slightly bloody, fragment of fried potato, two or three French beans—and he'd been saving it for last. But the dog, having made its entrance, was engaging him, as it always did at meals, in a battle of wills. It didn't beg. There was nothing pleading in its manner. It simply looked. The yellow eyes fixed him with the kind of stare he'd otherwise encountered only in starving children, an intensity of want that reminded him, in its singleness of purpose, of Kierkegaard's dictum: "Purity of heart is to will one thing." And perhaps this was why, he thought, he was generally the loser in these psychic struggles. The dog was pure in heart, and he wasn't.

"No," he said. "No way. This is the last bite, and it's mine."

From the corner of his eye he could see Vladek watching across the table, his head tilted slightly to one side, his look amused and slightly pitying.

"Who are you trying to kid?" Vladek said. "The pooch has your number, and he knows it."

Becker ignored him.

"Get lost," he told the dog. "You eat your food, I'll eat mine. OK?"

No response. No waver in the stare. No recognition, even, that he had spoken. Just the calm, unrelenting pressure of that will.

"Shit." He put the plate on the floor at his feet. "But one of these days . . . one of these days, my friend, it's you for the pound."

"He doesn't believe you," Vladek said. "And quite right. You couldn't fool anyone with that kind of threat. One of these days, baloney. He knows indecision when he hears it."

It was true, of course. He'd been saying the same for a month now, and the dog was still there, still eating off his plate. And though he'd refrained from giving it a name, precisely in order not to get attached, the fact remained that he was attached. Not by affection, he told himself—for the dog, a mix of terrier and bluetick hound, had neither the appearance nor the personality to inspire affection—but by logic. When he'd found it on the Beltway, wandering about, dodging cars, collarless and obviously abandoned, he'd acted to save it from an almost certain death. If he now condemned it to the pound, where animals not claimed within thirty days went automatically to the gas chamber, he'd be sending it back to what he'd rescued it from. So by the logic of charity—a logic, he'd found, apt to take one somewhat farther than one really wanted to go—he was obliged to keep it. And in the month he'd been doing so, he'd developed for it, if not affection, at least a sort of respect and fellow feeling. There was a bum's pride in its refusal to ingratiate itself, an integrity in the way, once it had thoroughly licked his plate, it returned to its favorite chair with no show of gratitude whatever. It took what life offered and made the best of it. There were lessons, Becker thought, to be learned from this dog.

Vladek got up and switched on the TV. The evening news was in progress. U.S. and Soviet arms negotiators were meeting in Geneva. Portly figures in diplomatic grey traded handshakes without warmth and smiles without conviction. The voice-over, a commentator, high priest of the obvious, expounded his specialty in loud, portentous tones.

"Shit," Becker said. "Not that. Not *now*."

Vladek turned off the sound.

"Pictures without words." He grinned. "It can be entertaining."

Background film clips followed. A missile launch was shown, then shots from the previous year's May Day Parade in Red Square—squad upon squad of goose-stepping soldiers, punctuated at intervals by tanks and armored cars, huge rockets reclining on what looked to Becker like military versions of carnival floats. On the reviewing stand, a phalanx of ancient dignitaries were surrounded by grim-faced security men. At the rostrum, their Supreme Leader, with a chestful of medals and a fur hat crammed onto his coffin-shaped head, stood rigid as a waxwork, receiving and returning the salute. His eyes under heavy brows stared fixedly ahead; his features, impassive, showed just a suspicion of strain.

"Brezhnev has just farted," Vladek said. "He's an old man and his innards are full of gas. The pressure has had to be relieved. There wasn't, thankfully, a great deal of noise, and though the smell is powerful, those in the affected area have managed to keep a straight face. But Brezhnev is worried. Another utterance is on its way. Suslov is standing right behind him, and Suslov is the Party theoretician. So what Brezhnev asks himself, as the might of the Soviet Army marches past and the pressure on his asshole inexorably mounts, is this: Did the Party theoretician detect, in this latest statement by the Party First Secretary, anything not quite ideologically pure?"

Becker grinned absently. Against his will his eyes were drawn back to the parade, his thoughts to the mortal lunacy that lay behind it. Without the voice of the commentator to give them sense and weight, the images on the screen seemed insubstantial, ghostly. Parade of the Grand Illusions, Becker thought, the hundreds of divisions and thousands of megatons enlisted on either side, all marching in the service of some mad geometry, a "logic" of computer-simulated doomsday scenarios devised by people who, for the most part, had never heard shots fired in anger or seen a dead body, and for whom the jargon of their ghastly trade—"preemptive strikes" and "megadeaths" and "circles of destruction"—was, therefore, never quite real, abstraction but not obscenity. But it was his trade too, and indeed it always had been. He was part of it, as much as soldiers or tanks or missiles. He too was marching to the beat of that idiot drum.

Vladek poured the last of the wine. Catching Becker's eye, he raised his glass in formal salute.

"To the triumph of the Revolution, the success of your sacred mission, and your own health and happiness . . . Tovarich."

"Tovarich?" Becker gave a sour smile. "Why not Lieutenant, if you want to get technical about it? Lieutenant Nicolai Ivanovich Beranski,

KGB illegal, code name Igor, at your service. As to the success of my mission and my health and happiness, screw you, too. May you marry your girlfriend's mother.''

Vladek grinned. ''A gruesome thought. My girlfriend's mother looks like Suslov. . . . But tell me, Comrade Lieutenant, now that they've called you to the colors, what will you do?''

''What are my choices?'' Becker shrugged. ''I can run or fight. Which would you suggest?''

Vladek considered, lips pursed, brow furrowed, fingertips pressed together and supporting his chin. His thin hatchet face—the high cheekbones, beak of a nose, eyebrows like circumflex accents—was, Becker thought, quintessentially Slavic, only saved from severity by the tolerant mouth, the eyes alive with humor and intelligence. Vladek, as someone had once said, looked like Kafka, but without the anxiety.

When Becker had met him ten years earlier, he'd introduced himself simply as ''Vladek.'' Asked whether this was his first name or last, he'd grinned enigmatically, shrugged, and said, ''Yes.'' Later he'd admitted to owning initials, but by that time Becker had learned other things about him: that he dealt only in cash, that his business—he ran a detective agency—was ''sometimes illegal but never immoral,'' that his apartment was rented in his girlfriend's name, that his car belonged to a company which existed only on paper, and that his driver's license identified him as Thomas Hannigan. It hadn't been much of a surprise, therefore, when he'd explained, solemnly but with a hint of that enigmatic grin, that the initials, which were A.K.A., stood for ''Also Known As.''

The conclusion that he was a fugitive from justice turned out, however, to be incorrect. It was perhaps true that justice—or at least the judicial and fiscal branches of government—would have *wanted* to lay hands on Vladek had they known about him, but they didn't know. All they knew was that the person Vladek had once been, a staff sergeant in the Joint U.S. Public Affairs Office in Saigon, to whom he now referred, with absolute etymological precision, as ''my predecessor,'' had ended his existence during the Vietnam war. The 1968 Tet Offensive, he'd explained to Becker, had blurred the distinction between ''absent without leave'' and ''missing in action.'' Given that, the rest had been easy. Some weeks of hiding in a girlfriend's apartment in

Saigon, a false passport provided at moderate cost by a contact in the consular section of the French Embassy, a flight to Singapore in the British air attaché's plane, which, during its owner's absences on leave, was operated by his staff on a charter basis, and Vladek had been done with the army forever. "Missing in action" had in time become "missing presumed dead," and not even the general amnesty pronounced subsequently by a magnanimous Uncle Sam had tempted the staff sergeant to a resurrection. The amnesty, Vladek explained, was for draft dodgers and deserters, people pissed off with the war but prepared, now that it was over, to kiss and make up. His own case was different entirely. He wanted no charity from Uncle Sam, to whom, in the diplomatic sense, he no longer extended recognition. He and Uncle, he said, were through with each other for keeps.

This confession of a shared outlook and predicament (both of them were sailing under very false colors), confided to Becker after several years of friendship, had reinforced the effects of a shared temperament and a common cultural background; Vladek was—or had been—second generation American, ethnically Czech. They'd developed, in time, an absolute loyalty, the type that between men will often outweigh all other loyalties. *Someone*, it had seemed to Becker, had to be trusted with his secret; otherwise there'd be no part of him that was real. And if he couldn't trust Vladek who'd trusted him, he couldn't trust anyone. So he'd trusted Vladek. In sixteen years of exile it had been his sole indiscretion. So far he hadn't had cause to regret it.

"What would *you* do?" Becker repeated. "Run?"

Vladek shook his head. "Run now and you'll run forever. Your whole life you'll be looking over your shoulder. Even with no one there, you'll always be looking. I wouldn't want to live like that."

"Nor me," Becker said. "But what's the alternative? . . . Fight?"

Vladek eyed him levelly. "In your place some people might spy."

Becker stared.

"Not again. Last time was enough. I'd sooner be dead."

I'd sooner be dead. . . . Hearing himself, he caught an echo of his father, that other reluctant servant of an all-demanding state: "Becoming a private person is going to heaven. But to get to heaven, you have to be dead." Vanya himself had achieved that privacy, had retreated into memory to linger there, a familiar, comforting ghost. But his words, remembered, summoned other ghosts: familiar too, but restless and unreconciled . . . Brodsky, Weiner, Salzman, Hasek, Blok . . . guiding spirits of the class of '68, University of Prague, whose memory, for Becker, invested his past with its particular shame.

"I'd rather be dead," he repeated.

"I don't mean forever." Vladek smiled wryly; he knew about Becker's ghosts. "And not for real. I'm saying fake it. To buy a little time."

"Time? . . . Time for what?"

"To figure out how to fight," Vladek said. "You can't do it blind. You need to know what they want."

"I can't do it anyhow." Becker shrugged. "Not with any hope of winning."

"I disagree," Vladek said. "Take history, for instance. How come the English always manage to make out so well?"

Becker shrugged. "I don't see what the English have to do with it, but the answer would be geography, I'd guess."

"Irrelevant," Vladek said. "Or at best a minor factor. The real lesson to be learned from the English is this: Always make friends with the biggest kid on the block."

"The biggest kid on the block? Who do you mean?"

"In their case the U.S.," Vladek said. "In yours, the FBI."

"You're telling me turn myself in?" Becker stared. "Admit I'm a Soviet illegal? Ask for protection?" He shook his head. "You've got to be kidding. Their first thought would be to double me. Instead of spying for one side, I'd find myself spying for both."

Vladek shook his head.

"I don't think so. If you went to the CIA, sure. Doubling you would be almost reflex. But the FBI's business is catching spies, not running them. They'll want you to give them what you can, of course, so they can nab your control, plus a few contacts—bagmen or whatever—but then they'll want to tell the world about it. . . . You'll be their mystery spy celebrity, their big success of the decade, doing the rounds of the talk shows with a ski mask over your face. Selling your memoirs for a high six-figure advance. And in six months you'll be forgotten. The FBI won't need you. The KGB will have written you off. You'll be able to go back to playing with your computer."

"The KGB will have written me off?" Becker looked dubious.

"Those guys have long memories and a nasty way with deserters. What makes you think they won't want me dead?"

"The Feds will look after you," Vladek said. "They have to . . . '*Pour encourager les autres.*' "

" '*Pour encourager les autres*'?" Becker made a face. Vladek's logic struck him as unsound. If, to reassure other potential defectors, the FBI would feel obliged to protect him, what, by the same argument, would the KGB feel obliged to do?

"Look," Vladek said, "the thing is simple. You don't want to run. You don't want to spy. And you can't hope to fight without help. So get help. What other choice do you have?"

CHAPTER FOURTEEN

THERE WERE TREES BORDERING THE REST AREA: STUNTED ALDERS AND a few brooding elms, leafless now and motionless as sentries in the still October air; but otherwise the landscape was open and exposed. Farm country, flat and featureless, the dark fields stretching their furrows to the horizon in every direction. No cover at all, Becker thought; not even enough for a fox to hide out in.

But even so, he had the sensation of being watched.

They'll never be content with a piece of your life . . . His father's words came back to him, an echo reaching him across the gulf of years. Becker could remember him saying it, lying on the hospital cot, helpless as a child amid the tubes and bottles. His hair had moulted, and the skin, sweaty and pale as lard, was stretched against the skull as though the bone were everywhere waiting to break through. Only the eyes, bright with intelligence and a lifetime's enjoyment of irony, still belonged to Vanya; and it had seemed to Becker that what life was left in him had retreated and gathered there, to stage amid the ruins of his body a last futile stand. . . . "They'll never be content with that," Vanya had said. But Becker had been eighteen and in no mood to listen. The KGB offered special privileges, access to the finest hospitals in Russia. A few months had seemed a small price to pay to make dying easier for his father. So he'd shrugged it off. "Just Prague," he'd said. "Just one quick mission, then out." But to Prague, when the mission was almost completed, had come Major Lem with new instructions, making clear to him what should have been clear from the start: that one didn't resign from the KGB. He'd remembered then something else Vanya had told him: "I don't think it's possible to sell *part* of your soul to the devil."

He took out the cigarettes and stuck one in his mouth. But he didn't light it, and he wasn't going to, no matter what they said. He wondered why, exactly, they wanted him to smoke. Perhaps it was their contribution to this little piece of theater, a stage direction issued on the doubtful assumption that a man sitting at a picnic table in a rest area off the Pennsylvania Turnpike, smoking, was inherently less conspicuous than a man sitting at a picnic table in a rest area, et cetera, doing nothing. Such attention to detail, he recalled, was typical of them. But it was somehow also typical that they had overlooked something, a fact that to him was of some importance: He didn't smoke.

Or had they, in fact, overlooked it? He was inclined to doubt it. They seemed to know everything else about him. Enough, at any rate, to insist that he leave the Porsche at home and rent, for this journey, a Ford Fairmont from a Hertz Agency on Massachusetts Avenue. Enough, also, to tell him to bring the dog. And the rest area was deserted, had been since his arrival; to be conspicuous, surely, you needed an audience. So the order to smoke, probably, was less an attempt at camouflage than a test of obedience, a reminder of the rule of his training, a twitch at the reins.

He didn't need it. He remembered the rule, even remembered the words, just as he'd first heard them, as if the years between had never happened, or as if they'd been simply a dream from which he'd this moment awakened. If he closed his eyes he could even *see* Yashin— erect bearing, bowlegged cavalryman's walk, cropped bullet head with the stubbled chin and skin like old leather, eyes like polished pebbles— and he could still hear the rasping tones that had struck him then, and still did, as the very accents of authority: "You are soldiers. Never forget it. You exist for duty, survive by discipline. And discipline is a reflex of unswerving obedience. You don't question your orders; you follow them. Only in that will you find safety. . . ."

He *had* followed his orders. Or most of them. He'd rented the Ford— odd that they'd specified the agency and make—and he'd bought a pack of Marlboros and stuck one in his mouth. And he'd wait here until three fifteen, unless contacted, and then he'd turn around and go home.

But he hadn't brought the dog. It didn't like long car rides, tended to whine and scratch the upholstery. And anyway, it was best to start as you meant to go on. He was their agent—or he was for now—but that didn't give them the right to control every last detail of his life, to pollute his lungs with filthy smoke or dictate what he did with his dog.

They wouldn't be pleased by this show of independence. The training was designed, among other things, to intimidate. Behind the stern prescription for survival (". . . discipline is a reflex of unswerving obedience") there lurked, as he'd always recognized, a threat. And that was, of course, what this was all about. Nothing else made sense. He was clean, wasn't he? . . . a U.S. citizen with papers to prove it and no blemish whatever on his record. In the sixteen years since he had left Prague with the fatherly blessing of the British ambassador and the more material assistance of M16, he'd had no contact with anyone, done nothing to arouse the suspicions of even the most paranoid security service. The surveillance, if there had ever been any, must by now have been withdrawn. The file, for there had to have been a file, must surely have been closed. So there'd been no need for their tradecraft, no need for the trouble and risk they'd taken by hacking into his program. They could have accomplished the same thing by sending a postcard. And likewise there'd been no need to drag him out here, to the middle of nowhere, to issue instructions they could as easily have phoned. What this meant, of course, was that they *wanted* him to be nervous. That was the purpose of this tiresome charade. They *wanted* him to pace around remembering Yashin, to feel watched, to start watching himself, to experience anew the shades of anxiety to which his profession was subject. They wanted it because, anxious, he'd be easier to control, which meant they expected him to be difficult to control.

Which in turn, of course, meant they weren't sure they could trust him.

They showed up when he was about to leave. A blue Fairmont pulled into the rest area, swung past the picnic table, drew up next to the restrooms. A man in sunglasses, beige twill trousers, suede ankle boots, blue turtleneck sweater, jumped out and marched into the building. He was balding, and his head, slightly flat on top, sloped sharply back from the brow in a way that to Becker suggested Hungarian. The sunglasses and the speed of his march from car to restroom combined to frustrate a more detailed inventory of his features, but Becker did notice, perhaps because it struck him as odd, that he was carrying a newspaper. A minute or so later—a minute Becker used to memorize the blue Ford's license plate number—he emerged and got back into the car. Again, he moved briskly and without appearing to notice Becker. This time, however, he was not carrying anything.

The newspaper was in one of the stalls: a week-old copy of the *Post* with several sections missing. There was nothing inserted between the pages, but at the foot of the second page, in very faint pencil, were scrawled the words "glove compartment." Examination of his rented Ford's glove compartment revealed a scruffy sheet of paper covered with what appeared to be the result of chaining a monkey to a typewriter—groups of numbers and symbols randomly interspersed with letters, some capitalized, some not. It took Becker no time at all to grasp the connection between these hieroglyphics and the newspaper, but rather longer to form the suspicion that this paper chase they had sent him on might have a purpose other than intimidation.

The deciphering took more than an hour. The newspaper was the key, of course, the hieroglyphics in the glove compartment the message. It was a cumbersome code, but foolproof unless you had the key. Digits, depending on their position, referred to page numbers, line numbers, or word positions; all other symbols were spacers. A cumbersome, stupid code, and all the more so for being unnecessary. Computer message to set up dead drop, dead drop to pass coded message, coded message to set up secret meeting: the obsessive tradecraft of paranoia, Becker thought, a ritual entirely without point.

Unless, of course, the point were distraction.

He got the idea from the dog. Or rather from their odd instruction about it. At some point on the drive home, he remembered Sherlock Holmes and the dog that *hadn't* barked in the night. It dawned on him then that could be what they were after: not the dog's presence at the rest area, but its absence from the house. And if that were the case, the conclusion was elementary.

He began his search in the kitchen, moving later to the den, then to the living room, the bedrooms, and finally, though this struck him as excessive, to the bathrooms. He found nothing. Not behind the pictures, nor in the telephones; not on the tops of door frames nor the undersides of bookshelves, nor in fireplaces, nor anywhere else that his educated ingenuity could think of looking. By ten o'clock it was clear his conclusion had been too elementary. It seemed he was wrong about the dog.

He was eating a late supper when it struck him that, since his return, he hadn't seen much of the dog. In fact, he hadn't seen it at all. And that was odd, because he'd forgotten to feed it. Normally, when he forgot, it sought him out to remind him. It wasn't one to miss mealtime, its own or his.

Then where was it?

He found it in the Porsche, stretched out across the seat as if asleep. But there was blood on the sheepskin seat covers and splashes were congealed on the dashboard. Not a lot, he thought. Less, under the circumstances, than he'd have expected. And what this meant, presumably, was that someone had first shot the dog in the eye, and only afterwards cut its throat.

CHAPTER FIFTEEN

"POETIC JUSTICE," SERAFIN SAID. "IGNORE ORDERS, YOU'VE GOT it coming. He'll know better next time, I'll guarantee you."

Volkhov regarded him without enthusiasm. Serafin, he thought, was a living reminder of the truth of a witticism Stein had once, in an unguarded moment, permitted himself: "If America didn't exist, we would have to invent it." He'd meant, of course, that whatever else it might or might not achieve, the Cold War did provide employment, and often for people who were otherwise unemployable. Like Serafin, for instance, whose instinct for violence would, in any well-ordered world, earn him a trip to instant oblivion, but whose talents, in the world as it existed in this Year of Grace, 1984, were always in heavy demand.

"Justice?" He shrugged. "Possibly. Poetic? Hardly. Poetry speaks to man's yearning for light and order. You speak to other impulses entirely. The truth is, my dear Grigori Petrovitch, poetry and you have nothing to say to each other."

"I wouldn't know about that." This was ignorance, to judge from Serafin's tone, that he didn't in the slightest regret. "What I do know is, it was stopping me getting into the house."

"So in your usual impetuous manner you stopped it stopping you," Volkhov said coldly. "And only afterwards realized that you couldn't go in anyway, because by that time you'd so fully advertised your intentions as to make it quite pointless to carry them out."

Serafin looked reproachful. "But that's where I was clever, don't you see? . . . Oh, he'll look, I grant you, but he won't find anything."

Volkhov stared. "You expect me to congratulate you for that? For not planting bugs you knew were sure to be found?"

"He'll look, and he won't find anything," Serafin repeated. "And he'll relax. And so later, when there is something to find, he'll forget to look."

Volkhov considered. It wasn't what he'd had in mind, but perhaps under the circumstances it was better than nothing.

"You may have a point."

"You bet I do." From Serafin's pleased expression, it struck Volkhov, you'd have thought he expected a medal. "And whatever else, from now on we'll have his full attention."

"Oh, indeed." Volkhov restrained a sigh. "I think we can count on that."

PART II

"Ask not what your country can do for you; ask rather what you can do for your country."

John F. Kennedy—Inaugural, 1961

"Don't bother to ask, they'll let you know."

Vladek a.k.a. Vladek—conversation, 1984

CHAPTER SIXTEEN

IN THE BEST OF CIRCUMSTANCES BECKER HATED WAITING. AND HE'D
been here, in a rented van in the underground parking at the junction of
K and 12th streets, for more than twenty minutes. There was nothing to
look at but cars and concrete, and the noise, a continual echo in which
the separate sounds, human and mechanical, were mangled by the
acoustics into a single muted roar, was starting to get on his nerves. It
was white noise amplified, he thought, only worse—grey noise, like
being imprisoned in a giant concrete seashell. But he knew it wasn't
really the noise that was getting to him, nor the inactivity, nor the
tedium. What it was, really, was fear.

Fear was their tool. They meant him to feel it. And he must use that
knowledge to fight it. That knowledge and his anger. Only not stupidly,
not like last time, when his childish gesture of defiance had cost the dog
its life. He must use his fear calmly, to teach himself discretion; his
anger coldly, for revenge.

Suddenly, from behind him, there came a noise. Soft yet distinct, not
quite muffled by the echo. It came again, on his blind side, recognizable
this time, the quick scrape of a footstep. Then other sounds, sounds that
for twenty minutes he'd been expecting . . . click of doorlatch at the
back of the van . . . creak of hinge. Harsh grunt of exertion followed by
a thud that made the van shudder a little. Click of latch again. Then, in
the darkness behind him, breathing.

Don't look. His instructions had been adamant about that. *Don't turn around*. But all the same he found it hard, now that the moment was here, not to. It made no difference that he'd been expecting this arrival, had been straining his ears, in fact, for just such sounds. Someone unknown was in the darkness behind him, and he was filled with the need to turn and confront, the old feral instinct to protect his back.

"Good evening." The voice behind him was calm and pleasant, the English almost unaccented, with only a faint suggestion of Slavic. "You may call me Yuri. I shall be your control."

"Good evening." Becker managed to sound equally calm. He paused. "May I start by asking you a question?"

"Certainly."

"What happens if I look? . . . Do I get turned into a pillar of salt?"

Pause.

"Ah, the Czech sense of humor. I enjoy that." The voice did sound amused. "But of course these are routine precautions. Necessary for both our sakes."

"*Not* necessary," Becker said. "Time wasting. Insulting. You hack into my program, send me halfway to Philadelphia when a phone call would have sufficed. Now you don't permit me to see my control face to face. So I'm wondering what you're trying to tell me. That you don't trust me, perhaps?"

Another pause.

"Not exactly." The voice was unruffled. "But look at things from our point of view. You've been inactive for sixteen years. Twelve of them in the United States. It seemed only wise to approach you circumspectly. And at the same time, of course, to remind you of the need for proper procedure."

"Remind me of the need for proper procedure? That was why you killed my dog?"

There was a risk, Becker knew, in taking this tone. But it was natural, wasn't it? They'd bullied him, jerked him around, made no secret of their distrust. It would surely be odd not to show some resentment. What was called for, he thought, was half-hearted outrage, a *cautious* resentment that stopped sensibly short of defiance.

"Ah, the dog." The voice became bland. "I regret about the dog. I didn't intend that to happen."

"I too regret about the dog." It wasn't hard for Becker to keep his tone chilly. He paused. "Would it be out of place to ask what you did intend?"

More silence . . . There wouldn't be an answer, Becker thought, and he didn't really need one. But again it would have looked odd—wouldn't it?—not to ask.

"Would it be out of place"—the response, when it came, was like ice—"to ask why you chose to ignore your instructions?"

"It was *one* instruction. A detail, for God's sake!" Becker permitted himself a moment of bluster. "And I didn't ignore it, I forgot it. To hear you talk, you'd think we were at war. What happened to your sense of proportion?"

Pause.

"We are at war. At least, you should act as if we were."

"Of course," Becker said. "For us it's always wartime. We are soldiers. We must never forget it. Discipline is a reflex of unquestioning obedience. Only in that will our dogs find safety."

"So you remember Yashin? . . . In my time an excellent teacher, perhaps the best. I'm sorry to hear you show him so little respect."

Becker thought. It was time, perhaps, to come to heel a little. "It's not that," he said. "I respect the teacher and the training, and I made a mistake. I just wish the dog hadn't paid."

"Would you rather have paid yourself? You may if you keep on making mistakes. . . . My friend, there are plenty of dogs. If you want a dog, in this nation of animal lovers, you have only to go to the pound. People, on the other hand, aren't so easy to replace."

Becker said nothing.

"And this, I think, is the lesson to be learned from the dog. I hope, for your own sake, you have learned it."

"Indeed," Becker said. "The lesson is perfectly clear. . . . And now, I imagine, you have instructions for me."

"It'll never work," Becker said.

"Oh?" Volkov queried. "Why not?"

"You've been watching too many movies," Becker said. "The kind where some kid with an Apple hacks into the Pentagon's system and just about sparks off World War III. And maybe, once upon a time, something like that *was* remotely possible, but times have changed.''

Volkhov shrugged. ''We hacked into *your* program.''

''I wasn't trying to keep you out. Systems like this CIA one are lousy with safeguards. You have to know the passwords. Start fishing around, you just trip the alarms.'' Becker paused. ''And the worst of it is you don't *know* that you've done it. You only find out when the FBI knocks on your door.''

This made sense, Volkhov thought. He didn't know much about computers, but it was inconceivable, to say the least, that the CIA would want a system that *wasn't* massively protected. His suspicions of Igor, on the other hand, were beginning to take definite shape. Though he might be correct technically, his attitude was distinctly unhelpful.

''Are you saying you decline to take risks on behalf of your country?''

Becker shook his head. ''I decline to take *pointless* risks. I decline— shall we say—to be sacrificed on a mission that, as things stand now, has zero chance of succeeding.''

''As things stand at present?'' Volkhov queried. ''Does that mean that in other circumstances you'd concede a chance of success?''

Becker considered. What they were asking was virtually impossible, and nothing, short of having the passwords, was likely to change that. If they got the passwords, moreover, they wouldn't need *him*. On the other hand, he hadn't learned much beyond the fact that the KGB knew of the existence of a new CIA system. If he was going to bargain with the FBI for protection, he'd need to offer them more than this. He'd need at least to be able to tell them how much the KGB knew about the system.

''In certain other circumstances . . . yes.''

''What circumstances?''

''I might be able to go *under* the safeguards. But you have to understand that I will get one chance at that, and one chance only. I shall have to write a program that will build a trapdoor into the system, empty out the data, erase the audit trail, and arrange for the time I use to be billed to other users. And unless it works perfectly the first time, the CIA will know that someone has attempted to penetrate their system, and of course they will change it. The total result of my efforts will be ten to fifteen years in a federal penitentiary." Becker paused. "If I'm to make this attempt with any chance of success, I need to know more about the system. For example, what hardware they're using, how to patch into it, what language the program uses. Get me that information at least, and I could take a crack at it."

Volkhov thought. This too made sense. And, assuming that at some point Marigold returned from his unauthorized vacation, he could perhaps obtain such information. If they gave it to Igor, on the other hand, they'd be handing a hostage to fortune. In the CIA itself there could be very few with access to that knowledge. So if the CIA learned that the KGB had it, they'd be that much closer to identifying Marigold.

"I see," he said. "Unfortunately we don't have that information. And we don't know how to get it. . . . Have you any suggestions?"

There was a pause. It was difficult to tell, but Volkhov had the sense that the answer to his question, or the problem of *whether* to answer it, was receiving serious thought.

"Look," Becker said finally. "Let's not play games with each other. You know that there's a system because someone told you about it. Why can't you get the information from him?"

"Good idea," Volkhov said. "The problem is that he's dead."

CHAPTER SEVENTEEN

BECKER LIVED ON RIVER ROAD, IN THE STRETCH WHERE SUBURBIA strives to achieve a suggestion of the rural. Lot sizes here average more than an acre. Houses are set well back from the road. Horses are sometimes to be seen, cropping the grass in neatly fenced paddocks. And the sanctity of property is everywhere asserted by sturdy walls and wrought-iron gates. It is the kind of neighborhood, as Vladek observed on an early visit, where the professional classes, relaxing from their labors, aspire, on weekends, to the condition of gentry.

Becker himself had no such aspirations. In spite of the years he had spent in America, he tended to be oblivious to social considerations. In shopping for a house he had looked for space, privacy, and a large basement. When he found them available in his price range on the upper reaches of River Road, he'd ignored his realtor's enthusiasm for local society ("Such a *select* neighborhood, if you know what I mean.") and had gone ahead and bought.

Grigori Petrovitch Serafin, about to pay Becker an unannounced call, found reason to approve his sense of priorities. Horsiness and its social implications were matters to which he, likewise, was indifferent; space and privacy, on the other hand, were not. He was especially grateful for the thick hedgerow that fronted Becker's property and for the eighty yards or so of wilderness that stood between hedgerow and house. He was even more grateful for the miles that separated the house and the underground parking garage at K and 12th streets . . . At least forty-five minutes each way, he figured. More in rush hour. So allowing forty minutes or so for the meeting (Volkhov, by design, would be late) he could promise himself a minimum of two undisturbed hours. He doubted he would need two—he would be in and out, he guessed, in under one—but it was always nice to have margin.

And at least this time he wouldn't have to deal with the dog.

Arlen was angry . . . also hurt. Though for five days now she'd thought almost constantly about Becker, he, all too clearly, had thought very little about her. Why, otherwise, hadn't he phoned? Why hadn't he returned her calls? And why, above all, on the one occasion when she had managed to get through, had he been so guarded, so patently *not* pleased to hear from her, so *not* eager to see her that, cutting him off in midexcuse, she'd hung up on him, furious? She'd had to work, afterwards, at holding back her tears.

He'd been using her. But it had felt so right, she thought. She'd been so taken with him. With the way he moved. With the way he thought (his mind spiralling in on the subject as if in the hope of taking it by surprise). With the way he insisted on taking the left side of the bed (his *querencia*, he'd explained, deadpan, that part of the ring the bull had established as its territory and where, consequently, it was most danger-ous). With the way he was plainly aware of his charm, but without seeming overimpressed by it himself. Above all, she'd been taken with his air of being different, of seeming to hold out the promise that he'd be able, always and often, to surprise her. And that was the real letdown—wasn't it?—the discovery that he wasn't so different or sur-prising after all, that, on the contrary, his instincts were all too familiar. He'd made a conquest to gratify his ego; now he was ready to move on to the next. It was standard male operating procedure, drearily and humiliatingly so.

But on the other hand, was it? It was natural, perhaps, in this kind of situation, to interpret it in the way least favorable to oneself, but intuition took issue. Could one really be that mistaken about someone? Had all the pleasure he'd seemed to take in her company been simu-lated? Had his tenderness, especially in bed, been faked? She couldn't quite bring herself to believe it. She was almost sure he had genuinely liked her, perhaps even more than liked her. And hadn't there been at least a moment in that last phone call when he'd seemed to hesitate, had seemed on the point of dropping the excuses? She thought she had sensed in his voice something that was more than merely guarded, an overtone, suddenly, of real regret. Then something must have happened to change him. Something had come between them. Perhaps something in his life had suddenly gone wrong.

But if so, so what? Her first instinct, a knee-jerk response of her pride, was to say "so nothing." Whatever his reasons, he'd chucked her. It was his decision, his loss. She wasn't going to pester him to change his mind. But on second thought, how important was pride? Weren't there other things more vital? For instance, peace of mind. She would give it one last try, she decided. If it failed, he could stew in whatever sour juice he chose. But since this was no conversation to have on the phone, assuming she could get him on the phone, she would need to talk to him face to face. To do that she would have to catch him at his house.

Arlen liked to act promptly on her decisions. If she were going to do this, she told herself, she'd better do it before her courage left her.

That meant now.

Actually, as Serafin conceded later to Volkhov, you couldn't really blame the screw-up on Fet. Fet had been working lookout, granted, but what happened had been an accident of timing, one of those inconvenient and actuarially implausible coincidences, which in the real world had a habit of happening more often than statistics might lead you to expect. When the woman's 280Z had come barrelling up the road, at a speed, Fet estimated, of well over sixty, Serafin had been on the point of making his exit. Because he'd had his hands full, he'd turned off the walkie talkie and put it in his bag. He'd expected to be out of contact with Fet for less than two minutes, and had thought—though "thought," in Volkhov's opinion, was perhaps a generous description of his mental processes at that point—that nothing much could happen in that time. What happened was that the 280Z, braking sharply, had turned without giving a signal and was halfway up Becker's driveway before its intentions had registered with Fet. When they did, he'd attempted to alert Serafin, but hadn't, of course, been able to raise him. All of which was why, as the woman was emerging from the 280Z, Serafin, tools in hand, was emerging from the house. One look at him had been enough to make her bolt, but she hadn't moved fast enough.

Impetuous. Overinclined to violence. In the postmortem these, once again, were the terms used by Volkhov to describe Serafin's actions. But as Serafin argued in his own defense: "She could have got us arrested. What the hell was I supposed to do . . . surrender?"

CHAPTER EIGHTEEN

CONSCIOUSNESS, FOR ARLEN, WAS AT FIRST A MATTER OF PAIN: SHE
was face down in gravel; there was grit in her mouth; her head hurt.
Recollection, following swiftly on pain, added fear. Someone had attacked her, knocked her out. Some man. Where was he? She raised
herself onto an elbow, looked around. The movement made her head
threaten to explode, sent shivers of nausea through her body, but the
pain now was accompanied by a flooding sense of relief. He was
nowhere to be seen. He was gone. She was safe.

She celebrated by throwing up.

Presently the nausea subsided. Her head cleared somewhat. Inspection confirmed that her injuries were slight, and memory supplied her
predicament with a context. This was *Becker's* driveway. She'd come
here to have things out with him. And a man, a man not Becker and
carrying what had looked like a toolbox, had been coming out of the
house.

A burglar? She didn't know why, but instinct told her not. The
toolbox, the look on his face when he'd spotted her, the fact of his
having attacked: these all argued forcefully that his business in the
house had not been lawful. But something, some recalcitrant detail,
which she couldn't at the moment quite put her finger on, seemed to
rule out burglary. She didn't for the time being pursue the question. It
didn't seem important. In any case, it wasn't her problem; it was a
problem for the police.

94

She should call them. Her first thought was to find a phone or, better yet, roust out a neighbor. The act of standing up, however, was enough to cast serious doubt on her ability to drive. Then she noticed that the front door was open. Easiest to call from Becker's phone, she thought. She could trespass on his hospitality, perhaps, to the extent of cleaning herself up in his bathroom. And afterwards, since she really was feeling rather wobbly, she'd lie down and wait for the police.

It occurred to her that Becker might be inside.

But he wasn't. And he hadn't, she was almost immediately sure, been robbed. Her intuitive objections to the burglar thesis were confirmed as soon as she entered the house. It was too tidy. She'd been burgled herself, once, and the memories of her first appalled perceptions of the fact were vivid. Burglars *trashed* places. Her apartment had looked as if a hurricane had hit it. Becker's house, though not exactly neat, showed only the normal bachelor disorder. No pictures broken, no curtains torn, no smashed crockery, no clothes scattered about, no books and records all over the floor. Nothing, moreover, appeared to be missing. None of the obvious things, anyway. The TV and stereo were present, likewise the VCR. And this all squared, she thought, with her recollection of the man who had hit her. He'd had the tool kit—hence her immediate suspicion—but he hadn't, or at least not visibly, had any loot.

But if not a burglar, then what? Her imagination, always active, could supply a number of ingenious hypotheses, but, absent evidence, they were worthless. Someone searching for something? Some industrial rival after Becker's work? Someone bugging the place? She didn't know, couldn't know. The only safe conclusion was that Becker, perhaps without knowing it, was involved in something extremely odd. And since it was Becker and not she who was involved, perhaps *he* should be the one to call the cops.

She would wait for him then. Explain why she was there and what had happened. It would give her, at least, an entry into the more delicate subject she had come here to broach. In the meantime, she would clean herself up. That and—now she was reminded of it, her head really hurt abominably—lie down.

She lay down for about an hour. When the throbbing in her head subsided, she was bored. She got up and wandered around. This made the throbbing start up again. Perhaps if she read something . . .

In the bookshelves she spotted an *Alice in Wonderland*, which Becker had mentioned as one of his favorites, an original English edition with the Tenniel illustrations. She pulled it out of the shelf and began to flip through it. On the flyleaf, she noticed, were several inscriptions, two in Cyrillic script and therefore presumably Russian, the third in German. The German appeared to be a dedication. It was addressed to "Kolya," dated "Kiev, 1967," and signed "Mutti."

This third inscription intrigued her. It was a link with Becker's past, a tiny rip in the fabric of the present, through which one might glimpse that other world where he'd once lived a wholly other life. It was a document, like some she'd run across in her research, whose few words—here in ink in a bold archaic hand—would be, to the right reader, radiant with meaning. It was one of those particles of irritant fact, like the atom of grit at the heart of a pearl, around which accretions of memory would gather. Not *her* memory, of course. Instead she would need logic and imagination. She didn't expect them to take her far, but they were better than nothing.

Kolya . . . The diminutive, she recalled of the Russian Nicolai. Or in German, Nicolaus; diminutive Klaus. So Kolya, presumably, was Becker, and the book a gift from his mother—secondhand, evidently, and very precious, for how easy could it have been in postwar Europe to find an English first edition of "Alice"? She had a vision of Becker's mother—whom for some reason she imagined as a kind of Chekhovian peasant, with a scarf round her head and bast leggings—scouring used bookstores for a gift for her son. But used bookstores *where*? The flyleaf said Kiev, but in 1967 Becker had been—or hadn't he?—in Prague, that city of baroque architecture and cobbled streets in which even then it had been possible to hear, or so she imagined, the distant rumble of tanks. So what had his mother been doing in Kiev? And why had she written in German? She'd been Russian, and Becker was fluent in the language; wouldn't she naturally have written in Russian?

It was a mystery. One of a series of mysteries, each small in itself, but in sum perhaps not so small, that seemed to be gathering around this interesting man. The burglary, for instance, that didn't look like one. The inconsistencies of detail in the accounts he'd at different times given of his past. (Was it, for instance, his mother or his father who'd been Russian?) Now this apparent discrepancy—only apparent, of course, since the inscription might not have been written to him—between those accounts and what seemed to be fact. And all of this, she was starting to believe, led up somehow to the larger mystery—in her priorities at least—of the abrupt change in his behavior towards her. It was more than ever clear, she thought, that she needed to have things out with him.

She was able to do so sooner than she'd expected. She was still standing there inspecting the flyleaf, when, from behind her, someone spoke. The words were Russian. The speaker—on hearing the words she instantly whirled around to confront him—was Becker.

She was good, Becker thought, very good; one had to give her that. Her start on hearing him was genuine, of course, but the rest, obviously, was acting and magnificent. The speed with which she slipped into her role was breathtaking. The startled turn, the look of apprehension that became, when she saw him, a smile of relief, the switch into puzzlement when he went on speaking Russian: It was all perfect. Better yet was her reaction, or lack of it, to his words. No flush of shame, no resentment in the eyes, no physical response whatever. One could almost believe she hadn't understood what he'd said.

He repeated it.

"What are you saying?" Her stare suggested he was out of his mind. "Why do you keep talking to me in Russian?"

"Of course." He smiled sardonically, switched to English. "You claim not to speak it. . . . I'd forgotten."

She continued to stare. "I *don't* speak it."

"Then perhaps I should translate. What I said was 'What are you doing here, you little whore?' "

She responded as if he had struck her. Her eyes flashed anger and resentment. Her head jerked back, bringing the left side of her face into the light. He saw the graze under her eye, the split lower lip, the purple bruise along the side of the jaw. *Somebody*—in part of his mind the knowledge provoked a tremor of uncertainty, but he was too angry to heed it—*had* struck her.

"How dare you?" she demanded. "How dare you call me that?"

He looked at her, shrugged. "A whore, in my understanding, is someone who uses her body for gain."

"You think I did that?"

He nodded.

Her eyes searched his face. The anger was out of them now. Replacing it was something he couldn't quite name, something steady, unselfconscious; not an emotion at all, perhaps, but instead a state of mind. She looked—he was reminded suddenly of his first impression of her —she looked like someone with nothing whatever to hide.

"I see. In that case perhaps you'll tell me what you think I did. . . . But first, if you don't mind, I'll explain what I'm doing in your house."

Anger, Becker thought, had made him stupid. Returning from the meeting with his control, he'd been naturally in the frame of mind where he *expected* the truth to be bitter. Now, calmer, he could ask himself how it was possible to be so dumb? How could he have overlooked—to hindsight it seemed almost wilful—so much that so obviously didn't square with his logic. But he'd been so disgusted, he thought, so depressed by everything, and especially by the futility, the sheer unforgivable *frivolity* of the scheme they proposed to involve him in, that when he'd seen her car in the driveway and the front door open, he had instantly leaped to a conclusion whose sheer unwelcomeness had seemed to guarantee its truth. It just figured, he'd thought; when you looked at the whole thing coldly, the pieces simply sprang into place. The timing, for instance. The fact that it was she, originally, who'd made the approach, she who since then had made most of the running. And the clincher, of course, was the meeting downtown to get him away from the house, the idiot business with the rented van, the elaborate, time-wasting tradecraft. The whole thing had been arranged so she could poke around at her leisure. And *he*—the irony of it had made him utterly savage—had been worried about *her*. He had tried to protect her, had wanted to spare her the deceit, and all the while *she'd* been the spy. It figured, he'd thought. It figured perfectly.

But now he could see problems. Not ones she had urged—she had urged nothing—but problems his own calmer thinking proposed: Why, for instance, had she let him catch her? Bad planning? It was possible, he supposed. But in that case, what about her undoubtedly genuine injuries? Self-inflicted, maybe, to give her a story if she happened to be caught? Hardly. Unless you were willing to accept the nonsense of her being smart enough to plan, but not smart enough, as she rummaged through the house, to take an occasional look at her watch.

In any case, he thought, it wasn't a matter of logic or evidence. Now that he'd recovered his wits, he just knew. There was something about her that went beyond acting; a quality of truth that reproached his suspicions, revealed them as paranoid, mean-spirited delusions and accused *him*, instead, for entertaining them.

"I seem to owe you an apology."

"An apology and an explanation." She nodded calmly. "The apology had better be abject, and the explanation had better be good."

CHAPTER NINETEEN

"ACTUALLY," ARLEN SAID, "YOU DON'T *HAVE* TO EXPLAIN."

Becker was silent. What he had to do, he thought, now that he'd got her out of the house and out of range, presumably, of whatever bugs they had planted, was find out how much she knew, or how much she thought she knew. Then he'd know how little he could tell her.

Arlen went on, "That man wasn't robbing your house. He was searching it. Or bugging it. When you found me there, that's what you thought I'd been doing. And that's why you spoke to me in Russian. You thought I'd . . ."—she faltered, coloring—"you thought I'd tried to get close to you so I could spy on you." She paused and stared at him accusingly. "Because that's what *you* are, isn't it? Some kind of spy."

He met this without blinking. "What *you* are is someone with too much imagination."

"Am I?" she challenged. "Then maybe you do have some things to explain."

"What, for example?"

"Your reactions, for example. . . . I tell you I've been mugged by a man coming out of your house, and you hardly bat an eyelid. You don't check to see if you've been robbed. And calling the cops, which would be any normal person's first reaction, doesn't even seem to cross your mind."

She waited, cocking an eyebrow. "You're used to people breaking into your house?"

He ignored this.

"You said *things*. . . . What other things?"

She shrugged. "How about this little nature walk we're taking? Your obvious anxiety over getting me out of the house? We could have talked more comfortably there. . . . Or couldn't we?"

The dusk was drawing in. Already the air held a nip of frost. Damp was soaking through the soles of Becker's shoes. He looked around. The lane was deserted, the surrounding fields apparently empty. But only for now, he thought; they wouldn't stick around after clobbering Arlen, but they'd be back. That was as sure as death and taxes. They'd be back.

"Explain that to me." Her voice was bitter. "Tell me I'm imagining things. Tell me I *wasn't* knocked on the head, you *didn't* think I was snooping back there, you *didn't* expect me to understand Russian." She paused, looked away, seemed to struggle for control of herself. "Go on, tell me. Tell me I haven't fallen for a spy."

Tell me I haven't fallen for a spy. . . . The words seemed to offer, for an instant, a glimpse of a different world, a world bright with possibility . . . a world where he wasn't a sleeper, code name Igor, where there wasn't a permanent KGB lien on his future, where he still had choices. In such a world, this woman and he might be left alone to explore the new continent of their feeling for each other. But it wasn't real, he thought. Or rather, the new continent might be there, but they'd never get to explore it. He was stuck in this shadow world that called him "Igor," and there was no room at all in it for her. In fact, he must get her out of it at once, for the house was now undoubtedly bugged, and enough had been said there, perhaps, to arouse the interest of his KGB masters. And if they ever got to know what she suspected about him, they'd kill her.

He reached out to take her in his arms, but she shook him off.

"I don't want to be hugged. I want to be told the truth."

"I can't tell you the truth."

"So it seems." She stared. "I wonder why."

"Couldn't you trust me?"

"*Trust* you? . . . You must be joking!" Her anger flared, then faded. "God, how I wish."

"Try. Listen, at any rate."

"Listen to you tell me the truth why you *can't* tell me the truth?"

"Just listen," he urged. "I can't tell you because it's not safe for you to know, because it's not even safe for you to be around me. You've got to understand. Those people are dangerous. If they heard me talking to you now they'd kill you."

She didn't seem to take it in. She was listening, he saw, but not to what he was trying to tell her.

"Then you are a spy."

He shrugged. "They want me to be."

"They . . . You mean the Russians?"

He nodded.

"And you don't want to be?" She thought for a moment. "That's it, isn't it? They've got some kind of hold over you. People in Czechoslovakia they'll harm if you don't help them?"

People in Czechoslovakia they'll harm . . . The irony stung him, summoning once more the ghosts of his past—Brodsky, Salzmann, Wiener, Blok, Hasek. People in Czechoslovakia they *had* harmed; people *he* had harmed. Ghosts who now surrounded him, accusing, forming yet another barrier between himself and her.

"That's not exactly it, but close enough." A small lie, he thought. A white lie. Or if not white, then grey. In any case, this was no time for explanations. "It's not important, anyway. What's important is you. . . . The way things stand, they've no reason to think you're anything but a bystander, someone who just happened to get in the way. So long as they keep thinking that, you're safe." He paused, steeled himself to say what, for her sake, had to be said. "What I want you to do is get in your car and drive off, forget you ever knew me."

She stared. "You want me to leave? Forever? Just like that?"

He nodded. "That way they won't even know who you are."

She thought for a moment. "And us?" she asked quietly. "What about us?"

"There is no 'us'," Becker said. "There can't be. Not now."

"And our feelings? . . . Don't they matter?"

He was silent.

"Feelings," she said. "You never mention them. It's as if you don't find them worth talking about. Or as if they don't exist. So I'll have to ask. Don't you feel anything?"

Don't make me say it, he thought, please don't make me say it. . . . But he knew he would have to. Because talking about the danger wouldn't be enough. Because in her pride, or courage, would always be stronger than fear.

"*Don't* you?" she insisted.

"No," he said. "Nothing real. . . . I'm sorry."

She didn't speak.

"Look." He forced himself to meet her gaze and hold it. "Don't get me wrong. It was good while it lasted, really good. But it was never worth dying for, and now it's over."

Her eyes continued to hold his. There might have been tears starting in hers, but if so she held them back.

"Then I guess I should thank you for your honesty," she said.

She looked at him a moment longer, then turned and walked off up the lane.

CHAPTER TWENTY

VOLKHOV REWOUND THE TAPE OF HIS CONVERSATION WITH BECKER, removed the cassette from the machine, dropped it into his pocket. On his return from the meeting with Becker, he'd found a note in his office instructing him to report immediately to the Resident. Though he'd wanted a word with Serafin first, he'd judged it wise not to keep his superior waiting. In her note, the word "immediately" had been underlined.

"You see," he told her. "He's not at all stupid."

She eyed him with displeasure. He seemed to be happy to be the bearer of bad news. Not that he let it openly show in his manner. Just, perhaps, in a certain smugness of tone, the suggestion that if this thing *were* to go wrong, it wouldn't be wholly unexpected by him, nor, indeed, wholly unwelcome.

"And what do you conclude from his not being stupid?"

"Mostly that we must handle him intelligently. We shouldn't count, in other words, on sheeplike obedience to orders. There may be a wolf in this sheep's clothing. Or at least,"—Volkhov smiled—"a fox."

She gave him a long stare. "I appointed you to control him, Major. Are you telling me now that you can't?"

Volkhov shook his head. "I'm saying it's not intelligent to back him into a corner, to force him into something he feels has no chance of success. If we do, I suspect he'll behave as I'd behave: nod my head and drag my feet; say yes and do nothing. And of course,"—Volkhov smiled—"in his place, I'd be looking for somewhere to hide."

104

She considered this. "You mean he might defect?"

"I'd expect it to cross his mind."

"But perhaps that expectation says more about you."

He looked weary. "I think what it says is that I, like him, am not stupid."

"So you're saying we have to get him the information he asks for?"

"If we want him to go after the CIA system." Volkhov nodded. "And of course the information will have to come from Marigold. And getting it, and giving it to Igor, will place Marigold at risk." Volkhov paused. "What I'm saying, Colonel, is it may be time to reevaluate your plan."

So *that* was his game: mishandling the sleeper so as to scare her into scrapping the operation. She studied him for a moment. The bland features gave nothing away. The habitual air of self-satisfaction, being here more than usually inappropriate, had been traded for one of mournful sincerity, but the eyes, little black marbles, were inscrutable as ever. It wouldn't work, she thought. Indeed, he'd played more than ever into her hands. It would be easy now to convince Moscow that he'd lost his judgement and nerve. There would be no more fleshpots for Major Volkhov. He'd be back to Dzerzinskii Street and a bit of real work for a change. And she would no longer have to endure his second guessing, this leftover from an earlier regime looking constantly and critically over her shoulder.

"What did you make of the sleeper, personally?"

Volkhov shrugged. "You heard the tape. . . . Personally, I don't like his attitude. He was unhelpful. Also, I think, insubordinate in tone."

"He was angry about the dog. To be frank, Major, I think you blundered there. I wouldn't call *that* intelligent handling."

She'd hoped to jolt him, at least into shifting the blame, but he just pursed his lips and nodded.

"In retrospect I agree with you. It's the sort of thing, of course, that either works well or fails badly. . . . With most people,"—he gave a faint smile—"it works very well."

"But in this case," she pressed the attack, "it might account, at least, for his lack of enthusiasm."

"That's also true." He was silent for a moment. "It occurs to me, Colonel, that this may have compromised my position as control. If we go ahead with this, it might be wise to replace me. . . ."

She ignored this provocation.

"Have you verified his technical objections?"

"I'm in the process of doing so. I've asked Kasparov to cable Moscow," Volkhov said. "I expect to learn that they're reasonable."

"Then, if so, it seems we must give him what he asks."

He nodded. "Either that or abandon the project."

She regarded him coldly.

"Let us understand each other, Major. I am assigning this project the highest priority. I have no intention of abandoning it. Nor do I propose to let myself be persuaded by foot dragging on the part of the sleeper or you. If Moscow confirms that the sleeper's requests are reasonable, you will immediately instruct Marigold to set about obtaining the information." She paused. "And for your sake, he'd better not drag his feet, either."

Which was all very well, Volkhov thought when he reviewed his situation later. Only Marigold was still missing. And he couldn't afford to tell the Resident so, because that would involve the admission that he'd previously kept her in the dark. The alternative of keeping his mouth shut and hoping that Marigold would show up involved, of course, an even greater risk. But it seemed to offer his only chance of coming through all this with his own career intact. He could put the sleeper on hold till he got the reply from Moscow, and then at least *shuffle* his feet a little by observing to the letter—under the circumstances, surely, no one could fault him for that—the normal procedures for contacting Marigold.

He figured it might buy him about a week.

CHAPTER TWENTY-ONE

SINCE DAYBREAK, UNDER COVER OF THE MIST, BURNSIDE'S MEN HAD been moving up. From Marye's Heights, you could hear but not see them—hear shouted commands, bugle calls, the rumble of gun carriages, staff officers' horses clattering through the streets. And beneath it all, like a pulse, the steady tramp of approaching columns—II Corps, Crouch's command, spearheading the assault, with Kimball's brigade in the lead: parallel columns in perfect order, weapons at the right shoulder, officers with drawn swords marching alongside. Then, about midmorning, when the regiments were all in position, as if at a prearranged signal, a breeze sprang up. The mist rolled back, and to the watchers on the Heights the whole magnificent pageant was revealed: Burnside's advancing army and the lines of waiting defenders spread out below like pieces on a chessboard. And that was the moment when Lee, torn between triumph and pity, was moved to turn to his staff and exclaim: "It is well that war is so terrible . . . We would grow too fond of it."

And that, Stoneman thought, was the moment he was after: that hushed pause before the onset, before order gave way to confusion, before poetry was lost in the arithmetic of battle, before Kimball's columns, reaching the bridges at the dike, encountered that concentrated, withering fire from the defenders dug in beyond the sunken road. . . . For a moment, in his mind's eye, he could see it all perfectly, every feature sharp, as if he'd actually been present. The topog-

107

raphy and terrain were exact down to the individual trees and bushes; the disposition of troops and artillery precise; the horses, weapons, uniforms accurate to the last detail. But then, as always, under the probings of his practical sense, the picture cracked, broke apart, and he was left with ill-matched pieces—and problems.

That question of scale, for example. Reduce *everything* enough for the whole battlefield to be fitted into the barn, and the figures would become insignificant, too tiny. Cheat with the scale, on the other hand, and there wouldn't be room for all the figures. Besides which, there was the question of time, the constraints imposed by his having only one pair of hands and rather less, under normal actuarial assumptions, than half his life remaining. Several thousand troops had been engaged in that one sector of the battle alone, and the arithmetical implications of that were daunting. At the present rate of progress, it would take ten or fifteen more *years*, at least, just for the figures. So realistically, he'd need to cheat with the scale *and* the numbers. Also, probably, on the detail . . . Compromises, he thought; how he hated compromises. They were reasonable, of course, necessary; but you could only compromise so much before you destroyed the whole point of the thing. Because the whole point was *not* to be reasonable. You wanted people to be stunned; first by the sweep of the thing, then by the sheer, preposterous wealth of detail. You wanted them awed into silence by the same arithmetic that had sandbagged you, not to be making allowances for the limitations of your stage. You wanted them to see what you saw, what Lee had seen on that crisp Virginia morning in 1862, when, at about the last moment in history before warfare lost touch altogether with chivalry and honor, he'd exulted in his coming victory and at the same time mourned the cost.

"Mr. Stoneman . . ." The voice of his secretary in the outer office snapped Stoneman out of his reverie, removed him from the battle of Fredericksburg and the model he was building in the barn on his property in North Carolina, and returned him to his office in Washington D.C., where the pile in his In-tray reminded him that he also was engaged in a battle, though a far less romantic one—a ceaseless struggle to monitor the activities of certain foreign diplomats in the city.

"Mr. Stoneman. I have this call on the line. Someone who won't give his name. Switchboard put it through . . . Do you want to take it?"

"Who is it?" Not, he instantly realized, the most intelligent of questions, but part of him was still at Fredericksburg; the words were out before he'd thought.

"It's Mister Anonymous, first name unknown." Her voice acquired an edge of irritation. "He won't even say where he's calling from."

"Well, will he say what he wants?"

"He wants to talk to someone responsible." Her tone suggested that this he—whoever he was—had in that case come to the wrong department. "He *says* he has information which may be of interest to us."

Becker didn't *think* he'd been followed. There'd been a green VW bug behind him part of the time on the George Washington Parkway, but it hadn't acted like a tail. It had made no effort, at least, to conceal the fact of its presence and had left him when he'd turned off at Key Bridge. Since then, though he'd kept an eye glued to the rearview mirror, he'd spotted nothing.

Which didn't mean, of course, that there *was* nothing. There could be a pack of them out there with two-way radios, boxing him front and back and trading places so that no car stayed in one place long enough to be noticed. He could take evasive action, of course. If it achieved nothing else it could force them, if there were a "them," into the open. But maneuvers such as doubling back or making an abrupt unsignalled turn on amber from the wrong lane might help resolve *his* uncertainty, perhaps, but only at the cost of also resolving theirs. To anyone watching, this part of the trip must look casual, innocent. Evasive action would not look casual or innocent. Evasive action, therefore, was out.

But in all probability there was no one watching. For while it was clear that they didn't trust him, it was also clear that their distrust, since he'd done nothing as yet to earn it, must mostly be based on instinct. And since, if they *had* decided to watch him, they couldn't know exactly what they were watching him for, they would need to watch round the clock and very carefully. But that kind of watching, given D.C. traffic and parking conditions, meant a minimum of three teams, each of at least four vehicles and twice as many men. And while their organization in Washington was no doubt very extensive, he seriously doubted it was quite as extensive as that. But on the other hand, he could be wrong. And since being wrong could be hazardous to his health, what he had to be now, as he approached his destination, was very, very careful. It was paranoid, perhaps, but better paranoid than dead.

And being paranoid meant doing things right. You learned to listen for the footfall at your back, for the over-profound silence. You learned to look back without turning your head, to loiter while seeming to hurry. You learned to notice everything, especially the inconspicuous. And you learned above all not to trust yourself too much; that your feeling of security was the surest indication of hazard, since it was what you didn't hear, didn't see, didn't sense, that in all probability would kill you. . . . You assumed, in other words, that you were always under surveillance. And if you needed not to be, you took steps to shake it. And if you wanted to shake it without seeming to know it was there, without even being able to risk finding out if it was, what your training prescribed was a filter.

He left the Porsche in the basement garage of an office building one block east of the hotel. There were four levels, and although there were spaces open in the upper levels, he descended to the lowest. Two women in a grey Volvo had been behind him at the entrance, but they parked, he noticed, on the third level. A bank of elevators connected basement and lobby, and when he reached it an elevator was waiting. At the third level it stopped to admit two women. Presumably the two from the grey Volvo, he thought, giving them a quick appraisal. They were expensively dressed and over made-up, had the air, characteristic of American women of a certain class and age, of being carefully gift-wrapped, though in their case, he suspected, the wrapping made promises on which the gift would not deliver. They eyed him in what stuck him as a predatory manner. They didn't *look* like members of a KGB surveillance team, but of course you wouldn't expect them to. In any case, he'd never dream of relying on looks.

In the lobby he made for the newsstand where he browsed through *Playboy* for a moment before buying a copy of the *Post*. The women, he saw, were waiting for an elevator. He paused in the entrance of the newsstand and flipped through the pages of his paper, glancing at headlines without really taking them in, listening for movement from the direction of the elevators and surreptitiously scanning the lobby. There was nothing new in the news, anyway. Tax reform blocked by objections from special interests; negotiations under way for the resumption of arms control meetings (talks about talks about reducing nuclear weapons to the point where each side had only twice the number needed to wipe out life on the planet); the NRA continuing to oppose pending handgun control legislation . . .

An elevator arrived and the two women got in.

He strolled over. When the next elevator came, he took it. A man in a grey pinstripe suit followed him in, also a young woman carrying coffee and doughnuts. The man's pinstripe suit was of polyester and slightly shiny, representing, Becker thought, a flat contradiction in sartorial terms. It was the sort of suit, perhaps, that a newly arrived KGB heavy might have bought, fondly believing it the last word in chic. On the other hand, since the cut was American, there were evidently natives with the same impression. The young woman was ruled out by her load; surveillance teams, after all, didn't go into action armed with coffee and doughnuts. He caught her eye and smiled. She smiled back. These people were no more KGB than the women from the Volvo had been. He'd have bet money, in fact, that there were no KGB within miles. He'd have bet *money*, but the stakes here were rather higher. In any case, his object was to eliminate gambling. The purpose of filters was to purify the air.

Polyester pinstripe pushed the button for the sixth floor, the young woman the ninth. Becker omitted to select his floor until the elevator was moving. When it reached the third floor, he punched the button for the fourth.

No one followed him out.

The fourth floor housed a secretarial agency and a law firm. No one was in the corridor. At the far end was a door leading to the emergency staircase. This, as a prior reconnaissance had informed him, led down to the alley that separated the building he was in from the back of the hotel. He made the emergency staircase without being seen and took the four flights of stairs at a leisurely pace but cat-footed. He met no one. The only problem now was the alley.

It was hard, after so long, to feel properly paranoid, to make himself treat it all—this tiresome business of loops and filters—with due respect. In Prague it had been different; he'd been just out of the training school. The conditioning had been new; the anxiety retained its edge.

And Prague itself had been a city of shadows, a maze of narrow streets and cobbled alleys in which it had seemed you could always hear behind you the echo of a footfall, dying into silence. In the summer of '68 the air had seemed charged with conspiracy and menace. Washington, by contrast, was too open, too modern. It lacked echoes. In its bland sunlight his maneuvers seemed silly, a melodrama without an audience, the solemn observances of an obsolete religion.

And of course there was no one in the alley, either. A delivery van drove off as he peered cautiously out from the fire exit, but otherwise the place was deserted. He strolled across to the service entrance. Vladek had obtained the key to Suite 314, so there was no need to stop at the desk or show himself in the lobby. He took the service elevator to the third floor, accompanied, part of the way, by a Hispanic-looking woman carrying blankets who smiled at him shyly but seemed to find nothing odd in his usurping her elevator. There was no one in sight when he reached the third floor.

Vladek had left the blinds drawn, the suitcase under one of the beds. The gun was in the suitcase, wrapped in a bath towel: a Spanish automatic, .32 caliber, silencer attached. Becker checked the magazine: seven shots, all present and correct. He replaced the magazine and sighted down the barrel at his own reflection in the mirror, aiming between the eyes and imagining how the image would shatter when he fired. But the thought merely heightened his sense of having wandered onto the set of a movie. It was hard to imagine circumstances in which he would actually use this gun, hard to think of himself as being engaged in anything other than a game. And it was dangerous, he knew, this mood of playing, because in the crunch it could make him hesitate.

They were not playing. To convince himself of that, he had only to remember the dog.

CHAPTER TWENTY-TWO

ARRIVING AT THE HOTEL, STONEMAN CONTINUED TO ENTERTAIN DOUBTS. Anonymous calls, most often, were crank calls. Most likely the guy wouldn't show, and he, Stoneman, would have wasted an hour of his time and $7.50, plus tip, in cabfare. On the other hand, there was something unusual about *this* anonymous caller. He'd spoken for one thing, with a certain authority. Though invoking no fears of wiretaps or assassins, he'd declined to discuss his business on the phone, had suggested instead that Stoneman show up, within the next sixty minutes, at Suite 315 at the————hotel, ask for a Mr. Hansen, and produce, upon arrival, convincing ID. The hotel, when consulted, had confirmed that Suite 315 was indeed rented to a Mr.Hansen. So Stoneman, doubts or no, had decided the thing was worth looking into. If it *was* a hoax, it would be no big deal. The nation would survive, at a pinch, the loss of an hour of his time, and the Bureau, last he'd heard, was good for the cabfare. And when you remembered that the Pentagon's annual budget was now close to three hundred billion, there wasn't much point, he felt, in worrying about waste.

Since he knew the room number, he bypassed the front desk, made his way through a lobby of gilt and crystal, leather and dark velvet, to the bank of elevators on the far side. Hoax or no, this was an interesting choice of hotel: discreet opulence rather than the noisy anonymity he'd expected. On the whole, this made a certain amount of sense. It was the kind of place, with the staff outnumbering the guests, where individual

113

comings and goings were likely to be noted. When you were worried about your safety, discreet opulence and an attentive staff were vastly preferable to noisy anonymity.

An elevator, operated by an old and dignified black attendant, took him to the third floor. This consisted of a single corridor, dimly lit and darkly furnished, serving, apparently, only four suites. The numbering system, in view of this, struck him as eccentric, but Suite 315, he discovered, was at the far end. The corridor was deserted.

He walked up to 315 and knocked.

No answer.

He knocked again.

This time he heard a noise behind him. Turning, he saw that the door to 314 had opened a crack.

"Looking for Hansen?" A quiet voice issued from the darkness within.

Stoneman nodded.

"In here," the voice said.

The door shut. From inside, there came the rattle of a chain. Then silence.

Stoneman went over and knocked.

"It's open." The voice inside sounded remote, as though it were coming from one of the inner rooms.

Entering, Stoneman found himself in a sitting room furnished in the by now familiar combination of gilt and dark velvet. Since the curtains were drawn, the only light came from a standing lamp on the far side of the room. Next to it were two gilt and plush chairs, in one of which sat a youngish looking man. He was dressed informally—Levi's, boots, and a dark blue polo-neck sweater—and his features struck Stoneman as faintly Slavic; they combined, at least, a broad face, strong jaw, and high, rather prominent cheekbones. The hair, a dark shock of it, fell into brownish-hazel eyes that were focussed, very intently, upon Stoneman. A pleasant enough face, Stoneman thought, and not, by the look of it, the face of a crank.

Nothing about the man suggested eccentricity, indeed, except perhaps for the gun he was pointing at Stoneman.

"Will you close the door please, and put the chain back on the hook?"

Stoneman looked at the gun. He didn't move.

"No," he said coldly. "I don't believe I will."

Silence.

"I don't like games," Stoneman said. "And I don't like guns. You want to talk, you'll have to put it away. Otherwise you'll find yourself talking to the wall."

More silence. The man seemed surprised, but not very. He looked, in fact, mostly embarrassed. He kept the gun where it was, however, and his eyes never moved from Stoneman's face.

"Let's compromise," he said finally. "if you're not who I think you are, I may need this. So how about I see some ID, and *then* I put it away?"

Stoneman reached into his inside breast pocket, withdrew his wallet, and pitched it over. It fell at the man's feet. The man reached down to pick it up, flicking it open to glance at the ID.

"This looks all right." He kept his gaze on Stoneman. "But IDs can be faked. Is there a number I can call?"

"Sure," Stoneman said. "But if I weren't from the FBI, you'd be dead by now. Since I got here you've made nothing but mistakes . . . sitting in plain view of the doorway, under the light, letting me go for my wallet . . . I mean, how did you know it wasn't a gun?"

Again the man looked slightly embarrassed. "That's true," he said soberly. "I remember now . . . Don't offer a clear shot. Make the other guy shoot with the light in his eyes. Don't let his hands out of sight. Make him lie down if you have to search him. . . . It's just hard to get back into it. Hard to make yourself take it all seriously. And that's the worst mistake of all, of course. They used to stress that all the time: 'Never relax. Never *ever* forget your training.' "

"Your training?" Stoneman queried. "And who provided this training?"

"The KGB, of course." The man looked surprised. "And now, perhaps we could call that number?"

"Let's be sure I have this straight," Stoneman said. "You claim you're a KGB sleeper . . ."

"*Was,*" Becker corrected. "I've never done any actual spying, here or in England. I want that on the record."

"Which record is that?" Stoneman asked.

"The one in that tape machine you're wired up to," Becker said. "The one with the microphone doubling as your tie pin."

"Got you." Stoneman smiled thinly. "You *were* a KGB sleeper. Never activated. You came here via England a dozen years ago with instructions to infiltrate the computer industry and lie low, pending instructions. You've done that, but in the meantime you've decided you don't want to be a KGB sleeper. So now you've been activated, you've come to us. That an accurate summary?"

Accurate but unsympathetic, Becker thought. Accurate but unfair. The description of his career in computers as "infiltration" ignored, at any rate, its spirit. But on the other hand, he thought, this attitude wasn't surprising. Any time now, the bargaining would start.

"Reasonably accurate."

"And of course,"—sardonically—"you can provide corroboration?"

Becker shrugged. "I've already given you facts you can check. . . . The SIS officer in Prague, presumably, kept a record of assistance rendered to dissident Czech students at the time of the Soviet invasion. There should be some mention of a certain Nikolaus Beckendorf, who was subsequently granted political asylum in Britain and given a scholarship to London University. . . . I can also give you the license plate number of the car that showed up at the rest area. I can even give you the section of newspaper I found in the john there and used to decode the message in the glove compartment. Also, of course, the message." He paused. "I'm afraid I can't show you the body of my dog. I buried him."

"No need to get snippy," Stoneman said. "You'd be surprised at the number of people who call us claiming to be KGB agents."

Becker shrugged. "I'm not offended. I just don't want to waste time. If I'm not what I claim to be, how could I know what I've told you?"

Stoneman gave another of his smiles. "You haven't actually told me much. And even that's subject to verification." He paused. "In any case, if you are a KGB agent, it creates a whole new set of problems. . . . I'm afraid, Mr. Becker, that you're going to have to get used to answering questions. Whether they seem pertinent to you or not." He shot Becker a sharp glance. "You understand why, of course?"

"Sure," Becker said. "You think I could be a double."

"Exactly . . . Under the circumstances,"—Stoneman smiled—"a not altogether unnatural suspicion. . . . So perhaps you won't mind, before we go any further, if I ask a couple of personal questions?"

Becker shrugged. "Go ahead."

"What made you change?" Stoneman asked. "You left Prague, you say, committed, fully intending to carry out your mission. . . . What brought about the change of heart?"

Becker had been expecting this. Vladek had asked the same question. But Vladek knew him, so with him the answer had been easy. He'd just said, "I saw my first computer," and Vladek had rolled his eyes, and no further words had been needed. But trying to explain to this Stoneman, with his disapproving manner and cynical smile, would be like trying to convey to a cash register the sensation of falling in love. Yet love was what it had been, he thought. Not with the computer itself so much, though even today he recalled it with affection—an antiquated affair of punched cards, vacuum tubes, and flashing lights that had occupied most of a sizeable room and had needed the full-time services of several tons of refrigeration equipment, to keep it from melting—but with the world it had drawn him into. What had really hooked him was the excitement, the almost audible fizz of exhilaration given off by the people who worked with those early machines. And those people, seeing the smitten look on his face and knowing immediately that he was one of them, had taken him in and thereby changed his life.

It had happened in England. That was where he'd learned the meaning of freedom. The true meaning, of course, not the conventional one; it had nothing to do, at any rate, with policemen who smiled or with idiots on soapboxes at Speakers' Corner. What he'd learned had been the freedom of the unrestrained intelligence; of people hacking cheerfully into the unknown, exploring this brand new world of fantasy governed by logic, and not in the expectation of any pay-off, but in pure curiosity to see where the journey would lead: people designing chess programs, people messing with robots, people devising elegant solutions to obscure problems in topology, people working thirty-hour days and subsisting on junk food and coffee in order to dream up, write, tinker with, and constantly improve programs that played Bach fugues, simulated cell growth or intergalactic warfare. Later, of course, money had come into it, and the innocence had been lost. But in the beginning, for all of them, it had been just love and playing. But he could never hope to explain this to Stoneman, because Stoneman belonged to what was known as "the real world," an accountant's world of cost effectiveness, and comparative advantage, where love was not an admitted motivation, nor was playing, where there was no such thing as a free lunch. So instead he said:

"America changed me. . . . I was nineteen when I left Prague. I'd been raised in Russia, brainwashed into accepting the system. I didn't know what I'd been missing. America showed me. It offered me freedom, opportunity, the chance to succeed through work and talent, to own my own house, to have a job I enjoy, to accumulate investments, to drive a Porsche . . ."

He looked at Stoneman. Stoneman was wearing his faint, fastidious smile.

"You find that unconvincing?"

"Not unconvincing," Stoneman said. "Unappetizing."

Screw you, Becker thought. Aloud he said, "Any more questions?"

"Just one." Stoneman paused. "You're offering information which, if genuine, may be useful. . . . Obviously you want something in return. What is it?"

"Help," Becker said.

"What kind of help?"

"Physical protection . . . short term. I don't flatter myself they'll bother me for long. But when they find out I don't plan to cooperate, I don't expect they'll be happy. . . . To judge from what I've seen so far, there'll be attempts at coercion, perhaps vindictiveness."

Stoneman considered.

"Physical protection . . ." He looked dubious. "That's not so easy. Not effective physical protection. It means a safe house, round the clock baby-sitters. Those things are expensive." He paused. "I'll tell you what I think you'd better do. For now, go along with these people. Let them think you're going along. Don't precipitate matters, in other words, until I've had time to talk to my people, see if we can work something out."

"Work something out?" Becker said. "Work what out?"

"I dunno." Stoneman looked vague. "What *else* can you do for us?"

"You'd want more? . . . More information?"

"Information?" Stoneman made a face. "Sixteen years out of date? I was thinking of something more practical."

"You mean help you nail some of them?" It was what Vladek had predicted. Becker thought of what his masters had done to Arlen, what they *would* do if they found out what she knew; what they'd do to him. "I'd be happy to do that."

"Good," Stoneman said. "That'd help . . . for a start."

"A start?" Becker stared. "What the hell else do you want?"

"Who can tell?" Stoneman shrugged. "You know the saying. There's no such thing as a free lunch."

And that, Stoneman thought later, having returned to his office and instructed his secretary to transcribe the conversation, had been exactly the tone to take with the fellow. For if his story could be believed, he was not just a spy but a mercenary to boot. And someone who'd been bought once could be bought again. In any case, there was no telling at all how far to believe him. He was a spy, after all, and spies, whether for you or agin you, were unreliable people. General Lee, he recalled, had held them in contempt.

CHAPTER TWENTY-THREE

"A COMBINATION OF UNLUCKY CIRCUMSTANCES."

Volkhov didn't comment. He had commented already, and at length, on Serafin's confrontation with the woman who'd seen him emerging from Becker's house, and saw nothing to be gained by repeating himself. More to the point, he'd also made a note of Serafin's personal file, with some cutting remarks about people who made a habit of being unlucky. He'd been conscious, at the time, that if things kept on the way they were, the same remarks would be made about him. Marigold was still missing—how much longer, one wondered, could the lid be kept on *that*?—and this business with Igor had been botched from the start. It was obvious that from here on they would have to regard him as hostile. Which didn't mean, of course, that he couldn't be used.

"Play the tape again."

Serafin did. It was like listening to Chekhov, Volkhov thought; a dialogue of intentions left unstated, significance packed into shrugs or pauses, the real action happening largely offstage. And to make it more difficult, you couldn't see the actors. Without faces, gestures, looks, body language to give them substance, the exchanges on the tape seemed curiously flat. But not altogether unrevealing. There had evidently been something between Becker and this woman. They'd been lovers, evidently, yet when he'd found her in the house he'd immediately questioned her motives. *And he had spoken to her in Russian*. But then, when she hadn't understood, the subject had been very promptly dropped. Or rather, not dropped, but shelved. But afterwards, when one might have expected a return to it, that hadn't happened. Or rather, it hadn't been allowed to happen. Instead, and almost physically it seemed, he'd hustled her out of the house.

"What do you make of it?"

Serafin shrugged. "At first, when he speaks in Russian, he seems to think she's working for us. Then after she tells him about me, he changes his mind. By that time, presumably, he's guessed what I was doing in his house." He paused. "What's interesting to me is what they *didn't* talk about."

Volkhov nodded. "Or what they didn't talk about there."

There was a short meditative silence. . . . One could say this for Serafin, Volkhov thought; he wasn't stupid. And there was often a serendipity to his bad luck. Perhaps that fact should also be placed on the record.

"I would remember her if I saw her again," Serafin said.

Volkhov considered.

"He may have confided in her, which would make her dangerous. And he appears to care about her, which could make her useful." He paused, nodding. "I think you're right. I think we must interest ourselves in her."

CHAPTER TWENTY-FOUR

"NICE OFFICE." HOLLISTER LOOKED AROUND. "BIG. COOL. HIGH High ceilings. Windows that open. Whatever did you guys do to get such nice offices . . . dig up some dirt on the chairman of Ways and Means?"

The admiration sounded almost genuine, but above it, barely audible, there were overtones of mockery. Stoneman, looking around himself, was assailed by a spasm of irritation. Normally he was oblivious, or indifferent, to his surroundings. But now, seeing them, so to speak, through Hollister's eyes, he found his attention drawn to their shabbiness, to the worn patch in the carpet near the doorway, the cobwebs festooning the ceiling fan, the dust on the bound volumes of *Law Reports* in his bookshelves, the streaks of grime on the walls and windows. Which, of course, was what Hollister had intended his attention should be drawn to; it was the reason for the touch of irony, or condescension, in Hollister's manner. Hollister felt himself to be slumming, so his manner indicated, slumming and being gracious. While he, on the other hand, was being hypersensitive, which he always was when he had to deal with Hollister. . . . Christ, he thought, how quickly the bastard gets under my skin!

"Nice, my ass." As he spoke he was conscious, though without knowing how to avoid it, that he was somehow playing into Hollister's hands. "Too hot in summer. Too cold the rest of the year. Crummy lighting. Plus the elevators never seem to be working. Actually, the place is a dump.''

And the worst thing about it right now is that *you*, Mr. Anthony Hollister III, are in it. But why are you in it? he wondered. What fetches you out of your rathole in Langley? . . . Fishing, he thought; somehow, the son of a bitch has heard something.

"Coffee?" he enquired.

"Is it decaf?"

"No," Stoneman said. "It's coffee."

"Then no coffee." Hollister shook his head. "Thanks anyway."

Candyass, Stoneman thought.

There was a short, meditative silence.

"So . . ." Stoneman said. "To what are we indebted?"

Hollister grinned. "Indebted is right. I'm here to do you a favor."

"Forget it," Stoneman said. "We don't want any favors."

"You want this one," Hollister said. "At least, your *boss* said you did."

Shit! Stoneman thought. Goddamn Borden again. He said nothing.

"I'm here to offer what you guys have always lacked," Hollister said. "Imagination."

"Imagination." Stoneman made it sound like herpes. "So *that's* what we've always lacked. Last time it was initiative."

"That too." Hollister grinned. "But chiefly imagination. I mean, here's someone hands you the chance of a lifetime, and what do you do? You start looking for ways to turn a small profit."

Stoneman said nothing. Goddamit, he thought. Why couldn't Borden, just once, resist the temptation to crow?

"Nothing wrong with a small profit. It's nothing to sneeze at. Not in these times of hardship. And better a small profit, as my dad used to say, than the goddamn Bay of Pigs."

Hollister gave him a pitying look. "Your dad. For Christ's sake spare me your dad. What was he? A dirt farmer in the Depression? . . . With that kind of philosophy, it's a safe bet he died broke."

Stoneman nodded. "He did, as a matter of fact. Started broke and ended up broke. Broke even, you might say. Whereas your dad . . .''
He paused, eyed Hollister with distaste. . . . Ur-CIA, he thought; the foundation pattern, correct to the last detail: winter suntan, pearly smile,

perfectly cut grey flannel suit, shirt of pale blue pinpoint oxford, paisley tie, and wingtip brogues with the kind of deep-down luster that only years of elbow grease, not Hollister's of course, could account for. "Whereas your dad, I would guess, inherited half of downtown Philadelphia and left *you* nothing but expensive tastes."

Hollister shrugged. "Might we suspend the discussion of ancestry and get on with the business at hand?"

"Fine with me," Stoneman said. "You had some point you were trying to make. About imagination, I think."

Hollister gave him a thin smile. "About your new defector, actually. About how, unless someone helps you, you're going to screw this one up, too."

Fuck you, Borden, Stoneman thought. Just fuck you. Someone should shove your umbrella up your ass and open it prior to withdrawing.

"*My* defector? What makes you think *I* might have a defector?"

"Your boss," Hollister said. "Your boss played golf with me day before yesterday at Congressional. And he mentioned you had a defector. So I thought for about half a second, and I realized that you guys, left to yourselves, would undoubtedly be boring and blow it. And I thought that would be a pity."

"So you made a suggestion to my boss."

Hollister nodded.

"And?"

"And your boss liked my suggestion."

"Doesn't he always?" Stoneman rolled his eyes. "And?"

"And . . ." Hollister paused, smiled with utterly infuriating smugness. "Your defector is now *our* defector."

"*Our* defector?" Stoneman had known it would be something like this. Had this been simply a fishing expedition, Hollister would hardly be looking so sassy. "Do you mean 'ours' as in 'yours and mine,' or 'ours' as in 'reserved for the exclusive use of the Central Intelligence Agency'?"

"The former, of course." Hollister looked hurt. "When have we ever been piggy?"

"Shit!" Stoneman said.

"Don't take it like that." Hollister grinned. "Look on the bright side. I know you wanted him all to yourselves. But now, instead of a hundred percent of nothing, you'll have half a share in a killing.''

"A killing?" Stoneman was reminded of the last time he'd dealt with Hollister, also about a defector, and of the outcome. Hollister's people had handled the debriefing, and the man had killed himself, whether from remorse or anxiety had not been clear. In any case, all the debriefing had netted was a handful of tapes of scant intelligence value and a corpse, slowly twisting on a length of extension cord in the stairwell of a safe house in Bethesda.

"I was speaking figuratively," Hollister said.

"Of course." Stoneman's voice was like chalk.

Silence.

"To be serious for a moment," Hollister said, "let me guess how you were thinking of using him. Straightforward counter-intelligence, right? Let him run for a while, set up a little discreet surveillance, watch what comes out of the woodwork? Then *maybe*, if you got a little lucky and nobody fucked up, you hoped to catch yourself a few spies. . . . That *was* it, wasn't it?"

Stoneman shrugged. "Something like that."

"*Something* like that?" Hollister queried. "Don't you mean something *exactly* like that? . . . The old tried and true. The classic Bureau game plan: grind it out on the ground, a yard or two at a time, never stopping to wonder why you never get into the end zone. Epitomizes what one might rightly call 'the small profit mentality.' "

Stoneman nodded. "I can see how it might. I guess we must seem kind of dull. Especially to you aerial circus types from Langley who make a habit of what one might rightly call the long *bomb*." He paused and gave Hollister a sardonic look. "I'm sure you know what I mean . . . the fifty-yard pass, just slightly underthrown, gets intercepted on the five and returned downfield for a touchdown. Seems to me you guys wrote the book on that one."

Silence.

"You know," Hollister said, "we might get done a little sooner if we cut some of this shit out."

Stoneman nodded. "That's sort of what I was thinking myself."

"Then perhaps we could start by taking a look at how many spies you can realistically hope to catch. Three, would you say? Maybe four? A bagman, maybe. A couple of spear carriers. The case officer, if you're lucky . . . Big fucking deal.''

He looked at Stoneman. Stoneman said nothing.

"And what happens then? The case officer has immunity, so all you can do is boot him. The Soviets find themselves short a cultural attaché, or whatever, and replace him in due course with an economic attaché or an extra member of the trade delegation or whatever, and we're all back to square one. And as for the bagman and the stooges, you can squeeze them a tad, I suppose, but *they* ain't going to give much because, as you know and I know and they know, we'll need to exchange them before long for some of ours. . . . I mean, let's face it, all you're doing is running in place. It's just a fucking joke.''

So what's new? Stoneman thought. All we *ever* do is run in place. Catch one spy, you just open a slot for another. Stop catching them, on the other hand, and the bastards bury you.

"So what's your idea? No, don't tell me; let me guess . . . You've come up with a scheme to end the Cold War.''

"Nah . . .'' Hollister grinned. "That's too easy—send Leonid and Nancy out on a date. Besides, why would I want to end it? You either, come to that? The Cold War pays my bills.''

It pays my bills, Stoneman thought, but then, I don't have a rich wife. I doubt it pays for your annual ski vacation.

"What is it then, this bright idea of yours?''

"Simple, really. Misinformation.''

"Misinformation? . . . Jesus.'' Stoneman looked disgusted. "Is *that* what you call imagination? Bigger and better lies?''

"Sure,'' Hollister said. "Instead of catching some low-grade spies they'll replace before you can blink, leave your guy where he is to feed them high-grade shit.''

"High-grade shit?''

"You know the kind,'' Hollister said. "The kind that if you eat it gives you food poisoning.''

Which was all very well, Stoneman thought later, but as he'd complained to Borden, not very specific. A small but tangible triumph for the Bureau, a chip you could bargain with at budget time, had been traded for some undisclosed benefit to the Agency, some pot of gold at the end of a very long rainbow. But Borden had gone along, of course, because Borden was an insecure snob, impressed beyond measure by Hollister's wife's money, his English suits, his membership at Congressional, his habitual air of superiority. In answer to Stoneman's hard-minded doubts, Borden had merely waffled about cooperation and the need to avoid a "narrow parochialism of interest" (and whose phrase was *that*? Stoneman wondered). In the end, Borden had more or less given the defector to Hollister. Hollister would run him, at any rate. Stoneman would hold "a watching brief."

A watching brief . . . Another of Hollister's phrases, no doubt. But apt, this time, because Stoneman, whatever Hollister's intentions, planned to watch this one very carefully. For among all the interesting things Hollister had told them, there had not been—Stoneman was almost sure of it—much truth.

CHAPTER TWENTY-FIVE

"YOU SEE," HOLLISTER SAID. "SOMETHING CAME OUT OF THE WOOD-work."

"He seems to be real." Sherwood nodded, handed Hollister the cable from London. "At least his cover is. We've confirmed the general outline of his legend for his time in the U.S., and for the years before that we applied to the Brits. Told them we were vetting him for a clearance upgrade and were therefore interested in the circumstances of his exit from Prague. His version checks with theirs at every point. He belonged to an anti-Soviet student group their Embassy had contact with. When the Russians invaded, most of the other ringleaders were arrested, but somehow he managed to make it to the Embassy. Later, when the heat had died down a bit, the local SIS man smuggled him over the border. Their people in London helped to resettle him." He paused. "*Somehow he managed to make it to the Embassy*. The Russians want to establish a sleeper, so they get the Brits to help write his legend. Jesus, is that typical, or what?"

"It's typical of the Russians," Hollister said. "They're good at taking what the situation offers. And the Czech situation in 1968 was, in certain respects, ideal. Wherever there's upheaval, there are always guys like us, dropping a line into troubled waters." He shrugged. "They arranged for us to catch something: an anti-Soviet student dissident who was actually a KGB sleeper. Saved them the trouble and cost of infiltration and more or less eliminated risk. Prague in late August of

128

'68 was utter turmoil. There must have been thousands of refugees like him. You can't blame the Brits for failing to spot what he was. I doubt we'd have done any better.''

"So here we have a genuine KGB sleeper, certified by the Brits. But still . . .'' Sherwood hesitated, decided to risk a flyer. "But does that mean, necessarily, that he's a genuine defector?''

Hollister looked thoughtful. "What else would he be?''

Sherwood thought. "Could he be simply a probe? The Russians weren't sure they should buy what we tried to sell them with Conlan, let's say, so they've sacrificed a sleeper to find out what's on our minds.''

"Is that *your* idea?'' Hollister's face was expressionless.

"Yes. . . . Is it dumb?''

"It's not dumb. In fact, quite the reverse. You're starting to think like a pro . . . in circles.'' Hollister grinned. "Vicious circles . . . In this case, however, I don't think you're right.''

"A good try. No points.'' Sherwood smiled wryly.

"He's too good to be sacrificed,'' Hollister said. "Or at least he's too good to be *merely* sacrificed. I mean, think about it. How many sleepers can the KGB have with Ph.D.s in computer science, and flawless, SIS certified legends stretching back sixteen years? There was no obstacle, none, to his ultimately landing some ultrasensitive job . . . with the NSA, for example, or a defense contractor. . . . I just can't see them wasting an asset like him on a probe.''

"Nineteen sixty-eight . . .'' There was awe in Sherwood's voice. "They've been planning this for more than half my life. Nineteen sixty-eight was my first year at summer camp. I was ten years old, still collecting baseball cards. This Becker was nineteen. . . . Do they *always* plan that far ahead?''

Hollister nodded. "They're incredibly patient. Unlike us, they think historically. Where we think in years, they think in decades.'' He paused. "They weren't planning *this*, however. With sleepers they seldom have specific targets in mind. They recruit them, train them, set them up with a legend, infiltrate them, then they wait. Sooner or later a target will come into view.''

"Like the Agency's new computer system.'' Sherwood grinned.

"I think so,'' Hollister said. "I think they must have bought into

Conlan just a little. The bait we offered was too juicy to pass up, and they happened to have this sleeper, ideally placed to go after it. He was valuable, but not nearly as valuable as their mole. So they risked the sleeper and protected the mole. Or, at least,'' he amended, ''they *thought* they were protecting the mole.''

''Thought?'' Sherwood queried.

''That's the beauty of this situation,'' Hollister said. ''If I'd planned it myself, it couldn't have turned out better. The sleeper has been ordered to break into the Agency system. To get under the safeguards without tripping the alarms, he needs, as he told his control, some basic information about the system. This information is highly classified, restricted access, and to get it they have no choice but to use their source in the Agency . . .'' He paused. ''Do you see what I'm getting at?''

''Sure.'' Sherwood nodded. ''We already have a short list of suspects. The information our sleeper needs is highly classified, so we simply put a watch on the file. If any of our suspects seeks access to the file between now and the time our sleeper hears back from his control, we'll know who to go after, won't we?''

''Elimination.'' Hollister nodded. ''It's usually the name of this game. Eliminate all of the suspects but one . . . then eliminate him.''

Sherwood considered. ''It's still a bit iffy,'' he objected. ''What happens if more than one of our suspects seeks access to the file. What happens if two or even three do? . . . We'll still have some eliminating to do. How do we do it?''

''Same way as before,'' Hollister said. ''The sleeper is a pipeline between us and the Russians. Through him we can know what they *want* to know about us, also what they *do* know. So this time we offer some information, let it slip inadvertently to someone on our new, reduced shortlist of suspects. If it gets to the Russians, we've trapped ourselves a mole; if not, we know we're looking at one of the others.''

''Offer them information?'' Sherwood was puzzled. ''But what information?''

''The sleeper,'' Hollister said. ''The sleeper is the information. We let them know, through the mole, that the sleeper has defected.''

''I see.'' Actually Sherwood wasn't at all sure that he did. ''But how will we know if they've received the information? I mean, they'll hardly tell the sleeper that they know.''

"Right,'' Hollister said. "They won't tell him, they'll tell us.''

"How?''

"Let me ask you a question.'' Hollister's face was a mask. "Knowing what you do about the KGB, how would you expect them to react to the news that their sleeper had been doubled?''

"How would I expect them to react? Oh . . .'' A great light dawned suddenly upon Sherwood. "I'd expect them to kill him?''

"Yes.'' Hollister said. "It's what I'd expect, too.''

CHAPTER TWENTY-SIX

WHEN BECKER ENTERED THE PHONE BOOTH ON F STREET IT WAS eleven-eighteen. At eleven-twenty—Stoneman had stressed the need to be exact about time—he dialed the number Stoneman had given him. It was not a local number, and the area code, he'd noted, was for Virginia, a fact which, though not necessarily sinister, had caused him a twinge of misgiving. After two rings, a recorded voice said:

"Digital Information Systems. Thank you for calling. All our lines are busy now. At the tone, please state your name and business, then stay on the line. Someone will be with you shortly."

"My name is Swanson," Becker said. "I'm calling about my credit application."

There was a pause, punctuated by squeaks and buzzes. Computer checking the voiceprint, Becker thought. Recorded music began to play, an irritating music-box tune that was no sooner finished than repeated and might have been chosen, Becker thought, precisely in order to discourage staying on the line. After a minute another voice, not recorded, said:

"Thank you for waiting, Mr. Swanson. Your credit application has been approved. The paperwork is ready for signature at our office at 43 K Street."

Becker hung up. Credit application? Paperwork? Who the hell dreamed these things up? he wondered. This business had hardly begun and already it was starting to get tiresome. While the meeting with Stone-

132

man's people, for instance, would take at most half an hour, the preliminaries to the meeting—consisting, in essence, of a casually elaborate obyssey that took him from his house to the center of Georgetown by a route designed to make life easy for the sweepers but not for him, and the phone call he'd just made to confirm that the sweepers had encountered no KGB surveillance—had already wasted the better part of the morning. Tradecraft, he thought wearily, was mostly elaborate bullshit dreamed up by a bunch of emotionally retarded clowns. It could strike you as funny, only while you were laughing the clowns would sometimes creep up on you and kill you.

Which was why, before he went to this meeting, there was one last bit of elaborate bullshit to attend to.

Vladek was already in the café, reading the paper at a table by the door. He didn't look up when Becker entered. Becker ignored him, went straight to the men's restroom. He was happy to see it was empty. Entering the third cubicle from the left, he locked the door, took a stub of pencil and a scrap of paper from his coat pocket, wrote "43K 1150" on the paper, licked one side of it, then inserted the paper in the cardboard tube that formed the center of a toilet roll. Then he urinated. On his way out—because it was always possible that when he got to the meeting he'd be searched, and writing implements were always viewed with suspicion—he dropped the pencil into the trash.

An unscheduled stop . . . But if they asked, he could always plead an unscheduled need to answer the call of nature. And since Stoneman's sweepers, in addition to checking for KGB surveillance, had surely been told to keep a sharp eye on him, an unscheduled pit stop at a nearby café was safer than leaving the note for Vladek in the phone booth, and a lot safer than making unscheduled calls on a line that might very well be bugged.

It might all turn out to be trouble for nothing, of course, but as Vladek said, in these days of herpes and AIDS it was always wise to know who you were getting into bed with.

Though they'd been in the van long enough to have driven halfway to Philadelphia, it was possible to wonder, Stoneman thought, just how far they had actually travelled. He'd met Hollister, by arrangement, in the bar of a Holiday Inn. They'd ingested a swift drink. A minion had stopped by to murmur that the area was "sanitized," then they'd taken an elevator to the second floor and the emergency staircase to the basement garage, where a van had been waiting. They'd sat in the back while, for close to an hour, they'd been driven somewhere. Quite where, Stoneman wasn't sure, since the back of the van had no windows at all, but he'd noticed that they'd seemed to turn a lot. Their tortuous journey had ended in the garage of what looked like a private house, but since they'd entered directly from the garage and gone straight to a room in which all the curtains were drawn, there'd been no way to guess their whereabouts. He'd been tempted to needle Hollister about all this, but in fairness he hadn't. Reverse the circumstances, he thought; there was no way he'd have given away the location of a Bureau safe house to Hollister.

The morning's only real mystery was what Hollister wanted with this defector.

Becker studied the two men confronting him. Stoneman, as before, looked professorial, disapproving. This new one, on the other hand, with his faultlessly cut pinstriped suit, cream silk shirt, paisley tie, and Gucci loafers, looked like a diplomat or an investment banker. But beneath the surface, you could sense, Becker thought, both a lot more intelligence than the surface suggested; and the predatory instincts of a shark. Though Stoneman had introduced him as a colleague, the antagonism between them was as palpable as the difference in style. If this one worked for the FBI, then he, Becker, was a Jehovah's Witness. It was not hard, on the other hand, to guess who he *did* work for. . . . "Pick powerful allies," Vladek had said, and this new one, whatever else, radiated power. But his power seemed unlikely to benefit Becker much. An alliance assumed mutuality of interest. In this case, it was clear there wasn't any.

"No," he said.

"No?" Pinstripe affected surprise. "What do you mean by *that*?"

"I mean no," Becker said. "As in 'negative.' As in 'I don't have any interest in working for the CIA.' " He paused. "That is what we're talking about, isn't it?"

Pinstripe ignored the question.

"You want help, in other words, but don't plan to do jack in return?"

Becker shook his head. "I plan to do plenty in return. I just don't plan to do *that*."

Pinstripe rubbed his jaw reflectively. "Trouble is, that's what we want."

"Well, the answer is no. . . . Look," Becker said, "I came to you guys because I didn't want to spy. Not for them, not for anybody. I wanted out of the whole stupid business. Now you ask me to spy for them and you too. That's not my idea of getting out of the business."

"We're not talking forever," Pinstripe said. "You'd be out of it soon. And afterwards you'd have complete protection."

"Oh sure . . ." Becker said. "*Afterwards*. But how much of an afterwards would I have, for instance, if the KGB found out about the deal?"

Pinstripe shrugged. "How would they find out?"

"How do they usually find out? I get unlucky. Somebody goofs. Or even," Becker paused, "somebody *doesn't* goof."

"Somebody doesn't? . . ." Pinstripe looked puzzled. "I'm not sure I follow."

"I think you follow just fine. You want me to stay in place, go through the motions of working for them, while actually working for you. You say you'll pass me enough genuine intelligence to establish my credibility, so that eventually you'll be able to sell them a bill of goods. But what I ask myself," Becker smiled thinly, "is just who else you're selling a bill of goods to."

"In other words, you're saying you don't trust us."

"Of course I don't," Becker said. "Because, in your place, I wouldn't trust me. I wouldn't confide *my* plans to some Soviet defector who'd just wandered in off the street, especially if he'd be in a position to cross me up. And there's another problem . . ."

He paused. Pinstripe said nothing, continued to watch him with the studied impassivity of a poker player.

"It's called defaulting on your obligations," Becker said. "Even assuming—which I don't for a second—that what you've just told me is true, why should I believe in your promises for afterwards? At that point, the KGB will have every reason to waste me. What reason will you have for seeing that they don't?"

Brief silence. Pinstripe exchanged glances with Stoneman.

"Well, well . . . What a nasty little mind we do have."

"We do," Becker said. "But on the other hand, it's a nasty business."

"Your trouble," Pinstripe shook his head as in disbelief, "is growing up in Russia. You'll find we do things differently here. We believe, for one thing, in looking after our people." He caught Becker's gaze and held it. "I can personally assure you of that."

There was another silence.

"Bullshit," Becker said.

Pinstripe frowned. His voice took on an edge. "Look . . . If you're not willing to trust us, why the hell did you come to us in the first place?"

Becker considered. "Well, setting aside the point that if 'us' is who I think it is—I didn't come to you—I'm inclined to agree: It was clearly a mistake."

"I see," Pinstripe said. "That makes things tricky, doesn't it?"

Becker shook his head. "I think it makes them easy. I came to you with a problem and an offer. You've made what you say is your best counter. It's unacceptable. But that's OK. So we *don't* make a deal. There's no harm done. I'll get along somehow without your help."

No harm done . . . He saw Pinstripe glance at Stoneman. No harm done? Like hell there wasn't. He was stupid to have come here, stupid to have thought he could deal on his terms with these guys. A defection was one thing. So was helping them roll up a network. Coups like that were always publicized, and defectors who helped were carefully protected, *pour encourager*, as Valadek had said, *les autres*. But for reasons they would never share with him, they wanted him to double. And doubles were the lepers of espionage, untouchables whose existence was surrounded by silence. And when their usefulness was over, they became embarrassments whose silence was apt to be deep and permanent. But he was trapped now, trapped by these bland-faced clowns with their Cold War, with their "misinformation" and "disinformation," their "black" operations, their espionage and counterespionage, their "legals" and "illegals," their double and triple agents. He'd been trapped from the moment he'd asked them for their help. But it went back farther than that, he knew. He'd been trapped, if the truth were told, since Kiev and Vanya's cancer and that day in Lem's office when he'd thought it was possible to sell part of his soul to the devil, not knowing that the devil didn't deal in fractions. He'd been in the trap always, he thought; he just hadn't felt the teeth.

"This makes it tough," Pinstripe said. "I'd hoped it wouldn't come to this. I'd hoped to appeal to your patriotism or gratitude or whatever." He shrugged. "But I guess it doesn't matter. See, the thing is, old buddy, mistake or not, you *did* come to us. Now you don't have any choice."

"So," Stoneman said. "Let's hear it for Uncle Sam's newest recruit . . . doesn't like us, doesn't believe us, doesn't want to work for us. But what the hell? We'll take him anyway."

"Sure we will," Hollister said. "Who needs enthusiasm? Give me a motive I can trust."

"One you can trust?"

"Intelligent self-interest. Also known as fear and greed. In this case, fear. Fear of what will happen if the KGB finds out. And they *will* find out if from here on in he doesn't do exactly what I tell him. As far as I'm concerned," Hollister said, "that's all the motivation he'll ever need."

"Mister Nice Guy," Stoneman said.

"Christ," Hollister said. "Who cares about nice? Do *they* care about nice? When I'm home I'll be nice. Here I'm not paid to. In any case,"—he paused—"who *says* he doesn't want to work for us?"

"Who says? . . . *He* says."

"Sure he does." Hollister's face was expressionless. "And therefore we should believe him. Right?"

"His story checks out."

"Well, that's reassuring," Hollister said. "Only if I were the KGB and wanted to plant a double in the Agency, the first thing I'd do is give him a story that checked out. Wouldn't I?"

"I guess." Stoneman shrugged.

"Look . . ." Hollister said. "They know that whenever we get a defector, the first thing we ask ourselves is 'Is he real?' What better way to answer that than send us one who says he wants to retire. If we buy his story, we won't let him retire. And if we don't, they really haven't lost a whole lot."

Just a man, Stoneman thought, a foot soldier. We've always got lots of those.

"That makes a certain sense, I suppose. Only getting him to double was your idea, wasn't it? How could they be sure that's what we'd want him to do?"

"They couldn't. But it's the rational thing to do." Hollister grinned. "I'd expect them to credit us with a modicum of intelligence."

A modicum of intelligence . . . That, Stoneman thought, was the problem, was why the profits of these operations were always so hard to assess. If you assumed your opposition was as rational as you were— and that, after all, was the only rational assumption—then you found yourself in an infinite regression of the "he'll think that I'll think that he'll think" variety, from which the only escape was a leap into the *ir*rational. A modicum of intelligence . . . If any of them had *that*, he was sometimes tempted to think, they'd devote their time to something useful—like chess problems.

"So you think he's a plant?"

Hollister shook his head. "Actually, I think he's real. There's something about him, a kind of innocence, that hits my intuition right. But of course, I'm not deciding on the strength of that."

"On the strength of what, then?" Stoneman asked. "How do you decide?"

"Slowly," Hollister said. "Circumspectly. After watching him a while."

"So for the time being, you're not going to use him?"

Hollister shook is head. "For the time being, we're going to let him twist in the wind."

Which was all very odd, Stoneman thought, because whereas previously Hollister had been all gung-ho to take over this defector, now he was marking time, claiming not to trust him. And this didn't make much sense, because, as Hollister must surely know, the defector was far too good to be merely a KGB plant. Which in turn, of course, confirmed his earlier suspicion that what Hollister had told Borden and him about using the defector for misinformation was a pile of horse manure. What Hollister did plan to use him for, he clearly didn't plan to share, but it evidently had something to do with this new Agency computer system the defector had been ordered to penetrate. . . . Not that you usually *wanted* to know what Hollister had planned, Stoneman thought, because working with the Agency, and especially with Hollister, was like looking under a flat rock: You never knew what you were going to find, but you could almost guarantee you wouldn't like it. But in this case, since the defector was part-owned by the Bureau and in some sense his, Stoneman's, responsibility, he was duty bound to try and find out what Hollister had planned. And especially in view of Hollister's history—despite all his talk about maximizing profits—of (so to speak) wasting assets.

And more especially yet, Stoneman thought, because among the strange vibes he was starting to get from the situation was a feeling that Hollister had somehow been expecting this defector.

PART III

"No logic is more compelling than the logic of a nightmare . . . until you wake up."
                    Colonel Vladimir Petrovitch Stein—conversation, 1983

"Logic is the art of going wrong with confidence."
                                                    Anonymous

CHAPTER TWENTY-SEVEN

"CIA? . . ." VLADEK MADE A FACE. "YOU'RE SURE?"

"He didn't produce ID, but he didn't need to." Becker nodded gloomily. "Now I'm really in the shit."

He was careful to keep any note of reproach from his voice. Certainly, it had been Vladek's idea originally that he approach the FBI, and even at the time he'd objected with the fear that what had just happened *would* happen, but in the end it was his responsibility. As it always had, his predicament now stemmed from decisions he alone had taken. And though he might claim, perhaps, that the first and most far-reaching of these, the original decision to get involved with these clowns, had been taken without knowledge of all the relevant circumstances (especially as to the precise nature of these clowns), this didn't, in his view, make any difference. In life, as in law, ignorance was no excuse; one paid in full for one's moments of carelessness. And people might very well argue—he thought of certain fellow students in Prague—that he hadn't yet paid nearly enough.

"I feel bad," Vladek said.

"No need to," Becker said. "You made a suggestion; I accepted it. It seemed to make sense. I think we just got unlucky. . . . What probably happened is, I wandered into something, some operation or other they already had in progress, to which they thought I might have something to contribute." He paused. "Did you get the shots?"

"I got the guy in the pinstripes." Vladek nodded. "The rest of them

143

left the way they came, in a van, which they entered in the garage. Pinstripe stayed and was picked up later by a young guy driving a dark brown S-class Mercedes.''

"I think it's a CIA safe house," Becker said. "They don't want Stoneman's people to know the location. Pinstripe, clearly, is now in charge. Stoneman was merely there on sufferance.''

"But what does Pinstripe want from you? Did he tell you?''

"Not really," Becker shrugged. "He had transcripts of my conversations with Stoneman. Asked a couple of technical questions about how I'd responded when the KGB gave me my target—he seemed happy about that for some reason—then he told me he wanted me to carry on as I was. 'Keep on sleepwalking,' was the way he put it, and report any contacts to him. In due course, he said, they'd have further instructions for me.''

Vladek considered. "Sounds as though they're planning to use you for misinformation.''

"Or as a pipeline . . . the fuckers!" Becker spoke with sudden anger. "They're planning to *use* me, is the point. They don't give a fuck that I don't want to be used. I told them I wanted out, so now I'm working for *two* spy networks. Three, if you count the FBI.'' He paused. "My father had a saying about working for the government. If I didn't before, I'm starting to see what he meant.''

" 'Heaven is becoming a private person' . . .'' Vladek nodded. "I remember your telling me about that. And I remember there was also a punchline: 'To get to heaven, you have to be dead.' ''

"My father knew what he was talking about. However," Becker smiled ruefully, "I'd like to think there was some alternative.''

"There is," Vladek said. "Counterattack.''

"How?" Becker said. "Counterattack where, and with what? Show me a weapon. Show me a point of weakness. . . . I'm dealing, remember, with powerful organizations. Some of the most powerful in the world.''

"I disagree," Vladek said. "What you're dealing with are people. And people, as anyone in my line of work can tell you, not only *have* areas of weakness, they actually consist of little else.'' He paused. "I'm not suggesting you attack the CIA; I'm suggesting you attack Pinstripe. Or actually," he amended, "that *we* attack Pinstripe.''

"We? . . ." Becker frowned. "Look, Vladek, I've imposed on our friendship too much already. I don't want to involve you any further."

Silence.

"You're not imposing," Vladek said. "And you're not involving me, either. I volunteer, you see. I enter this war of my own volition. For reasons of friendship, but also others. I see more at stake here than Becker and his right to life, liberty, and the pursuit of women, though these, naturally are important to me. I see this war as a kind of crusade, a jihad against organized folly, against psychopathology in pinstripe suits, against the evil that lurks behind soothing abstractions and sets of euphemistic initials. Besides,"—he grinned—"without me, you don't stand a chance."

Becker considered. The last part, at any rate, was probably true. Without Vladek, without Vladek's expertise and the resources of his detective agency, his chances of winning were practically nil.

"This is going to get rough, Vladek," he said gently. "These people are not used to being crossed. I think if we lose this, we will end up dead."

Silence.

"So?" Vladek shrugged. "We will end up dead anyway. To get to heaven, you have to be dead."

Becker ignored this. "And assessing our chances objectively, I also think," he held Vladek's gaze and spoke very deliberately, "that we probably will lose."

Vladek looked skeptical. "If you think that, why fight?"

"Because in my case the alternative is intolerable," Becker said. "You don't have that excuse."

"No, I don't," Vladek agreed. "My excuse is better . . . I think we can win."

"How?" Becker queried. "Maybe we are dealing with people, but they're people *backed* by the power of organizations. How can we expect to match that power?"

"Power?" Vladek queried. "Their power is unimportant. What's important is their weakness. *You* will fight to the end regardless of cost, because, as you say, the alternative is intolerable. *I* will fight because I have chosen. But tell me this: When we start to hurt them, when we make them feel the cost of this war personally, in their own lives, what will *they* find to fight for?''

What will they find to fight for? A good question, Becker thought. In the end it was a matter of commitment. He recalled his first encounter with the unarmed combat instructor at the Kiev training school. The instructor—a small flat-faced Estonian with a body on which there was no fat whatsoever, a voice that never seemed to modulate, and eyes that seemed to focus on no one and yet to take the measure of them all—had told them that in combat the important qualities were mental. What counted more than speed, strength, coordination, or skill even, was will; and will, in combat, was nothing more or less than the ability, in the interest of killing or maiming your opponent, to absorb and ignore pain. All of which was just fine, Becker thought—he himself had never been better than average at unarmed combat—provided you had at hand the means of maiming or killing your opponent.

"But how do we make them feel the cost?" he queried. "It's easy to talk of areas of weakness, but how do you know that Pinstripe, for instance, has any?"

Vladek looked at him for a moment without expression. "Everyone has weaknesses," he said.

"But how does one find them out?"

"You're being unusually obtuse this evening." Vladek raised one of his circumflex eyebrows. "In order to find them, you have to look."

"Set people to watch Pinstripe, you mean. But isn't he likely to know they're there? It *is* his area of expertise."

Vladek shrugged. "He's probably a desk jockey. Fieldwork won't be his forte. With good people and a big enough team, I think we can get away with it. Remember"—Vladek paused, favored Becker with his pirate's grin—"this is my area of expertise too."

Becker considered.

"You're determined to be in this thing with me?"

Vladek nodded. "Actually, I insist."

"In that case, wait. I'll be back in a moment . . ." Becker disappeared, returned a few minutes later with glasses, corkscrew, and a dusty bottle of red wine. He set the glasses on the table between them, opened the wine, performed in silence the ritual of sniffing and tasting. Then he poured a glass and gave it to Vladek.

"Stag's Leap Cabernet, 1973. I bought two cases in 1975 and still have a few bottles left. I think we should drink it," he paused, "while we can."

He raised his glass, caught Vladek's eye and held it. "To you, my friend."

"Sentimentality . . ." Vladek made a face. "I propose instead a proper, warlike toast."

He raised his glass. "To our enemy's weakness."

CHAPTER TWENTY-EIGHT

"ECCE HOMO." VLADEK HANDED THE PHOTOGRAPH TO BECKER. "This *is* him, isn't it? Or, as my high school English teacher at the Prague Gymnasium would have said, 'This is he.' "

Becker examined the photograph. Staring back at him was the face of the man from the safe house, whom Vladek had evidently snapped entering his car. The prints were grainy, had obviously been much enlarged, but unquestionably it was the same man. Becker recalled the regular, slightly heavy features, the perfect self-confidence of their expression, the look of arrogant appraisal in the eyes.

"Her name was Wedekind, in case you were wondering. . . . My English teacher, I mean." Vladek's voice took on a nostalgic note. "Fräulein Theresa Wedekind. She had those beautifully muscular runner's legs and heart-stopping breasts that jiggled when she walked. We called her Fräulein Wunderbar and we worked like slaves at our English just to bask in the sunshine of her smile." He sighed. "Dear Fräulein Wunderbar. I owe her several utterly delirious wet dreams and my present mastery of English grammar."

"Do you know who he is?" Vladek's storehouse of sexual memories was in Becker's experience unequalled, but he refused to be drawn in. "Who he is at the CIA, I mean."

"I know everything about him." Vladek sounded offended, as if the question implied a slight on his competence. "I have this journalist friend, a professional Agency watcher. I showed him the photographs,

148

and he was able to get me the inside scoop. The man you're looking at is a bigwig. Anthony J. Hollister III, Chief of Counterintelligence. An aristocrat, or what passes for one in this shrine of democracy; the kind who's been running things from behind the scenes for so long it's come to seem an inalienable right. And I think," Vladek paused, "actually I very much *suspect* he has something to hide."

"Something to hide?" Becker queried. "Something personal, you mean?"

Vladek nodded. "Almost everyone does. Almost everyone has some guilty little secret tucked away in some closet or other. Dig it up, you've got them by the balls. And the balls"—Vladek grinned—"are what I think we have Anthony J. Hollister by."

"You mean he's screwing around?" Becker frowned and shook his head. "I doubt *that* would give us much leverage with him. Almost everybody's screwing around. Trouble is almost nobody's feeling guilty about it."

"There are, however, different degrees of screwing around," Vladek said. "There's the ordinary screwing around most people do, then there's the screwing around on a wife who inherited forty-five million, who regularly pays most of the household bills, and who won't if she finds out you're screwing around." He paused. "Let me put it this way. If Anthony J. Hollister has nothing to hide, why is he going to so much trouble to hide it?"

"Do I gather you put a tail on him?" Becker asked. "Treated him like one of your wandering husbands? You're telling me you put the CIA's Chief of Counterintelligence under round-the-clock surveillance?"

"Why not?" Vladek shrugged. "The advantage of owning a detective agency is one has the means to indulge one's curiosity. And these big government guys can be very arrogant. It never occurs to them anyone will dare mess with them, especially on their own turf. . . . The thing is," he paused, "it actually did occur to this Hollister that someone might be tailing him. Or it did, at least, whenever he was driving the Mercedes and happened to turn *left* at the Beltway . . ."

It had been pattern, Vladek explained. Hollister, they'd discovered, owned two cars, a red Lotus and a dark brown Mercedes. When he drove the Lotus, as he did relatively seldom, he turned right at the Beltway and drove sedately home, invariably using the same route and taking no precautions against being followed. When he drove the Mercedes, which was several years old and somewhat scruffy, far less noticeable than the Lotus, the pattern was less predictable. If he turned right, as he did most days, he went home. If he turned left, on the other hand, things got interesting. . . .

He drove erratically, constantly switching lanes and varying his speed, signalling exits he didn't take, not signalling the exit he ultimately did take. Then there was the business of his using the rest area of the turnpike as a filter and doubling back with an illegal U-turn across the median strip. All of this would have been more than enough to detect and/or shake any ordinary tail, but to Vladek's four-car team of professionals it had succeeded only in conveying that Hollister wanted to avoid being followed. This conclusion was confirmed by what had happened at the parking garage in Alexandria.

"He pulled a switch," Vladek said. "There were two of us still with him at that point, and I think he'd more or less convinced himself he was clean, for he drove the last stretch without pulling any tricks. But anyway, when he got to the garage, I couldn't follow him in, obviously, so I sent my partner round to the exit, just in case our friend was using *it* as a filter. I parked outside and went in on foot to cover the elevator in the lobby."

Vladek paused. Like the veteran storyteller he was, he waited for Becker to prompt him.

"Go on. . . . What happened next?"

"We lost him." Vladek produced this with an air of pulling a rabbit from a hat, which struck Becker, under the circumstances, as inappropriate. "He didn't emerge from the elevator, nor from the vehicle entrance. He didn't emerge from the exit, either. At least," Vladek amended, "not in his own car."

"In someone else's car?"

"In an old green Plymouth Fury." Vladek nodded. "Or that's what he came *back* in. When we realized he'd given us the slip, we parked inside on the same level as the Mercedes and waited . . . *three hours and twenty minutes.*" Vladek paused to bestow on Becker a look of grave reproach. "Have you any conception at all of how *boring* it is to sit in a parking garage and wait for someone to show up?"

"Quite a good conception." Becker thought back to his meeting with the man who called himself Yuri. "I did it only last week. No doubt I shall have to again, before this thing is over." He paused. "I'm very grateful for this, Vladek. I insist you bill me for the time."

"I shall not bill you for the time," Vladek said. "For one thing, I run a very lucrative detective agency. For another, I see this as my war too, 'part two' of my vendetta with Uncle Sam, and with organized stupidity in general."

"Well . . ." Becker smiled gratefully. "We'll leave the question open for the moment. I think of this as a debt, at any rate." He paused. "I don't see why you think he was cheating on his wife. I mean, the man works for the CIA. Couldn't what you've been describing have been in the line of business?"

Vladek shook his head. "It was too amateurish. If this had been an Agency operation, they'd have expected professional surveillance, taken more thorough and less obvious precautions. They'd have sent him out, I'd have thought, with a team of sweepers—or someone behind him, at least, to watch out for a tail and run interference. He had nothing like that. No help at all, unless you count the woman. . . ."

The woman had been in her mid to late thirties. Attractive, Vladek said, in a heavyset kind of way, though not, when one came right down to it, his type. He'd have tried for a photograph, he said, but there'd not been enough light. Flash, of course, had been out of the question. In any case, what had happened was this: Hollister had returned in the green Plymouth at five of ten. Once he'd made sure no one was around, or once he *thought* he'd made sure—the glass in Vladek's van was heavily tinted—he'd switched back to his own car and departed, leaving the keys to the Plymouth in the tail pipe. The woman had arrived at about eleven and on foot. She'd retrieved the keys from the tail pipe and driven off, followed, at a safe distance, by Vladek's partner.

"It was the key in the tail pipe made me wait," Vladek said. "It told me someone would be coming for the Plymouth, so I thought I might as well wait and find out who."

"And did you?" Becker asked. "Find out who, I mean."

"I think so." Vladek nodded. "According to her mailbox, at least, she's a Mary Lou Vickery, of 43 Larchdale Road, Annandale. She's also, I'm convinced, Anthony J. Hollister's piece of spare time ass."

"You're convinced?" Becker gave a sceptical smile. "Maybe because you judge everyone by yourself. I mean, granted Hollister's business with her was confidential, does that mean that he had to be screwing her?''

"Not necessarily. I've only been doing divorce work for more than ten years. My instinct does sometimes let me down. . . . But tell me this, if he wasn't screwing her, what *was* he doing with her from seven o'clock to ten? I mean, maybe you can tell me.'' Vladek paused to favor Becker with the blandest of smiles. ''How else does one pass that kind of time with a hooker?''

''A hooker.'' Becker stared. ''Are you sure?''

''She gives a lifelike imitation if she's not. Goes to lots of motel rooms with lots of different men. But don't take *my* word for it. Next time come see for yourself. Next time we'll find out exactly what she gets up to with Anthony J. . . .'' Vladek shrugged. ''I'll bet you a hundred it ain't backgammon.''

''Thank you, no.'' Becker smiled. ''But what makes you think there'll be a next time?''

''It's got to be a regular deal,'' Vladek said. ''You don't go to all that trouble for a one-night stand.''

''I guess not. You're saying, then, that on the nights they've arranged to meet, she leaves her car for him in the parking garage. So next time we can follow him from there?''

''Not follow,'' Vladek said. ''We won't have to. Next time he'll *tell* us where he is.''

''Tell us?''

''Sure,'' Vladek said. ''These days the detective racket is high tech.''

Becker smiled. ''I should have guessed. You put a beeper in her car.''

''His, too. After all,'' Vladek said, ''how else was I going to pass those lonely hours in the parking garage?''

CHAPTER TWENTY-NINE

MARY LOU VICKERY WAS NORMALLY INDIFFERENT TO SEX, BUT THERE were times, she thought, when she actively hated it. Not men, of course. Men, in her experience, were mostly like her father, well-intentioned but weak, victims rather than villains. What she hated was the urge that took men from whatever was good and admirable in themselves and put them at the mercy of their hormones. She hated to see them reduced that way, to vehicles, simply, of their complicated passions. She'd hated it in her father, who in most respects had been kind and decent, and she hated it in the rest of them. And that was why, as she often told herself, she tried to do what she could to help them. She liked to think of herself as a kind of therapist, an exorcist of men's recurrent demons, and though part of her recognized this for the rationalization it was, something that enabled her to hold on to a little self-respect, there was also a part of her that felt it to be true. Why otherwise—she mulled the question over in the taxi ride back to Alexandria, always the most tiresome part of this weird little melodrama she found herself involved in—why otherwise did this one, who insisted on all the cloak and dagger, with his sad little fantasy of his sister's nanny or whatever, why otherwise did he make her feel so bad?

It brought him so low, she thought. In his other life he was obviously sober and responsible, the head of a corporation, perhaps, the father of a family, someone with authority and a proper hold on himself. With her, on the other hand, he was almost infantile—abjection combined with a quirky appetite. A hunger was released from the deepest part of himself, which, appeased, fell back and left him feeling diminished. And he hated her, of course, for the part she played in delivering him from his ghosts. So afterwards—the thing seldom took very long, a one-act play, she thought wryly, and sometimes not even that—when what she wanted was to console him in his defeat, he avoided her eyes as much as possible, just paid her the money, a good deal more, unfortunately, than she could afford to turn down, and slunk away.

The cab drew up to the curb, interrupting, for the moment, her train of thought. She paid and got out, giving the driver a larger tip than was necessary. Spread it around, she thought; spread it around and hope that some of it comes back. . . . She noticed that the clock on the building across from the parking garage said nine-thirty. She was earlier than usual tonight, but the garage would still be dark and deserted, and the prospect of entering in search of her car made her think uneasily about muggers. As she exited from the elevator, she asked herself, as always, if this stuff with the cars and the keys in the tail pipe were really necessary and, if so, why? Was it just paranoia, or part of an even stranger compulsion, an unusual twist to a kink that was otherwise routine? And this in turn led her, not by any means for the first time, to speculate about men and the odd relationship they always seemed, when left to their own devices, to insist on establishing with the world. Was it boredom, fear, or reluctance to abandon childhood that compelled them to their various evasions? And just what the hell was it, she wondered, that they hoped to achieve with their games?

Her car was on the third level—why did he always make her *leave* it on the second?—and he'd parked, as usual, at the end where it was darkest, away from the elevator and lights. There were more cars tonight than usual. She noticed a van with tinted windows beside the Plymouth, and for some reason that reassured her. But the echo of her footsteps on the concrete still struck her as vaguely menacing and she stopped once, though she knew it was silly, to check that what she heard *was* an echo, not someone else's footsteps.

She heard nothing, of course. But when she got to the Plymouth, there were no keys were in the tail pipe. . . . He forgot, she thought, the jerk went and forgot. . . . Then she heard a noise, a faint electronic whine, from the van beside her. The window opened. A face emerged, and next to it a hand. The hand was holding a bunch of keys.

"These are yours, I believe?" It was a man's voice—what else?
—light, pleasant, faintly amused.

"Who are you?" her voice, amazingly, came out strong, unterrified.
"And what the hell are you doing with my keys?"

"Who *I* am doesn't matter. The question is, are you Mary Lou
Vickery?"

She nodded. "I am, and those are my keys. If you don't give them to
me, I shall scream."

"We're not planning to hurt you." The tone was almost offended.
"If we were, we'd have done it by now, don't you think?"

"What do you want, then? Money?"

"Certainly not." Now it *was* offended. "If anything we're givers,
not takers. We're here to make you a business proposition."

Later she would wonder why she agreed. Money was part of it, of
course. Five thousand dollars was an utterly extravagant reward for her
consent, as they'd delicately phrased it, "to co-star in a movie." But
what they were asking was not quite as simple as that. They were asking
a betrayal, and though she felt no particular loyalty to the man whose
eccentricities had involved her in these dealings, the act itself stuck in
her throat. Or it would have done, she thought, but for something that
was perhaps, in the end, even more important to her than money. They
hadn't tried to *bully* her. There was some vendetta, clearly, between
these two and her weirdo, and the movie they wanted to make would
give them a leverage with him they evidently desperately needed.
They'd be thrilled, she thought, when they saw how *much* leverage their
movie would actually give them. But they hadn't threatened or tried to
scare her. Rather (to be completely accurate), when she'd asked what
would happen if she didn't do what they wanted, the one with the heavy
eyebrows, who'd up to then done the talking, had glanced in silent
enquiry at the other one, and the other one had shaken his head and
said: "*He'd* do that." And that was exactly right, she thought, he *would*
have threatened. He would have bullied her and scared her, then despised her for giving in. And perhaps that was the reason, she thought—
that and of course the money—that in the end she'd decided, though not
without a twinge of misgiving, to sell him out.

CHAPTER THIRTY

VOLKHOV SWITCHED OFF THE TAPE RECORDER AND SAT FOR A MOMENT, thinking. It wasn't easy to know what to make of this sleeper, it wasn't easy at all. These phone calls, for instance. Presumably, since the woman must have told him of her encounter with Serafin, he'd have thought about what Serafin had been doing in his house and figured out, since he wasn't stupid, that his phone had been tapped. One would have expected, therefore, that when using this phone, his manner would be awkward, or at least show signs of constraint. Any normal person, even if he had nothing to hide, would tend, knowing that someone was listening, to cut down on his calls, to reduce them to essentials, and to eliminate the social element almost entirely. This Becker, however, had done nothing of the kind. There were seventeen calls on the tape. *Seventeen* in twenty-four hours. (A measure, possibly, of how deeply enslaved to bourgeois institutions the sleeper had become.) Most of them had been purely social, more than half had been instigated by him, and several (the ones to this Vladek, whoever *he* was) had been protracted. One, indeed, had consisted mostly of a half-hour exchange of sexual reminiscence, which Serafin and Kasparov, since they'd peppered the entry in the log with exclamation points, had evidently found fascinating. Volkhov had found it fascinating too, though not for the same reasons, he suspected, as his colleagues. What interested him, or what interested him most, was what it appeared to tell him about

156

Becker. Either the man was a kind of exhibitionist, the conversational equivalent of the perverts who enjoyed sex most when someone was watching, or else he was someone trying to act natural—and overdoing it, of course, because acting natural, especially when you had something to hide, was the hardest thing in the world to do.

Especially when you had something to hide . . . That, of course, was the crux. One had to guard, Volkhov reminded himself, against circular logic. The knowledge that you were being watched was enough by itself to make you feel suspected. That in turn might make you try to look innocent by acting natural. And since trying to act natural was a virtual guarantee that what you'd succeed in doing would be exactly the reverse, it was hardly reasonable to build much on that foundation. But did that analysis necessarily hold here? he wondered. If you were going to assume that Becker would conclude, on the basis of Serafin's encounter with the woman, that his telephone had been tapped, shouldn't you also assume (since Serafin could be expected to report the encounter) that Becker would also conclude that you'd figured out what he'd concluded? In which case, Volkhov thought, this lavish use of the phone took on, possibly, another significance. It amounted, perhaps, to saying: "Since we both know you're listening in on my phone calls, the least I can do is make it entertaining." It amounted, in fact, to a kind of civilized insolence. And that told one very little, except perhaps about Becker's character. And what it said about Becker's character was just this: that he was still, in spite of his years of exile, very Russian.

But if the psychological evidence was, as usual, inconclusive, there were—were there not?—some awkward facts. . . . The woman, for instance, had disappeared from view. She was conspicuously absent from the log of phone calls and the audio surveillance transcripts, and had been since that first fragmentary conversation. This could mean, of course, no more than that Becker had dumped her. But since that first recorded conversation was both the only recorded conversation between Becker and the woman and the only recorded conversation in which Becker had seemed at all anxious about a tap, it seemed reasonable to contemplate—not suspect, Volkhov thought; suspicion at this point would be going beyond the evidence—a connection between the two facts. In other words, Becker had either dumped the woman, *or* he'd made very sure their contacts were not monitored, presumably because he didn't want the woman to come to his control's attention.

If so, why not?

It was worth asking, Volkhov thought, and especially in view of awkward fact number two: Becker had done nothing about carrying out his mission. In more than two weeks now he had taken no positive action, but had merely reiterated his request for the information he claimed he needed in order to plan his assault on the CIA's computer. Here again, this was not necessarily suspicious. Volkhov had understood almost nothing of the talk about "multi user level security," "audit trails," "trapdoors," and the like. But the gist was that Becker needed to write a program that would break into the system, obtain the user codes, erase all evidence that the system had been broken into, arrange for the computer time his activities had used to be billed to other users of the system, and all this in one fell swoop because there would be no second chance. This had made sense both to Volkhov and to the computer experts in Moscow he'd been able to consult by telex (none of them close to Becker's caliber, alas). But if Becker's inactivity wasn't in itself suspicious, it was nonetheless disturbing: a) because the information Becker needed, or *said* he needed, could only come from Marigold, b) because Becker knew about Marigold, had figured out, at least, that there must be a Marigold, and c) because once Becker had his information, he'd be a serious and abiding threat to Marigold's security. If he decided to defect, for instance, he'd have that vital prerequisite for any successful defection: something worthwhile with which to bargain.

All of which, Volkhov was careful to remember, didn't mean he *had* decided to change sides. What it did mean, though, was that the whole issue of his loyalty had become too important to be left to the kind of speculation that had occupied—Volkhov was tempted to think that a better word might be "wasted"—the better part of an hour. He couldn't afford to speculate; he had to find out. And he couldn't find out in the obvious and convenient way (by hauling Becker in for a polygraph test) because Becker—Volkhov was starting to find this sleeper tiresome—was, of course, polygraph resistant. He would therefore have to be put under total round-the-clock surveillance, which would mean three surveillance teams (four hours on, eight hours off) with a minimum of four to a team, or in other words, a massive disruption of normal routine and a severe strain on available manpower resources.

In these circumstances, Volkhov thought, it was perhaps just as well that Marigold was still AWOL.

But at the same time, it was very ominous.

CHAPTER THIRTY-ONE

THE MOMENT HOLLISTER ENTERED THE MOTEL ROOM, HE KNEW THAT this time it wasn't going to work. The woman was dressed in her usual outfit. She stood up and turned to accuse him as she always did when he entered, but the chemistry was wrong. It was how she was holding herself, he thought. She looked awkward, as if she were playing her part against her will. Her body language was uneasy. Her expression was almost apologetic, a mixture—it struck him suddenly as ominous—of guilt and something akin to compassion.

When he heard movement from behind him, he knew it was not just the chemistry that was wrong.

"You may as well sit down," Becker said. "The chair in front of the TV would be good. We've something we want to show you."

He had a gun . . . pointing at Hollister's stomach. Hollister sat. The man with Becker, he now noticed, had a video cassette recorder, which he proceeded to hook up to the TV. The woman collected her coat and purse, made her way to the door. At the door, she paused.

"I'm sorry," she said. "I didn't want to. They forced me."

"Bitch." Hollister didn't spare her a glance. "They forced you with money, I bet."

She hesitated a moment as if she'd have liked to dispute the point, but instead she shrugged and left. Becker locked the door after her. He put the gun in his pocket, produced from it instead a video cassette.

"I'm sure you can guess what this is."

Hollister nodded. "What's your price?"

"I think you should see it first," Becker said. "You know the old saying, 'a picture is worth a thousand words.' The sound track is also compelling."

"I don't *want* to watch it."

"So turn your head." Becker shrugged. "Cover your eyes if you like. We can't make you watch, but we can make you stay while we run it. And that's what we're going to do." He paused. "My bet is you'll end up watching. After all, you are the star."

It seemed to Hollister that he'd been psychically flayed, then, with every nerve end exposed, plunged into brine. He'd started by trying not to watch, but the effort, of course, had been self-defeating. Imagination had supplied his mind with the very pictures his eyes denied it. Indeed, it had been easier to let go, to surrender himself entirely to the shame and hope to pass through it to a kind of numbness. He'd achieved, this way, a division of himself, one part of his mind detaching itself and observing the other from a distance, the way a sleeper in the grip of a nightmare will sometimes be conscious that it *is* a nightmare even as he goes on submitting to the terror. In the end he'd watched in a sort of trance, as if the whole scene—the room, Becker and his assistant, the TV, the shameful images on the screen, himself watching those images of himself—were not quite real, could, in due course, be banished by an act of will.

The film ended. Becker got up and turned off the TV. Hollister found himself trying to hold onto his trance, knowing that when it ended the nightmare itself would persist. He could feel the pressure of the other men's eyes upon him, but couldn't for the moment bring himself to meet them.

"You shouldn't feel bad." Becker himself sounded almost embarrassed. His voice was unexpectedly gentle. "It's probably a fairly common phenomenon. A matron at school, no doubt, a housemaid or maybe a nanny . . . A masochistic experience so intense it dominated the sexual response thereafter, inhibited the development of normal feelings. An enlightened person would pity, not condemn you. The question is, though, how many people can you count on to be enlightened?''

Silence. Hollister tried to feel anger. He tried to imagine how he'd feel if someone he knew saw this movie, but he couldn't. It seemed that, at some point in the last half hour, his capacity for feeling of any kind had died.

''Your employers?'' Becker persisted. ''Your wife? Your kids, perhaps?''

''My kids?'' An image of his daughters forced its way into Hollister's mind. A stab of pain like a knife in the heart showed him he'd been wrong about his capacity for feeling. ''You're telling me you'd show that film to my *kids*?''

''I won't show it to *anyone*,'' Becker said. ''Not unless I have to.''

''Unless you have to? Unless I do what you want, you mean.''

Becker nodded. ''But I'm very modest, you'll find, in what I want.''

''You want me to spy.'' Grimly Hollister pronounced sentence on himself. ''You want me to work for the KGB.''

Becker stared. ''Now that's a thought. . . . But you don't listen much, do you?'' He shook his head in disbelief. ''You're so enslaved to your own habits of mind that you can't seem to hear me when I say I'm not interested. I don't want any part of your nasty little games. I want you guys to carry on your Cold War without me. *I* don't want to spy. I don't want *you* to spy. I don't want anything to do with you guys . . . with the CIA, the FBI, or the KGB, or with any other set of deliberately misleading initials.'' He paused. ''Is that clear enough for you?''

Hollister shrugged. ''I'm clear about what you don't want . . . but what is it you do want? Money?''

''Jesus . . . You don't get it at all, do you?'' Becker sighed, looked over at his companion and rolled his eyes. ''I want you guys off my back. You and the FBI. Now and always.''

''That's all?'' Hollister was amazed. ''Nothing else?''

Becker nodded. ''Nothing else.''

Hollister thought. . . . In the Agency, he himself, Cartwright, and Sherwood were the only people who knew about Becker. Cartwright and Sherwood would be easy enough to square, but there was also the problem of the FBI. The head man, Borden, he could lead around by the nose, but he wasn't so sure about Stoneman. Stoneman didn't like him, for one thing, and Stoneman had displayed, on occasion, disturbing independence of mind. But he could stall Stoneman, he thought, could stall him at least until he'd figured out how to turn the tables on this Becker.

"That's not as easy as you think," he said. "I can speak for my own people, but you defected to the FBI. I can try and persuade them, of course, but I don't have any way to make it stick. Those guys won't take orders from me. They do what they want."

"That's your problem," Becker said. "Deal with it any way you like, just deal with it." He paused. "It's like this . . . You guys get off my back and stay off my back, and the film stays lost in decent obscurity. You guys *don't* get off my back, and copies get mailed to your wife, your kids, the Director of Central Intelligence, and anyone else I can think of, including, since you were kind enough to suggest it, the local chapter of the KGB."

"Got you." Hollister nodded.

"Do you?" Becker queried. "I certainly hope so. I expect it's crossed your nasty little mind that you can solve your problem by getting rid of me, so let me make one last thing clear . . . A copy of the film is in a safety deposit box, and a duplicate of the key has been left with my lawyer. If, within the next ten years, I happen to die from any cause whatsoever, the film gets delivered, but only to the KGB. This instruction can be countermanded only by me, and only in person . . ." Becker paused. "I'm sure you can guess what the Russians would do with that film."

Silence.

"But that's not fair," Hollister said. "You could have a heart attack or get hit by a bus. You could die tomorrow from perfectly natural causes. Are you saying, if you did, that the film would go to the Russians?"

"If I thought I could trust you, I'd be fair," Becker said. "But if I thought I could trust you, we wouldn't have a problem, now would we? . . . And who's to be sure that I died from natural causes? Who knows what techniques you guys have devised for inducing heart attacks or infecting people with anthrax?" He shrugged. "We'll have to leave it like this . . . You offer prayers for my continued health and safety, and

I promise to eat right, get plenty of exercise, and take good care crossing the street.''

Hollister stood up, summoned what dignity he could still muster. ''May I take it there's no longer an objection to my leaving?''

''Feel free,'' Becker said.

At the door, Hollister paused, turned back to Becker.

''There's something I'd like you to tell me. I just want to know what kind of man you are. . . . Would you really show that movie to my kids?''

Becker looked at him for a moment without expression. ''You don't get it, do you? And you, of all people, should. There's nothing personal in this at all. I've nothing against you or your kids. We're at war, don't you see? And war makes people expendable. I'm expendable, you are, everyone is. Why should we make an exception for your kids?''

CHAPTER THIRTY-TWO

"So . . ." Stoneman shifted his gaze from Borden to Hollister and back again. He raised an eyebrow. "First they said they only wanted to share him. Now they're telling us they want to run him alone?"

It was typical Hollister, he thought. To bypass him and go over his head to Borden because Borden was easier to snow. Because Borden was weak, unsure of his authority, and therefore, having once been snowed, would dig his heels in with a stubbornness, so characteristic of the weak, designed to convince himself that no one could push him around. Stoneman wondered why he was even surprised. Perhaps at how easily it had happened, he thought. Perhaps only because he'd believed there were depths of ineptitude, or spinelessness, to which even Borden couldn't sink. If so, he thought grimly, he'd been sadly mistaken. From the moment he'd walked in the door and seen the pair of them, Hollister wearing his Cheshire Cat smile, Borden defiant and at the same time slightly anxious, it had been obvious that Borden had given away the store.

Now it was just a matter of learning how badly.

"It's a question of administrative convenience really," Borden said. "Security too, of course. After all, we've agreed to let him be used against an Agency designated target. It doesn't make sense for us to keep looking over their shoulder."

We agreed? . . . Stoneman inspected his superior in silence. . . . You mean *you* agreed. And as for the Agency designated target, he thought, it was only too clear that, like him, Borden hadn't the vaguest notion of what the designated target was. Whether, indeed, there was a target at all.

"And what do *we* get out of this?"

"Get out of it?" It was Hollister who interposed the query. His tone was edged with distaste, as if, when he'd thought he was dealing with gentlemen, he'd found himself confronted by Lebanese carpet merchants. "You mean as in 'rewarded'? As in 'How will the Agency repay the Bureau for this small contribution to the national interest?' "

"I'm talking reciprocity," Stoneman snapped. "As in 'one good turn deserves another.' As in 'What have you ever done for us?' "

Hollister said nothing. Stoneman turned back to Borden.

"Tell me if I've got this right," he said. "A defector walks in off the street. Gives himself up to the FBI. Becomes, therefore, a Bureau asset. But because he claims to be a KGB sleeper, you, as a matter of professional courtesy, inform the CIA. The CIA then decide, for purposes which they haven't so far condescended to explain, that they wish to take over this Bureau asset." He paused. "And we're going along with this? Just like that? No questions asked?"

But even as he heard himself speak, he knew he was making a mistake. The tone was wrong, too close to insolence. And arguing— at least in front of Hollister—was in any case pointless. A more selfconfident man, he thought, might disregard the tone, might look beyond the fact of a subordinate's opposition to ponder at least briefly its substance. Borden would see nothing but the need to assert himself.

"We happen, though it's something you seem to overlook, to be on the same side and fighting the same war." Leaning forward, Borden asserted himself. He was frowning, his tone was snappish, but his eyes were anxious; his body language expressed discomfort. Asserting himself was something he hated, Stoneman thought. What he really wanted was to be mild and reasonable. He wanted you to be mild and reasonable too, to understand him. And that was the trouble with Borden, Stoneman thought, the cause of his spinelessness, the source of his crippling weakness: He wanted to please people, to go through life without making enemies. "It's juvenile to talk about our assets or their assets; they all belong to the U.S. of A."

Stoneman regarded him bleakly. If you believe that, he thought, if you truly believe that, we're really in the shit.

"They belong to the U.S. of A.," he agreed, "but there's still a question as to how they should be used. Do we even know what they want him for? I hope you do. I sure as hell don't."

Borden blinked. "Misinformation. I thought you'd been told about that."

"Oh, I was." Stoneman's face was expressionless. "I just was never quite sure *who* exactly was being misinformed." He paused. "Did they happen to share with you any of the details? . . . The target, the time frame, any of that sort of thing?"

Pause. Borden hesitated. "I understand this is somewhat sensitive. . . ." He glanced uncertainly at Hollister.

"It is more than somewhat sensitive," Hollister said coldly. He turned to Stoneman. "The need-to-know applies here absolutely. I presume you know what that means."

It means you, Mister Stoneman, Stoneman thought. You, your boss, the entire FBI, the Senate Oversight Committee, and anyone else I, Anthony J. Hollister III, decide in my wisdom to exclude from that knowledge, up to and including the President.

He smiled faintly. "The national interest wouldn't be served by the FBI knowing what the CIA is up to? Somehow I'm not surprised."

"Jesus . . ." Hollister sighed. He turned to Borden. "I think I'll leave you to pursue this squabble in private. Perhaps when you've sufficiently hashed things over, you could let me know your decision?"

He made no move to leave, however. And, though with this not very subtle suggestion that Borden was indecisive he'd effectively ended the debate, it struck Stoneman suddenly that there was something uneasy about him. Not that his manner was any less arrogant than usual, but whereas normally the arrogance seemed natural, proceeding from assumptions of superiority so automatic as to be not really conscious, here it seemed deliberate, almost willed. As if the confidence it normally built on were lacking, Stoneman thought, as if Hollister were relying on manner alone to carry him. As if, for some reason, he were nervous.

Nervous?

Why would Hollister be nervous?

*   *   *

Returning to his office from his meeting with Borden and Stoneman, Hollister was conscious, for the first time in two days, of a lifting of the spirit. Though the little shit, Stoneman, had caused him some anxious moments, the situation, as he'd always been confident it would be, had been neatly brought under control. The defector would now be allowed to fade quietly from the scene (at least until he, Hollister, could figure some way of arranging a more permanent departure), and the video would be left where it belonged. Sherwood and Cartwright might wonder about things, of course, but Sherwood and Cartwright were his minions and would not question his bidding. The problem had always been Stoneman, and Borden, with his usual mix of vanity and weakness, had taken care of that. Hollister thought of Borden with a kind of gratitude. If not grateful *to* him, he was grateful *for* him. Borden, he thought, was a man P.T. Barnum would have loved.

He felt no guilt for his decision about the defector. The important thing here, he thought, the *only* important thing, was relevance. It boiled down to a question of the national interest: Who meant more to it, this Russian or himself? And once the question was reduced to these terms there was, to be utterly objective about it, no contest. The Russian might well be useful (and only "might," Hollister thought; the conditional was appropriate, surely, because usefulness depended largely on willingness, and the Russian's recent behavior had put that substantially in doubt). But he, on the other hand, was essential. He was the CIA's chief of counterintelligence, by general agreement an extremely able one, and the first since the shake-up of the early seventies to enjoy the unqualified confidence of his colleagues. And now, more than ever, an able, trusted, counterintelligence chief was what the Agency imperatively needed. There was a traitor in its ranks, a traitor whom only he—at least with the necessary quickness and cleanness—could identify and remove. Someone else, a successor, could mount some sort of investigation, no doubt; but probably not without creating the kind of public hue and cry that would drive the traitor deeper underground and might damage the Agency as much as, or more than, the treason. Objectively—and the demands of objectivity, he thought, outweighed those of modesty—it would not be exaggerating to say that, in terms of the national interest, he was vital.

And the video would finish him in the Agency, no question. He'd have no choice but to resign. He might claim that by resisting this present attempt, he had shown he was proof against blackmail, but doubts would always linger. And even if security were not a problem, there would still be people—the envious, the sanctimonious, the conventional, or the just plain stupid—to say the whole thing reflected on his judgement; that while what he did in the privacy of the bedroom was, whatever one might personally think of it, his own business, getting caught was inexcusable. But in any case, if the thing became common knowledge, staying on would be unthinkable. The contempt, real or imagined, of his colleagues and subordinates would be more than he could live with. Their smiles, their surreptitious glances, even their silences, would drive him crazy.

His wife, of course, would divorce him. That he could live with. But she would also be vindictive. It was one thing—he could hear the cool indifference she would summon for the pronouncement—to be burdened, so to speak, with a semi-functional partner, but something else entirely to have the fact made public, to have it known by her friends that her husband suffered from some dreary, juvenile hang-up on his nanny. There would be, therefore, no cozy financial settlement. He would have to live on his salary, and there would be no salary.

And then there were the girls. Amanda might be vindictive about them, too. And not only Amanda. That bastard had seemed serious about his threat to show them the video. They would be forced to watch their father . . . their father with . . . that woman. The prospect made his mind cringe. Some things were unthinkable; this was one of them.

But the girls weren't relevant here. Amanda wasn't relevant. What he personally wanted or felt wasn't relevant. There was only one thing relevant here.

The national interest.

In the analysis of intelligence, pattern is everything. It was only afterwards, when he was mulling over the meeting in Borden's office, that the significance of Hollister's nervousness, the full extent of its departure from pattern, hit Stoneman. Hollister was *never* nervous. And why? Because Hollister, paragon of bureaucratic virtue, never took risks. Not personal risks. He would never try to persuade when he could order. He would never enter an argument, moreover, at least with an equal in rank like Borden, unless the outcome were already assured, unless he knew that, if he lost at this level, he could successfully go higher. But here he *had* argued. He'd come over from Langley to persuade Borden, and had stayed afterwards, exploiting the chink in Borden's psychological armor (Chink? Call it a gateway, Stoneman thought wryly) in order to make damn sure Borden stayed persuaded. *And he'd been nervous about it.* He'd been worried that Stoneman might make Borden change his mind. And this, of course, meant not only that he *hadn't* already taken this to higher authority, but also that he didn't want to. That if he was forced to take it to higher authority, he was scared he might not win. Why?

Hollister always won. At least, Stoneman thought, in any turf battle with the FBI, the CIA always won. It was a matter of glamour, partly, of social and intellectual prestige, also a question of administrative focus. The CIA was an instrument of foreign policy, and foreign policy was where this Administration, given its lamentable domestic record, had been forced to pin its hopes. More importantly, it was an issue of personalities: the Director of Central Intelligence was a personal friend of the President; the Director of the FBI was not. So in any normal squabble about the handling of a KGB defector, the CIA could expect to get its way without much trouble.

What was different about this squabble?

It was sometime later, when Stoneman was home, working on his model and ostensibly pondering, therefore, a different set of problems entirely, that his unconscious conjured up a face and, instants later, a name to go with it.

Alex Kontarski.

Kontarski had been a KGB defector, subject of an earlier turf battle. Hollister had won that battle, taken Kontarski over. Hollister's people had done the debriefing. And the debriefing had ended before it had properly begun with Alex Kontarski—who at that point had yielded up little of real intelligence value—hanging by the neck from a length of extension cord in the stairwell of a safe house in Bethesda.

Suicide, they had said.

Now Hollister was taking over another KGB defector.

There were differences in circumstance, of course. Kontarski had been a member of the regular KGB establishment, with presumably a good working knowledge—not that he'd succeeded in sharing much of it—of current personnel and operations. This Becker, on the other hand, was a sleeper, by his own account years out of touch. But Hollister, who had seemed to be expecting this sleeper, seemed nevertheless very anxious to cut all contact between him and the FBI and, indeed, to ensure that no use was made of him. His only stated intention so far, after all, was to let the sleeper "twist in the wind."

It all made you wonder, Stoneman thought. It made you wonder about Hollister's reason for wanting to take over this KGB defector, and why he wasn't willing to share this reason, *apparently even with his own people.*

Which in turn could make you wonder who his own people were.

It was all speculation, of course; uncomfortable suspicion that was also, so far, unfounded. But there were enough unanswered questions here (Un*answered* questions, hell, Stoneman thought. In Borden's case they were also un*asked.*) to make anyone who cared about more than just keeping his job and not rocking the boat profoundly uneasy. So Borden could go fuck himself. He, Stoneman, was going to get to the bottom of this thing, make damn sure that this time the defector wasn't wasted. And since Hollister wouldn't tell him what was going on, that left him only one option.

Reestablish contact with the defector.

CHAPTER THIRTY-THREE

SERAFIN WRIGGLED DOWN IN HIS SEAT TILL HE WAS MORE OR LESS sitting on his shoulder blades and his knees were wedged against the dashboard. In this position he couldn't see the entrance to the restaurant, could see little, in fact, but sky and the tops of the houses across the street. But this didn't, he told himself, really matter. Kasparov (doing his isometrics again) looked reasonably alert, and in any case, Serafin thought, nothing was going to happen. Apart from the fact that the route of a white Toyota had coincided with their own for the final half-mile of the drive to the restaurant, a fact which, in spite of Kasparov's insistence on noting it in the log, he, Serafin, was confident in attributing to chance, nothing remotely suspicious or even interesting had happened yet—not on their watch, not on anybody else's. He was aware, of course, of the logical pitfalls involved in this kind of projection from the past—each moment of his life up to now, after all, had been a moment when he'd managed not to die, and one couldn't build indefinitely on *that*—but it was hard to resist the conclusion that, in ordering this round-the-clock surveillance of the sleeper, Volkhov had for once been mistaken. The sleeper, at any rate, had conducted himself like a man with nothing on his conscience, and he, Serafin, after five days of watching—and there was nothing quite so tedious, surely, as watching a man with nothing on his conscience—was not only convinced the man *had* nothing on his conscience, he was also profoundly, exquisitely bored.

He reached into his pocket for the bag of candy (Was it his third or fourth today?) and noted, in passing, that the burgeoning spare tire at his waist had caused him to pop a shirt button, revealing around the navel an expanse of flesh that was covered with coarse black hair and was roughly the color and consistency of lard. Lard, of course, was exactly what it was. One developed strategies for dealing with the boredom. His was overeating.

"M&M? . . ." He offered the bag to Kasparov.

"Sugar." Kasparov wrinkled his nose in distaste. "Poison. Attractively colored capsules of pure poison. I have more respect for my body than that."

"Yet you smoke." The argument was a stale one, but still preferable to silence. "You poison your body with tar and nicotine?"

"I smoke in moderation." Kasparov, ever suggestible, abandoned the isometrics and started to rummage in his pockets. "And I exercise to keep myself in shape. I don't sit on my shoulder blades all day, gorging on sugar. I tell you, Grigori, you're starting to look like a maggot."

"I feel constipated." Serafin nodded gloomily, popped an M&M into his mouth. "I think it comes from the sitting. I feel like something you'd find under a rock. It feeds on garbage and hates the light."

"*They* feed on Tournedos Rossini." Kasparov, sourly, voiced a recurrent complaint. Ever conscientious, he continued, while complaining, to scan the approaches to the restaurant. "We sit here and ruin our digestions, but our colleagues, Dobrinin and Dolgushov, dine in style. I tell you, Grigori, their luck is uncanny. When it's their turn to go in after him, he eats someplace fancy. When it's our turn . . . McDonald's."

Serafin popped an M&M. The same thought had occurred to him. There was nothing like a protracted surveillance for making you question life's purpose and fairness. But questioning that only made you unhappy, which in turn made the time pass more slowly.

"Imagine we were eating in there, what would we order?"

Kasparov considered. "Sturgeon to start, I think, followed by Tournedos Rossini. The sturgeon washed down by ice-cold schnapps, the tournedos with a bottle of Chateau Lafite."

"Sturgeon . . ." The thought made Serafin homesick. "Where the hell would they get sturgeon? This is Washington we're talking about, not Moscow."

"And this is an imaginary meal we're talking about." Kasparov lit his cigarette. "I can order whatever I want. I can imagine, for instance, having the sturgeon flown in from Moscow. I can also imagine," he grinned, "the look on your face when they hand you the check."

"But since it's an imaginary check," Serafin riposted, "I imagine myself signing it with a careless flourish and telling them to send it to Volkhov." He paused. "What is Tournedos Rossini?"

"Beef tenderloins. The most expensive cut. Served on toast with a rich wine sauce, the whole thing topped off with a slab of foie gras. . . . I actually had a glass of Lafite once. At a reception in Oslo when I was babysitting the general." Kasparov sighed. "It was like drinking velvet."

Serafin popped another M&M. Wine bullshit again. Drinking velvet would make you gag. He tended to doubt this tale of the Lafite. Soviet embassies didn't serve fine French wines to people like Kasparov and him. Most likely Kasparov, scavenging after the party, had finished the dregs from glasses left the bigwigs. In any case, they were back to food. It was their standby, the sturdy backbone of their conversation, more reliable than sex because there was more to talk about and less temptation to lie. The essence of sex, after all, was repetition.

"I'm imagining that sturgeon," he said dreamily, "the flesh white and flaky, delicately smoked . . ."

Kasparov was not listening.

"The camera." His voice was suddenly urgent. "Is the camera loaded?"

"The camera?" Serafin's mind was dragged protesting from the region of his stomach. He felt under the seat for the Nikon. "Of course it's loaded. Why?"

"So you can take a picture, stupid, earn your salary for a change. Stick the camera out of the window and get a shot of that man."

"Which man?"

"The man going into the restaurant," Kasparov said. "Who'll be gone if you keep asking questions. The one who five minutes ago was driving that white Toyota."

When Becker saw Stoneman, hunched over a martini at the counter of the restaurant bar, his first thought was that Hollister had decided to resist his blackmail. Second thoughts, however, told him this was unlikely. Hollister, when he'd last seen him, had looked incapable of resisting anything. And Stoneman didn't work for him directly. He worked for the FBI, and between that organization and Hollister's no love whatsoever was lost. So perhaps Hollister had been unable to square Stoneman. Or perhaps Stoneman's presence in the restaurant was merely chance.

This last hypothesis, half an hour and two martinis later, was the one Becker tended to favor. One was always running into people. And the fact that one wasn't happy to see Stoneman didn't necessarily make the encounter sinister. In a universe governed by the random, the chances of running into someone one wasn't happy to see were as great as (or, given the makeup of one's circle of acquaintance, even greater than) the chances of running into someone one was. Stoneman, moreover, had made no effort whatsoever to communicate, didn't, in fact, seem even to have registered Becker's presence. His seat at the bar, admittedly, was at roughly two o'clock from Becker's table, so he'd have had to turn clear around to spot Becker. But the fact remained that, to Becker's knowledge, he hadn't. He'd shown no interest in his surroundings, paid no attention to anything but his newspaper and his martini. He was there—the conclusion was irresistible—for the simple purpose of drinking lunch.

This conclusion survived Stoneman's departure from the restaurant. It survived, indeed, until Becker himself was in a taxi and three quarters of the way back to his office. At that point, he discovered in his right-hand overcoat pocket a rolled-up copy of *The Washington Post*, which, he noticed, was one day out of date. It had not been there when he left his overcoat at the coatrack in the restaurant.

The message was on the front of the sports section. A faint pencil scrawl at the foot of the page: "We need to talk. Please contact soonest."

CHAPTER THIRTY-FOUR

"IT'S HARD TO BE SURE WHAT WAS GOING ON." VOLKHOV HANDED the Resident the first pair of photographs. "What started out looking like surveillance ended up looking like a contact. Either way, the tradecraft was incredibly careless. If they'd done things properly, Kasparov wouldn't have noticed." He paused. "It just points up what they tell you in the training. Sloppy tradecraft is worse than none at all."

The Resident examined the photographs: a three-quarter profile shot of a grey-haired man in a tweed overcoat entering a doorway, and a full-face shot, presumably taken later, of the same man leaving it. For a moment, searching them for what Volkhov found significant, she could find nothing. She was about to submit to the irritation of having to ask, when a small discrepancy, a detail, jumped out at her.

"I take it you're referring to the newspaper. In the first shot it's protruding from the right-hand pocket of his overcoat. In the next shot, though both overcoat pockets are visible, it's not there."

Volkhov nodded. "The textbook procedure is to *exchange* newspapers. The target goes in, let's say, leaves his overcoat at the rack with a copy of the newspaper in the left-hand pocket. When the contact arrives, later, with an identical issue of the paper, he hangs his coat next to the target's, slips *his* copy of the paper into the right-hand pocket of the target's coat. When he leaves, of course, he takes the copy from the target's left-hand pocket."

The Resident stared. "I'm familiar with the textbook procedure. Perhaps you'd be kind enough to tell me what actually happened."

"What actually happened was this," Volkhov said. "This man arrived with a newspaper, but left without it. Becker, on the other hand, arrived without and left with. And the contact appeared to *follow* Becker to the restaurant. At least, he was recognized by Kasparov as the driver of a white Toyota that might have been shadowing Becker's taxi the last half-mile or so of the drive. That too, of course, was a breach of accepted procedure. A pursuit vehicle should never stay close to the target for anything like that long." Volkhov paused, pursed his lips in disapproval. "Incredibly sloppy tradecraft."

He passed the Resident a photograph of Becker leaving the restaurant, the rolled-up newspaper clearly visible, sticking out of his right-hand coat pocket. She studied the photograph with detached, faintly sceptical interest. She would look at his pictures, her manner implied, but preferred to draw her own conclusions.

"Perhaps it wasn't tradecraft." Her eyes, he noticed, flicked to the photographs he hadn't yet shown her. "It's quite possible—isn't it? —that the white car seemed to be following the taxi because it happened to be going to the same restaurant, that it disappeared when the taxi stopped because, unlike the taxi, it had to find somewhere to park. And it's equally possible that the newspaper this man took in and the newspaper Becker took out were not, in fact, one and the same. Perhaps the man just happened to leave a paper, and Becker just happened to pick one up. It wouldn't be a very remarkable coincidence." She paused. "Did anything take place *inside* the restaurant? Since you took it upon yourself to order this surveillance, I'm presuming someone thought to follow him inside."

"Dobrinin and Dolgushov. They claim to have had him under observation the whole time he was in the restaurant, and they have a receipt for seventy dollars and thirty cents to prove it. They swear they ordered the least expensive items on the menu." Volkhov smiled faintly. "Apparently he ate alone, met nobody, talked to nobody. They didn't see his contact make the switch."

"So?"

Without speaking, Volkhov passed her the final pair of photographs, isolated details from the earlier shots. In each, an overcoat pocket with a newspaper sticking out of it was blown up to the point where the headlines could be read.

"We were able to identify the papers. We compared the headlines showing in these photographs with recent back issues of local newspapers. In both photographs it's the same newspaper, *The Washington Post* of November the fifteenth."

"That doesn't surprise me." The Resident looked down her nose. "In fact, it's just what I'd expect. Copies of *The Washington Post,* Major, aren't exactly uncommon in Washington."

He shook his head. "These photographs were taken yesterday, Colonel. And yesterday was November the *sixteenth*. Now perhaps this man just happened to leave his one-day-old newspaper in the restaurant, and perhaps Becker just happened to pick up a quite separate copy of the same one-day-old edition, but I myself find that difficult to believe."

He paused, regarded her gravely.

"Our training teaches us to distrust coincidence. Especially when it passes a certain point. The man in this first photograph, Colonel, has been identified by the Photo Archive in Moscow as an official of the counterespionage section of the FBI."

Silence. What made her invariably such a bitch? Volkhov wondered. Why did she always need to be fighting him, reminding him who was boss? Was she trying to prove she had balls? . . . That was probably it, he thought. And the effort to deny her identity had led to sexual frustration. Probably she needed to be fucked. He tried to imagine doing it. The notion was not unpleasurable; hostility between sexual partners often lent a certain spice to the proceedings. The problem was, he thought, she'd always want to be on top.

"You're saying you think that the sleeper has been turned?"

He shrugged. "I think there are questions, at least, as to his integrity."

"Questions?" She stared. "You seem to be a specialist at questions, Major. I prefer answers. They're easier to work with."

"Of course." He nodded. "The problem is how to obtain them."

"It's simple, surely. You have questions, ask them."

"Interrogate the sleeper?" He looked dubious. "He's polygraph resistant. We could question him forcefully, I suppose, but that would destroy him as an asset. If, on the other hand, we could establish that he's been turned, but without his knowing that we know, we could still use him. Not for the original purpose, of course, but for something."

"I do realize that," she said frostily. "And I know how much you hate to waste assets. I'm not suggesting you interrogate the sleeper. Interrogate the other one."

"The other one?" It was his turn to stare. "But that means . . ."

She cut him off. "I'm perfectly aware of what it means."

He continued to stare. If she knew what it meant, she *did* have balls. Balls where her brains should be.

CHAPTER THIRTY-FIVE

STONEMAN NEVER SAW HIS VISITORS ARRIVE. FOR A MOMENT HE thought he'd heard what might have been a car coming up the driveway, but since the barn where he was working was some distance from the house, he hadn't been certain, nor indeed much interested in finding out. He was busy, wasn't expecting a caller, didn't have time for casual chitchat. People who just dropped in unannounced would have to take their chances. If they tracked him down to the barn, OK. If not, that was fine with him too. He'd put the subject out of his mind and returned his attention to Volume Ten of *The Photographic History of the Civil War*. What he needed right now was not visitors but a decent picture of a private in the 7th Michigan.

He wasn't really aware of them until they entered. He heard the side door creak, looked down from the loft where he was working, and there they were, three of them, a woman and two men, standing in semi-shadow by the doorway. An impulse made him switch on the floods—the lighting console was next to where he was sitting. For a moment they stood, blinking in the sudden glare, focussing, when their eyes had adjusted, on the half-finished model of Fredericksburg (circa 1861) that suddenly and startlingly had sprung into being all around them. Only afterwards—it seemed to him almost minutes—did they turn their attention back to him. His curiosity, too, was at first preempted by pleasure at the amazement (you could call it stupefaction, he thought) that had evidently seized them at the sight of the model. It was not till the woman spoke to her companions in a language he recognized as Russian that his memory, starting to function, discovered in its files at least two of the faces now turned in his direction. His satisfaction gave way to disquiet. These people were not casual callers. The shorter of the two men, the one in the camel hair overcoat with the plump shiny face and thinning hair slicked back from his forehead, was Pavel Volkhov, familiar from dozens of photographs, officially Assistant Cultural Attaché with the Russian Embassy but in fact almost certainly KGB. And the woman—he couldn't immediately recall her name—was officially the new Soviet Counsellor for Economic Affairs but most probably, in view of the near coincidence of her arrival with his departure, Stein's replacement as Washington Resident. The other man Stoneman couldn't identify from memory but didn't, on the other hand, really need to. The man was bullet-headed, coffin-faced, built like a truck. His presence was heavy with physical menace, albeit a certain blankness in his look that suggested he had long ago and willingly surrendered to others the responsibility for anything his presence might seem to threaten. He was clearly (behind whatever elaborate facade his masters had contrived to disguise his essential function) just muscle.

"You are Francis Stoneman." Volkhov was the speaker, his words a statement, not a question, and therefore, Stoneman decided, not in need of an answer.

"What do you want?" Not in need of politeness, either.

"We wish to talk." Volkhov again. The file described him as bilingual, Stoneman recalled, but it was not quite accurate. There was a hint of accent in the voice, something overcareful in the phrasing. "Will you come down, or shall we come up?"

Politeness, but a limited choice, Stoneman noted; where but not whether. For a moment he thought of the lighting console. He could throw the main switch, plunge the place into darkness, rely on his knowledge of the ground to get him out. Common sense, however, rejected the notion. There might be others outside. And the three below, much more to the point, might blunder around in the dark and damage his model. In any case, he asked himself, why so anxious? Granted these were KGB, but at least two of them were of the diplomatically accredited variety. And diplomatically accredited KGB were the plotters and planners of espionage, not its spear carriers. They would hardly risk

their health, or their carefully elaborated cover, by engaging in scuffles
on enemy turf. A remark made by Wellington at Waterloo floated to the
surface of Stoneman's consciousness: "It is not the business of general
officers to be *firing* on one another." A troubling question remained in
that case: What *was* their business?

No doubt they would shortly tell him.

He beckoned them to come up, sat waiting while they clunked up the
spiral staircase. Instinct prompted him to put down the book, however,
and get to his feet to meet them.

"What do you want to talk to me about?"

"My name is Smyslov." It seemed for a second that Volkhov would
offer a handshake, but instead he merely inclined his head and bent
slightly from the waist. He nodded at his companions. "These are
associates."

"Your name is Volkhov." As soon as the words were out, Stoneman
realized he'd made an error. Depriving them of their fictions might
make it impossible to maintain his. But it was too late now. He plunged
ahead. "You work for the Soviet Embassy, allegedly as a cultural
attaché. The woman is allegedly the Counsellor for Economic Affairs.
I'm afraid I can't remember,"—gesture to the other—"what this
gentleman allegedly is."

His gaze locked onto Volkhov's. Volkhov held it for a moment then
shrugged, nodded his head at the model. "What are you playing here?
War games?"

"It's a model of Fredericksburg. A Civil War battle. One of our
greatest general's greatest victories."

"Lee?" Volkhov cocked an eyebrow. "You admire Robert Lee?
Personally, I prefer the other one. Ulysses Grant. Robert Lee was on the
side of slavery. Also,"—pause—"on the side that lost."

"Lee disliked slavery," Stoneman said. "He released his own slaves
long before the war. And he knew he couldn't win, but he fought
anyway. For honor and duty, concepts you may find unfamiliar."

"Romanticism." Volkhov made a face. "Futile gestures. I don't
believe in them. All they achieve is unnecessary pain. Is that what you
believe in, honor and duty? Fighting anyway? Losing?"

Stoneman stared. "Was this what you wanted to talk to me
about?"

"Possibly not." Volkhov shrugged. "I *hope* not."

Pause. Volkhov used it to take a photograph from the large manila envelope he was holding. He handed the photograph to Stoneman. Stoneman examined it—a head and shoulders shot, three-quarters profile, of a man emerging from a doorway. It was Becker, Hollister's defector.

"We wish to know about your contacts with this man."

Stoneman took a few more moments inspecting, then shook his head, handed the photograph back. "I'm afraid I can't help you. I have no contacts with him. To the best of my knowledge, I've never met him."

"We believe otherwise." Volkhov made a show of consulting a sheaf of notes he'd removed from the envelope along with the photograph. "We know you are Francis Stoneman. You work for the Counterespionage Section of the FBI. On November sixteenth, at approximately one-twenty P.M., you endeavored to make contact with this man in a restaurant at 13th and K streets, by means of a message concealed in the newspaper you placed in his overcoat pocket. The newspaper was an out-of-date copy of *The Washington Post*. It was in your possession when you entered the restaurant, in his possession when he left." Volkhov paused. "Permit me to say that your tradecraft was rough."

Pause. Stoneman tried, successfully he thought, to hide his dismay.

"Permit *me* to say that your imagination is overactive."

"We know you work for the FBI," Volkhov said patiently. "How else would you have known my name? We have photographs of you entering that restaurant with the out-of-date copy of *The Washington Post* and leaving without it. We have photographs of your contact leaving the restaurant with a similarly out-of-date copy of *The Washington Post*. So tell me, what is left for me to imagine . . . the message?"

"I have no recollection of the events you describe. Since you say you have photographs, they presumably took place." Stoneman found himself copying the Russian's habits of speech. Their exchanges, as in all interrogations, were moves in a duel. It was a drama with conventions, formal, ceremonious, potentially deadly. "But if I happen to leave a newspaper in a restaurant, someone, surely, can happen to pick it up."

Volkhov shook his head. "Your contact sat at a table. You at the bar counter where, incidentally, you drank three dry martinis in less than an hour. You did not have your newspaper at the counter with you. He did not go anywhere near the bar.''

"Then I guess I discarded the newspaper at the coatrack."

"So you remember there was a coatrack? Your recollection improves, I see." Volkhov looked gravely at Stoneman, flicked a glance to the thug who stood beside him, imperturbable as a boulder, following these exchanges with no evident comprehension or even interest. "Look, Francis Stoneman, we need to know about your contacts with this man. We need to urgently. Do you understand what I mean?''

"You're making a very serious error." Stoneman understood perfectly, but he met Volkhov's gaze without blinking, managed to keep his voice steady. "I don't know this man. I don't know how he came to have my newspaper, if he did. All I know is, there was no message in it.''

Volkhov sighed, stepped back, said something in Russian to his henchman. The big man took a step towards Stoneman, stood for a moment in front of him, inspecting, then hit him in the face.

It was a loose-wristed blow, not a punch but a kind of contemptuous backhanded flick that caught Stoneman on the bridge of the nose. As his head jerked back, he felt cartilage give, and his vision blurred and swam. It was only by grabbing the table that he was able to stop himself falling.

"Stone . . . man." Volkhov pronounced the word as separate syllables. "A suggestive name. Are you, in fact, made of stone?''

Stoneman said nothing. There were tears of pain in his eyes; blood was running from his nose, but he felt oddly detached. He knew they had only started, that this would get much worse. But he could, he thought, at a pinch, take it. It was as if his body were somehow expendable, an outlying province whose temporary invasion could be viewed from the center with a certain indifference, as in no way compromising the integrity of the whole. He braced himself to be hit again, but before it could happen, the woman spoke. She spoke to Volkhov in Russian, sharply it seemed to Stoneman, and pointed to the model.

Volkhov shrugged and nodded. He turned back to Stoneman.

"My colleague accuses me of using unsound methods. She reminds me, correctly, that people are most vulnerable through what they love.''

Stoneman looked down at his model, the landscape bisected by the river, the half-ruined town on the high ground above it. It took up a good three-quarters of the barn. An inherited bias had prompted him, when the ground and buildings were finished, to people them first with the Confederate forces. So the figures for the town and the heights above the river were now largely completed and in place, but the Union positions were unoccupied. Lee's army seemed poised to fight off an enemy that had not yet materialized. But even now, in his mind's eye, Stoneman could see Burnside's forces, mustering for their gallant, futile attack. What was it, he wondered, that had kept him patiently at it? What explained its unslackening hold on his imagination? He supposed "love" was as good a word as any.

"It's a hobby." He shrugged. "Something to occupy my leisure."

Volkhov said something to his henchman. The big Russian stepped forward and picked up the chair on which Stoneman had been sitting. It was a wing-backed chair, upholstered in leather, a solid, old-fashioned, heavy piece of furniture, but he raised and held it above his head as if it were weightless. Then he pitched it over the balcony.

It landed like a bomb in a company of artillery, tearing a crater in the landscape, scattering and smashing the delicate, vulnerable figures, the men, gun carriages, and horses, each one of them perfect, whose making had cost Stoneman so many hours of labor.

"How long would it take you to rebuild?" Volkhov spoke conversationally, as if pursuing a mutual scientific interest. "What you've done so far, I mean. . . . Three years? Maybe five?"

Call it ten, Stoneman thought bitterly, if indeed he could ever rebuild it. And in fact he knew he wouldn't. He wouldn't have the energy to start over, nor the will. He said nothing.

"We were speaking before of futile gestures," Volkhov continued. "The thing to remember, of course, is that they are futile. They achieve nothing. Your labor of love will be ruined, your body perhaps broken, but sometime, sooner or later, but probably sooner, you will tell us. . . . You really ought to think about that."

He sounded concerned, his voice almost gentle. But it was standard procedure, Stoneman knew, one he himself had used on occasion. You offered your subject the foretaste of a violence both mechanical and utterly ruthless, then proposed yourself as an ally, a voice of sympathy and reason, interceding between him and it. It was an old technique, but effective, and he found himself wondering why he didn't just go ahead and tell them. The sleeper, after all, was as good as dead anyway, and effectively ruined for Hollister's purposes. And Hollister's purposes— though it now seemed clear that at least they were not treacherous— were ones in which he, Stoneman, had never placed much faith. In any case, he thought, when it came right down to it, he lacked the conviction for futile gestures, whose virtue, if any, consisted in their assertion of values above and beyond the strictly practical. He thought of Lee, lucid and unyielding, starting, for simple duty and honor, down the road it was clear even then would lead to Appomattox, and he knew not only that he was not of that temper but also his cause was not worth that devotion. There was nothing much real at issue here. To give his life, even the ten years he'd put into the model, to this sordid and tortuous chess game, whose object, probably, even the principals had long since lost sight of, would be a travesty of sacrifice, a sick joke of duty. It couldn't be loyalty that kept him from telling them.

What was it then?

That telling them wouldn't save him. . . . The truth hit him suddenly, like a kick in the stomach. The question that had nagged at him for the last few minutes—why it wasn't Becker they were kicking around—was clearly, chillingly, answered. It was obvious, wasn't it? If, without Becker knowing, these thugs could establish that he had been turned, they could still use him. Not as originally planned, but as a pipeline (unwitting, because it was clear he couldn't be trusted) for feeding their enemies false intelligence. But only, of course, so long as Hollister and his cohorts were unaware of the deception. Once the CIA realized the Russians knew their sleeper had been turned, his usefulness to the Russians, or indeed to anyone, would be history. . . . It made perfect sense, he thought. It explained, as nothing else did, why the Russians were asking *him* what their agent, Becker, was up to. And it also meant, of course, that if he told them what Becker was up to, they couldn't leave him in a position to reveal what *they* were up to. And it was even worse than this, because they already had grounds for suspecting Becker had been turned. If he stonewalled from now to doomsday, he would never convince them otherwise. So unless he could think of some way out, he wasn't just going to lose his model or be kicked around, he was going to be dead.

He had to get out of here . . . How?

Perhaps the lights . . . His original notion now seemed to make more sense. The master switch (he was careful not to look at it) was close to his left hand. The three Russians were facing him in a rough semicircle, the woman to the left between him and the staircase. If he hit the switch and went for the woman, pitching her sideways into the others, he might make it down the staircase before they got untangled. In the dark, his edge would be knowing the ground, both in the barn and outside. If he made it to the house, to the telephone and the twelve gauge, the odds would be in his favor.

The thug picked up the other wing-backed chair.

"Well?" Volkhov asked.

Stoneman waited till the chair was on its way. When the Russian thug's weight was into his follow-through, and the others, drawn to the prospect of destruction, had turned their heads to watch, he threw the master switch and, leading with his shoulder, hurled himself at the woman.

The darkness was absolute. He had the sensation of launching into the void. But he had gauged the distance perfectly. His shoulder slammed into the woman, the impact slowing his own momentum, imparting it to her, pitching her sideways into Volkhov with a gasp of pain and outrage his mind was able to register and fiercely relish, even as his hands grasped for and found the handrail of the staircase. Then he was down the staircase, half running, half falling, in a series of heart-stopping leaps of faith in which only his death grip on the handrail saved him from disaster. At the bottom, he cut right, not hesitating nor even really thinking, spurred by the sounds of incipient pursuit from overhead, his memory judging the distance to the wall, his feet by instinct dividing it into paces. Getting it right, too, the wall where it should have been, coming out of the darkness to him at just the moment he reached for it, so that even as his fingertips made contact with the planks, he was swerving left, down the alley that separated wall and model, and racing for the side door and safety. It was here, going almost full out, that he barreled into the metal folding chair he had somehow forgotten he'd brought down from the house and had therefore omitted from his mental map of the terrain. His feet were swept out from under him. His momentum cannoned him forwards and sideways, hurled him headlong into one of the posts that marked the boundary of the model.

It seemed to him that he was only out for a moment, but it must have been more like a full minute. When he came to, the lights were back on. The big Russian and Volkhov were standing over him, and he was looking into the muzzle of what memory, accurate but irrelevant, identified as a .45 Colt automatic.

PART IV

"Soles occidere et redire possunt.
Nobis cul semel occidit brevis lux
Nox est perpetua una dormienda."

Catullus

("Suns may set and rise again.
For us, once our brief light is spent,
there is one perpetual night to be slept through.")

CHAPTER THIRTY-SIX

THE NEWSPAPER REPORTS WERE BRIEF AND SHORT ON DETAIL. THE *Post,* in a story headlined "FBI MAN DIES IN FIRE," which it ran on page three, confined itself strictly to the facts. The body of Francis Stoneman, a senior member of the FBI, had been found by firemen in the burnt-out wreckage of a barn on his property near Raleigh, North Carolina. Fire had broken out in the barn late Saturday night, November 17. The local fire department, alerted by neighbors sometime after the fire had taken hold, had arrived to find the barn almost totally gutted. Stoneman's body, charred beyond recognition but later identified from his dental records, was discovered only when the blaze had been put out. Death had been caused by smoke inhalation. The barn had housed a scale model of the Civil War Battle of Fredericksburg, which, according to friends, Stoneman, a bachelor, had been building for several years. The cause of the fire was unknown, but fire department sources had speculated that it might have been sparked by an electrical fault in the extensive system of floodlights apparently used to illuminate the model, which was built largely from balsa wood and model cement and was therefore intensely flammable. It seemed likely that Stoneman, trying to fight the flames with the fire extinguisher found next to his body in the wreckage, had been overcome by smoke and toxic fumes from the paint used in the model.

The Washington Star, reporting essentially the same set of facts, found a possibly sinister significance in Stoneman's having worked for

191

the counterespionage section of the FBI. Its account of the incident, which ran at the foot of page one under the headline "SPYCATCHER DIES IN BLAZE," and which, to the annoyance of his immediate superior, Borden, overstated Stoneman's government service rank, included a statement from an FBI spokesman that the Bureau "found no reason whatsoever to suspect that Frank Stoneman's death was in any way connected with his work, or indeed that it was anything but a tragic accident." This statement, though acknowledged by the *Star* to have been made in response to a direct question, was printed otherwise without comment, an omission, presumably, intended to speak volumes to the *Star*'s discerning readers.

Hollister, unquestionably a discerning reader, though not normally of the *Star,* greeted the news—he read both of the newspaper accounts—with a mix of relief and misgiving. The relief was natural and unalloyed with regret. Stoneman had always been a pain in the ass, and in this latest business with the KGB sleeper he had threatened (for Hollister had not been convinced by his show of complying with Borden's orders) to be a *royal* pain in the ass. The misgivings sprang from the fact that, after fifteen years in the counterespionage business, Hollister found it hard to believe in the Tooth Fairy. If Stoneman's death was convenient, it was also way too coincidental. Stoneman, Hollister was certain, had died for reasons in some way connected with the sleeper. Either the sleeper himself had murdered him, or the KGB had. And if the latter, there was more going on here than had so far met the eye. Hollister would dearly have loved to know what it was that didn't meet the eye, but since showing interest would merely draw unneeded attention to himself, there was nothing he could do for the moment except button his lip and sit on his hands—and pray.

Becker, another discerning reader, was also a sceptic about coincidence. His reaction was simple dismay. Stoneman had forced a contact, demanded a meeting, and now, before Becker had had a chance to respond, Stoneman was dead. It was possible—Becker was inclined to think it probable—that he'd been murdered and by someone who had known about the contact; that the two events, in fact, were connected. If so, the candidates for killer were either Hollister or the KGB, and though he wouldn't have put it past Hollister to choose this decisive and permanent method of getting Stoneman's cooperation, he tended to favor the KGB. The murder, if it was one, had a KGB flavor about it. And the implications, of course, were alarming: Just at the moment when the CIA had seemed neutralized, the KGB had discovered that their sleeper had been turned. Their reaction, though not predictable in detail, was likely to be violent and harmful to his health. He must therefore find some method of neutralizing the KGB—soon.

The Resident read the newspaper reports—she'd had Volkhov prepare a translation of them, allegedly to catch any nuance of the English she might miss, but actually for the pleasure of employing him in a task he was bound to regard as demeaning—with satisfaction. It was clear that at least officially (which was all she cared about) the authorities had bought the scenario offered to explain Stoneman's death. And since, prior to beating him senseless and incinerating what was left of him in the wreckage of his model, her minions had succeeded in extracting the admission that the sleeper had defected to the CIA, the KGB was admirably placed, she thought, to exploit the new situation. Igor could no longer be used, of course, to penetrate the CIA's new computer system, but he could serve as a channel for misinformation and also perhaps as a decoy to distract the CIA while *Marigold* penetrated the system. Indeed, as she remarked to Volkhov, while things were perhaps not working out exactly as planned, they were nevertheless working out very nicely.

Volkhov received this remark, as he'd received the order to prepare the newspaper translations, in silence. His reaction to events as they were presently developing was like that of an expert observing a chess game by beginners: a reluctant, slightly appalled fascination at moves so inept they created, in the end, their own perverse logic. Since Marigold was still missing, he could not be used to penetrate anything. So Becker, serving as decoy, would be serving no useful purpose. Moreover, since he, Volkhov, had less confidence than ever that the CIA's new computer system was anything but a fiction, there was, he was almost certain, no useful purpose to be served. Thus Stoneman's interrogation, not to mention his subsequent murder, had achieved little but the confirmation of facts that, in Volkhov's estimation at least, had not stood in need of confirming.

The whole business, in short, had been unnecessary and distasteful—stupid.

CHAPTER THIRTY-SEVEN

THE SAKS ON WISCONSIN WAS JAMMED WITH SATURDAY SHOPPERS, and Arlen, drifting listlessly through the menswear department, found herself wondering, not for the first time, about the trick of character that seemed to impel her, whenever she was seriously unhappy, to go out and spend a bunch of money. Was it, she asked herself, what she bought that mattered? Was the acquisition of things an attempt to compensate for psychic deprivation? Or was it the act of spending that was vital, an assertion that, however bleakly she might view it at the moment, the future existed and must be provided for, for instance by buying Christmas presents? Or was it just that being in stores and spending money had always given her a lot of pleasure, and when most other pleasures were letting her down, she instinctively turned to the tried and true? She didn't know. And it didn't, of course, really matter. There were only two things here that really mattered. The first was that, in her experience, going out and spending a bunch of money was always at least mildly therapeutic—a kind of spiritual equivalent to Maalox, she thought wryly, fast temporary relief for a bad case of heartburn. The second, that thanks to the generous provisions of her grandmother's will, she had a bunch of money to go out and spend.

So far, in the space of twenty minutes, she'd spent six hundred dollars.

She'd bought boots (to add to the five or six pairs she had already), a pair of French sunglasses (to protect her eyes against a sun that hadn't,

it seemed to her, shone in weeks), a set of six champagne flutes
(champagne to celebrate what? she asked herself), some silk scarves,
and a jerkin in soft Italian leather, which in spite of a price tag that
boggled the mind she hadn't been able to resist. In the interest of
staying solvent, she thought, she needed to get out of here. There
remained, however, the problem that ostensibly had brought her in the
first place: What to get Uncle Max for Christmas?

Some kind of sweater? He probably had dozens already, but another
wouldn't hurt. She wandered over to a table display and started to pick
through the selection.

"Can I help you with anything?"

The store assistant was young and good-looking. His smile conveyed,
along with an occupational eagerness to please, the recognition that she
also was young and good-looking, and the suggestion that they might,
therefore, find they had other things in common.

"I'm looking for a sweater." Her own smile was merely polite.
Though normally she enjoyed flirtation, it was not what she needed at
present. "Cashmere, maybe . . . In navy or brown, I think. With long
sleeves."

"Crew neck or V? Or perhaps a polo?"

"V, I think . . . Or maybe a polo. I'm not sure." She tried to
visualize her uncle, but could call to mind only a generalized image of
silver-haired distinction. "I'd better take a look at what you've got.
Men are so hard to buy for, I find."

"Perhaps I can help. Would this be for your husband? . . . A boyfriend, perhaps?"

A boyfriend? Fat chance. Impossible, however, not to think of Becker.
He kept lurking just below the threshold of her consciousness, quick to
respond to exactly such a summons. She could picture him now in the
navy polo neck being offered for her inspection, a fringe of hair falling into
his eyes, his head tilted slightly to one side, the lean face with the high
Slavic cheekbones wearing its customary look of amused provocation.
A clever face, she thought, a game player's face, the face of a man who
might argue—*had* argued, in fact, and with cogency and wit—that by
far the most interesting character in modern fiction was Spiderman.
Becker the educated spook. She wondered what he was doing right
now. Was he really a spook? Or had that been just bullshit he'd

dreamed up (under *her* prompting of course) to cover a strategic withdrawal? . . . But these questions, too, she thought, didn't really matter. What mattered was that, for whatever reason, he'd dumped her. She missed him, and her pride was hurt, but she'd get over that.

Screw him.

"Navy not doing it for you?" The salesman's voice cut in. "Maybe the brown?"

She hardly heard him. Her attention, recalled to the present, somehow bypassed the salesman entirely and focused instead on someone behind him, a man on the far side of the counter, looking at ties in a rack. Or rather *pretending* to look at them, for though his eyes had instantly flicked away when she looked, what he'd actually been looking at was her. Not casually either. Their eyes had met only for a moment, but his, she was sure, had not just been girl-watching. And almost at once, she knew that she'd seen him before, and where. She'd met him coming out of Becker's house. He'd attacked her and left her unconscious.

"Should I show you the brown?"

But Arlen's gaze was riveted on the man at the tie rack. He seemed more than ever intent on ties, but she was sure he had recognized her, too. Why, otherwise, had he looked away so quickly?

"Miss?"

She turned back to the salesman. "I'm sorry . . ."

"Are you feeling OK? You don't look well."

She stared at him vacantly. His smile had given way to a look of wary concern, as if he thought she might be going to faint, but still she barely registered his words. What she heard instead were Becker's, the last time they'd been together. . . . *Those people are dangerous. If they knew I'd been talking to you, they'd kill you. . . .* The salesman's question, his tepid concern, the whole world of cashmere sweaters, charge accounts, Christmas presents seemed suddenly irrelevant, unreal. . . . *Those people are dangerous . . .* The man at the tie rack was real. He belonged in Becker's world, and he was dangerous. It was clear, whatever else he had lied about, that about this Becker had been telling the truth.

She looked back to the tie rack. The man had gone.

She looked around wildly, spotted him almost immediately, picking through the shirts at a table near the main exit. . . . The *other* exit, she thought; if she took the far exit, she'd have a head start. . . .

She snatched her packages from the counter.

"I'm sorry," she stammered at the salesman. "It's . . . the heat in here, maybe. I'm really *not* feeling very well. I need fresh air."

She had to get out. To go home. Or maybe not home. Maybe to the police. Or at least, she thought, away from the man at the tie rack and his ilk.

Somewhere safe.

Where?

Serafin watched her departure with satisfaction. He'd gotten lucky again. Lucky to have spotted her in the first place. Lucky also to have spotted her before she spotted him. Lucky above all to have been with Kasparov when he'd spotted her. A chase that would otherwise have been problematic would now be as simple as beating game. He, having spooked her, would drive her towards Kasparov and let himself be lost; and she, having assured herself she'd lost Serafin, would then lead Kasparov straight to her car. This time they would get the license plate number.

They should have got it the last time. Volkhov had been scathing about that. License plate numbers, he'd patiently explained, enabled vehicle owners to be identified and contacted.

And not necessarily by the police.

CHAPTER THIRTY-EIGHT

THE POSTCARD ARRIVED IN THE MORNING MAIL AT VOLKHOV'S APART-
ment. This in itself was unusual. Volkhov didn't normally receive much
personal mail. What personal mail he did receive was usually from the
Soviet Union, and it came to the Embassy in the diplomatic bag. The
postcard, however, was clearly personal; the message and address were
handwritten and the picture was of some tropical beach populated by
women in bikinis. The postmark said St. Lucia.

Volkhov had never been to St. Lucia. He didn't know anyone there.
He couldn't recall knowing, or even having met, anyone whose plans
for the second week of November had included a trip to the West
Indies. Someone in St. Lucia, or someone who'd been there on the 13th
of November, knew him, however, (or knew someone who knew him)
for the postcard was clearly and unambiguously addressed. Perhaps a bit
too unambiguously addressed, Volkhov thought, for the use of his
military rank, given the allegedly civilian nature of his job, was something he discouraged. Exactly who—among the small number of his
acquaintances who knew of his military connection—had sent him a
postcard from St. Lucia was not immediately clear, however, since the
postcard was unsigned.

Nor was the message immediately clear. . . . "To a poet, the words
of a poet must always be pregnant with meaning: NAL. R&J. III, i,
108." It referred him to a work of literature presumably, but which
work? Reflection suggested Shakespeare (*Romeo and Juliet*, Act Three,

scene one, line one hundred and eight?) but this failed to account for the initials, NAL, which formed part of the reference and were therefore, apparently, important. In any case, the line in question—Volkhov looked it up in a massive *Collected Works,* the only edition of Shakespeare in the Embassy library—was disappointingly *un*pregnant with meaning, being neither a complete sentence nor relevant, so far as he could see, to any of his current preoccupations. It was only after a lunch spent moodily trying to recall what he could of an English literature course he'd taken at the university that his memory came up with a potentially helpful fact: The texts of Shakespeare's plays were all more or less corrupt; no version was generally accepted as authentic, and different editions—a prime example was *Hamlet*—could vary by hundreds of lines. To refer precisely to a line of Shakespeare one needed, therefore, to specify the edition. In the light of that recollection, and with help from the glossary of *Books in Print,* "NAL" ceased to be a problem. Line one hundred and eight of Act Three, scene one, in the *New American Library* edition of *Romeo and Juliet* was, he found, alarmingly pregnant with meaning.

So much so that he felt obliged to request an immediate meeting with the Resident.

" 'A plague a both your houses' . . ." The Resident looked at the quote and back at Volkhov. Her expression was both sceptical and unfriendly. "I don't get any message out of this. It doesn't even make grammatical sense."

"It's a matter of context." Volkhov worked to keep his look neutral, his tone properly subordinate. The Resident's grasp of English, adequate for most purposes, was not, apparently, equal to Shakespeare. But this was clearly no time to be showing off his own superior knowledge. The citadel of his security had fallen. The walls had been thrown down. He stood naked to the freezing winds of his superior officer's hostility. It would be wise to conciliate, come across as the humble technician, possessed of a specialized and limited expertise which, she, with her broader talents and duties, had not been able to spare time to acquire. "The play, Colonel, deals with a feud between noble families. The speaker, a supporter of one family, has been mortally wounded in a brawl with members of the other. He is uttering, in effect, a curse upon both.'' He paused, then added as a kind of peace offering, ''The language, of course, is archaic and colloquial. 'Houses' in context means 'families.' The second 'a' is a corruption of 'on.' ''

Silence. The Resident let her gaze rest on him just long enough to make him uncomfortable. It occurred to him that his display of erudition had achieved the effect he'd hoped to avoid, that part of his problem was he'd lectured her too much. He received this insight with a mental shrug. It wouldn't have made any difference. At this point, a miracle wouldn't make any difference.

''And you think that because Marigold has refused contact now for . . . What is it? Three weeks? . . . Four?''—her voice had a latent menace, like a folded razor—''that therefore this message must be from him?''

He shrugged. ''I don't know who else it could be from. Marigold has failed to respond to repeated requests for a contact. He knows my real position here, my military rank, also that in my spare time I write verse. The situation of the speaker in the play at least superficially resembles his. . . .'' Volkhov shrugged. ''It all seems to fit.''

''The situation in the play resembles his? Are you suggesting he's telling us he's dying?''

He considered. This was an aspect that hadn't occurred to him. ''It's possible. I don't know. But if that's what he wanted to tell us, I doubt he'd do it in such a roundabout way. I think he's telling us he's quitting. That he no longer wishes to take part in this feud.''

She considered him coldly. ''Feud? Is that how you regard the Worldwide Proletarian Struggle against Imperialism and the Forces of Reaction?''

She was speaking in slogans again, which probably meant she was taping the conversation. This in turn, of course, meant she was back to collecting evidence for The Case Against Volkhov. It was as well, therefore, that he also had thought to take precautions. He shook his head. ''I was using the terms of his reference to the play. I'm saying I think that's how *he* might regard it. The tone of his message, given the recent developments, strikes me as perhaps deliberately insubordinate.''

''I'm quite sure you're right.'' *Her* tone suggested that when it came to deliberate insubordination, she considered him an authority. ''The assets recruited by you and Stein, I've noticed, tend to be lacking in ideological commitment.''

Mere provocation. He let it pass. Motive was important, of course, but only as a means of control. Most agents just wanted revenge or money, though the few who laid claim to ideological conviction might also look for gratitude and respect. In the last analysis, however, though this woman would never put off the blinders of dogma for long enough to recognize the fact, what *brought* people to treachery was unimportant; what was important was what *kept* them there. And what mostly kept them there, the ideological and the venal alike, was fear. But fear hadn't worked with Marigold, he thought, or not in the normal way. Marigold had been that rare phenomenon, the existential risk taker. Like Philby, or Sorge, or any of the great spies, his motive had been mostly the thrill of living on the edge. For him, fear had acted as a drug. Then why had he quit? Perhaps, Volkhov thought, the woman for once was right, and the quote from *Romeo* was apt in more ways than one; perhaps Marigold was indeed dying. Volkhov hoped not. Though Marigold's recent actions have placed Major Volkhov's career at considerable risk, he found himself worried for his former agent, not just as an asset but as a man. To the limited extent that their contacts had allowed them to know one another, he'd liked him.

"If I might have your attention, Major . . . ." The Resident's voice, it's edge quite naked now, cut into these reflections. "What steps have you taken to verify your hunch? Have you, for instance, placed surveillance on his house? Are you sure he's left the area? Do you even know whether he's still at his desk?"

Oh naturally not, Volkhov thought savagely. Of *course* I've taken none of the obvious steps. It's because I'm an idiot, you see, because I've been fifteen years in this profession, most of them in the field, and managed in that time to learn absolutely nothing. . . . Aloud, he said:

"When he failed to respond to his call sign, Colonel, my thought, of course, was that he'd somehow been blown. The impulse to try and verify this suspicion by placing a watch on his house was curbed, however, by an instinct for caution. Were he, for example, merely under suspicion, then the presence of our surveillance, if detected, would only compromise him utterly." Volkhov paused. He was lecturing again, but the bitch appeared to need it. And since the conversation seemed destined to be part of the evidence against him, he might as well score some points for the defense. "I did, however, take other action. I was able to confirm, for instance, that he wasn't to be seen in any of his haunts: the local restaurants, for instance, or his club. I found out he'd cancelled his subscriptions to newspapers and magazines. My provisional conclusions were, therefore, that he'd gone away somewhere, and that his departure had been voluntary, not the reverse." He paused again. "These conclusions, I suggest, are confirmed by this message."

This was reasonable, he thought. This would look good in the transcript. Not her transcript, of course. His.

The Resident, however, seemed unimpressed.

"Did you cable Barbados to send someone to check in St. Lucia?"

Volkhov shook his head. "It seemed to me, Colonel, amidst so much that was speculation, one thing at least could be taken as reasonably certain. If Marigold was at *any* time in St. Lucia, he is surely not there now."

"That's speculation too, Major. As usual, you are betting on a hunch." She paused. "It is one of the things I find inexcusable in your conduct that you persist at crucial times in making these errors of judgement. I want an immediate trace put out for Marigold, the search to start in St. Lucia. And when I say immediate, I mean 'starting the instant this meeting is over.' Do I make myself clear?"

He nodded stonily. "Quite clear, Colonel."

"Another thing I find inexcusable. . . . And this I find *truly* inexcusable, for while your other failings can perhaps be put down to incompetence, this I can only attribute to disloyalty. . . . What I find truly inexcusable is this: that when a major asset disappears without trace, it takes a month before I hear about it."

Disloyalty. A serious word. She had him at her mercy and she planned to disembowel him. "Errors of judgement" could derail a career; "Disloyalty," as she well knew, could kill you. But that was like her, he thought; her kind was never content with winning.

"I did plan on telling you, Colonel, but delayed in the hope of getting more information. In the hope, also, that Marigold would resume contact and spare me the need to worry you with the matter." He paused. "These hopes were clearly misplaced. Permit me to say, however, that my motive was the opposite of disloyalty."

She stared at him without expression.

"And permit *me* to say, Major, that for close to one month you conspired to keep from your head of station that a vital asset under your control had disappeared without trace. Permit me to point out also that of the two major assets asigned to your control, one has defected and the other appears to have quit. Your protestations as to motive notwithstanding, the facts will speak for themselves, I think.''

He received this in silence. His only hope, he thought, was that she would somehow overplay her hand. Perhaps in her eagerness to nail him she would falsify the record, lay herself open to his countercharge that for reasons of egotism she was running a private vendetta against him. It was for this reason, at any rate, that he'd taken the risk of coming to this meeting wired for sound. There would be two records of the conversation, and one, at least, would be accurate.

"So . . ." She leaned forward, suddenly brisk, signalling by her change of manner a change of topic. Major Volkhov's shortcomings could evidently keep for the moment. Major Volkhov's shortcomings would be served up later. Cold, he thought, the way revenge was proverbially best eaten. "What is your analysis of this situation? Given that my original plans have been botched in the execution, how do you think we should proceed?''

How did he think they should proceed? He thought they shouldn't. He thought they should never have started. And Stoneman's revelations —an otherwise regrettable episode had at least achieved something, Volkhov thought—had surely confirmed that. For the CIA's insistence on leaving Igor, against his own expressed wishes, where he was, suggested they planned to use him chiefly as a means of learning about KGB intentions with regard to the computer system. And that suggested they weren't at all worried about the computer system. Which in turn suggested that the computer system, as he had argued from the start, was just the bait with which they hoped to lure Marigold into the open. But Marigold had bolted, thus rendering the maneuvering on both sides pointless. The KGB might be able to find him, of course, but as the postcard indicated, at least to anyone who knew him, Marigold was through. No amount of persuasion, friendly or otherwise, was likely to make him change his mind. As for the sleeper . . . From what Stoneman had told them about him, he might as well have co–signed Marigold's postcard. They might *try* to use him, but as his actions had made clear, he objected to being used. He was intelligent, resourceful, resentful, unreliable; more likely, therefore, to prove a liability than an asset. They should let him go.

Or kill him.

Volkhov thought about this. He had no particular objection to killing, if it achieved something, but what would this achieve? What, indeed, had the whole operation to date achieved? Some people had been killed. . . . Why make it more?

"Well? . . ." the Resident demanded.

"I think we should cut our losses."

"By which you mean abandon the operation?"

He nodded. "That and find Marigold, if we can. Find out what danger he poses to us. If necessary, eliminate him." He paused. "On second thought, since he will always be in a position to reveal to the CIA which of their secrets he has passed us, he will always be somewhat of a danger to us. Perhaps it would be safer to eliminate him."

"And Igor?"

"In his case, I think we should sever the connection. Let the CIA, if it wishes, imagine it has an asset."

"You mean just let him go?"

He nodded. "Anything else, it strikes me, would be wasted effort."

For a moment she said nothing, just looked at him. When she spoke, her voice was dangerously mild.

"Igor was—was he not?—a Soviet citizen and a KGB officer."

She paused for his response. He nodded.

"And while actively employed by the KGB, he not only refused to carry out orders but engaged in treasonable contacts with the enemies of the state. Am I correct?"

Silence.

"Am I correct, Major?"

Reluctantly, he nodded.

"Then what, in your view, does that make him?"

In view of his own predicament, there was only one possible answer. "It makes him a traitor."

"It makes him a traitor. Which is one very good reason why we cannot just let him go. Because traitors, Major Volkhov"—she fixed him with a stare like an icepick—"traitors must be punished."

CHAPTER THIRTY-NINE

ALONG WITH THE MANY THINGS BEQUEATHED HER BY HER GRAND-mother—three quarters of a million dollars in cash and marketable securities, seventy acres along a creek in northern New Mexico close to the Colorado border, a house and its contents in Alexandria, Virginia—Arlen had inherited an obligation. A great-grandfather and two great-uncles had died in Dachau. Their arrest, in a roundup of Jews of which they'd had some advance warning, had resulted, so Arlen's grandmother claimed (she and her mother had been visiting cousins in France), from delaying their escape in order to assemble that bare minimum of material possessions they conceived to be necessary for starting life in exile. "Steenie's getaway valise," as it was called by those family members who didn't share her sense of history, had its origins in that family tragedy. Transplanted to a United States where, she was assured, such things could never happen, Steenie was nonetheless subject to attacks of anxiety. To allay them she had resolved that, for one family and in one respect at least, history should not be permitted to repeat itself. "Steenie's getaway valise" had been packed and repacked every month for thirty-five years. It had passed from a family secret to a family joke to something close to a family icon, a symbol of their history and will to survive. And Arlen, on her grand-mother's death, had found it entrusted to her care, not just because she was her grandmother's heir, but also, as the will expressed it, because

205

she'd been "the only one loving enough to be trusted to respect an old woman's wishes and the only one smart enough to understand the need."

In fact, the second part of this judgement had somewhat flattered Arlen. Or perhaps it had flattered Steenie's own judgement. Arlen, at any rate, had kept the valise intact, and from time to time checked the contents, more from the wish to honor her grandmother's memory than from any conviction of real need. She herself was remote enough from Dachau that it, and the impulses that had given it being, had taken no hold on her imagination. The Holocaust was a part of her inherited consciousness, and pictures of the death camps would always make her shiver, but it was a detached kind of shiver, born both of a natural sympathy for the victims and an equally natural conviction that the Holocaust was history, and history was what happened to other people. This conviction had not survived her encounter in Saks with the man from Becker's house. History, it seemed, was suddenly camped on her doorstep.

The terror of that encounter hadn't left her. She was sure she'd given the man the slip, but the conclusion that she was therefore safe had survived no more than a moment's reflection. There could have been others. And though no one, so far as she'd been able to tell, had followed her home, someone could have noted her license plate number. She was *not* safe. There was someone out there—the conviction grew stronger the more she thought about it—tracking her down.

But what to do? . . . Her first instinct, to go to the police, was almost immediately rejected. The police wouldn't believe her. She could imagine the patronizing smiles, the unconcealed scepticism with which they'd receive her hysterical woman's tale of an ex-boyfriend who worked for some secret outfit or other and an encounter (in *Saks,* of all places) with foreign agents. Though she'd willingly have endured their scepticism to obtain their protection, since they wouldn't give her protection there was just no point. Her other obvious option, to get out of the country, keep moving, make it harder for them to track her down, was at first glance more promising, but suffered the drawback, fatal in her eyes, of adding to the uncertainty and prolonging the terror. When would she know she was safe? And how? And wouldn't she, in the meantime, though the danger might be imaginary, be haunted by a fear that was constant and real? A single day sitting in her house, pretending to read or watch TV, and all the time listening for God knew what—suspicious noises or suspicious silences—had convinced her of how little of that sort of thing she could take. The only choice she was left with—she was forced to it, she told herself, pride would just have to defer to her need—was to get in touch with Becker, tell him what had happened, and find out from him the real extent of the danger and what exactly was going on. At least this way she'd know what she had to deal with, whether there was anything to be gained by flight. And his former objections to seeing her, surely, were answered by what had happened. On his own admission, he was responsible for her predicament. He could hardly refuse to help.

She'd sent him a note by messenger service. Since his house was bugged, his phone presumably tapped, this had seemed the one means of getting in touch that was quick and also reasonably secure. The note had said enough, or so she hoped, to convince him her need was real. "The people you warned me about have been back in touch. I'm scared. Please contact. Arlen." She had hesitated over that "I'm scared," thinking perhaps that the appeal to his pity was too naked. But it was true, wasn't it? She was more scared than she'd ever been in her life.

As she'd sat in her apartment, waiting for the call from Becker that might or might not come, it had seemed to her that, apart from the flimsy brass chain and far from impregnable mortice lock on her door, she was defenseless. If they traced her to her house and decided to break in, she had nothing at all with which to resist them, except—a notion so ludicrous that in other circumstances it would have made her smile—a kitchen knife.

It was then she'd remembered the getaway valise.

Or rather, what she actually remembered was Steenie's Luger.

The Luger—how she could have forgotten it?—had always been at the heart of arguments over the getaway valise. The financial assets, the three one-carat diamonds sewn into the lining, the fat wad of greenbacks (later replaced, as a result of Steenie's well-founded fears for the future of the dollar, by rolls of gold Krugerrand), had at various times been subject to objection on the grounds that stashing them in a valise was a waste, like burying money in a jam jar. But since it was Steenie's money, and since the diamonds at least had answered by increasing astronomically in value, these objections had never been forcefully urged. The Luger, on the other hand, had provoked outrage.

We are not violent people. How often Arlen had heard the argument: her uncles asserting that ownership of a gun—a German gun at that—amounted to the adoption, tacitly, of principles that ran counter to everything they had ever held sacred, principles which, if you examined them closely, led straight to Hitler and the philosophy of the death camps; her grandmother telling them to come down to earth, to recognize the world for what it was, and admit, accordingly, the need for precautions. . . . *We are not violent people.* Though accepting this assertion of her culture's essentially pacific nature, Steenie nevertheless insisted on adding a rider: *But we are if we have to be.*

We are if we have to be. Arlen had never taken much part in these debates. Her belief about guns had always been that, in the hands of the inexperienced, they were more a source of risk than of safety. She'd been sure that if it came right down to it and her life were on the line, she wouldn't be able to pull the trigger. But now, sitting in the bedroom alone with her fear, the contents of the valise laid out on the bed, she felt different. The Luger and its magazine of bullets—the oiled wood, brass, and blued metal forming a composition of spare, functional beauty—seemed set apart from the extra clothes, the coil of rope, the pile of emergency rations. It seemed to belong to another order of existence, to radiate somehow promise and power. She picked it up, cocking it as Steenie had shown her, and worked the safety. Then, uncocking the action and checking that the safety was on, she fitted the magazine into the butt and slapped it into place with the heel of her hand. Hefting the weapon, she seemed to feel some of its power flow into her. She heard an echo of her grandmother's voice . . . *We are if we have to be* . . . and understood that for her, too, violence was not a question of nature but of choice, that if it came right down to it, she *could* pull the trigger.

Just then, from downstairs, came a knock at the door.

She crept downstairs and approached the front door on stockinged feet, Luger at the ready. It occurred to her that if she ended up letting someone in, the Luger might be difficult to explain, but at this point she was past caring about embarrassment. In any case, she wasn't going to let anyone in. Not anyone she didn't know.

She looked through the peephole.

She saw a face, white and male, apparently young, not altogether clean-shaven. Its expression, so far as she could make it out, seemed innocent of menace. In other circumstances she'd have described it as stoic. It seemed to belong to someone patiently waiting, someone, moreover, accustomed to patiently waiting.

He knocked again. For the fourth time, wasn't it? Shouldn't he have given up by now?

"Who is it?"

"Messenger service. If you're Arlen Singer, I got something for you."

"I'm Arlen Singer. Can't you shove it through the letter slot?"

Pause.

"Won't it fit?" she enquired.

"It'll fit, but I need you to sign a receipt. I'm not s'posed to deliver without it."

"So shove the receipt through the letter slot too."

Another pause, longer this time.

"Look, lady, why not just open the door? You scared of something?"

"Yes," Arlen said. "As a matter of fact, very scared. Push the receipt through the letter slot and I'll sign it and send it back. Then you can make your delivery."

"I was told to wait for an answer: 'yes or no.' "

"So wait. I'll give you an answer . . . and a tip."

Promptly, the receipt came through the mail slot.

Arlen's purse was on the hall table. She placed the Luger within easy reach and rummaged in the purse for a pen and a five-dollar bill. Signing the receipt, she shoved it and the five dollars back under the door. A manila envelope came through the slot. Inside, a single sheet of paper gave detailed instructions for a meeting downtown that afternoon. It was signed: "Becker."

"What's your answer?" Five dollars, it seemed, did not buy gratitude or much of the messenger's time. "Yes or no?"

Arlen hesitated. This might be a setup designed to lure her out of the house. Maybe they'd intercepted her message and were faking Becker's response. But they couldn't know—could they?—that she always addressed Becker by his surname. And, anyway, what about the postscript? . . . "P.S. I still think the most interesting character in modern American fiction is Spiderman."

"Jesus, lady . . ." The messenger was getting impatient. "Do you need six months to make up your mind? Is he asking you to marry him or something? Do I tell him yes? Or do I tell him no?"

"Tell him yes," Arlen said.

CHAPTER FORTY

When the van arrived in front of Becker's house, the man named Garland, who was pruning fruit trees in the orchard, took a moment to glance at his watch. It was two-thirty. Another half hour, he thought, and he could maybe justify getting off this damn ladder and taking a coffee break. He shifted the ladder to another branch, one that happened to afford a view of both the front and back of the house, and went back to his pruning. He worked, as he had all morning and indeed for the past three days, deliberately; more deliberately than another employer might have been willing to tolerate and more thoroughly than the state of the trees perhaps warranted. But gardeners, he'd observed, were deliberate people (and much given to coffee breaks). In any case, he wanted to drag out the pruning because, whatever you might think of pruning, it was at least better than pulling weeds. He despised pulling weeds.

He saw that two men in white overalls had gotten out of the van. They walked towards the front door and disappeared from view. After two minutes, they reappeared at the back from around the far side of the house. They rang the back door bell, tried the door, and finding it locked, wandered back towards the front, completing in the process a full circle of the house and pausing en route to look in the downstairs windows. When they reached the front again, they caught sight of him and came over.

"You work here?"

Garland looked down from his perch on the ladder. The speaker was the taller of the two, blond and thickset, his features slightly flattened in a way that struck Garland as Slavic or Central European. Not typically American, at least, but then what was? His companion was of medium height and dark-skinned. Mexican maybe. Or Cuban.

"*I* like to call it work."

Pause. Exchange of stares. The blond man's eyes narrowed.

"I meant regularly. . . . Do you work here all the time?"

Garland shook his head. "Contract job. Prune the trees, weed, and clean up, generally. Take maybe two, three weeks."

Pause. The blond man's gaze wandered over the garden.

"I wouldn't have thought it would take that long."

"You wouldn't?" His shrug implied lack of interest in the other's opinions on gardening or anything else. "Can I help you with something?"

"I was wondering if he was in."

Garland gazed down without expression. "I couldn't say. . . . If he didn't answer, I'd guess not."

"That's strange. We had an appointment, see." The blond man wrinkled his brow, made a show of consulting his watch. "Two-thirty, Tuesday."

"Tuesday?" Garland shrugged. "Today's Wednesday."

"I meant Wednesday. Didn't I say Wednesday?" The blond man frowned. He paused, struck by a sudden thought. "This *is* Mr. Wanamaker's house?"

Garland let a moment go by before he answered. "Your appointment was with a Mr. Wanamaker?"

"Yeah."

"Then *that* must be why." A look of dawning enlightenment passed across Garland's features.

"That must be why what?"

"Why he's not here." Garland paused. "This isn't Mr. Wanamaker's house."

He watched them till the van was out of sight then descended the ladder and sat down on the grass with his back against the tree. He took his lunch box from beneath his neatly folded coat—gardeners, he'd noticed, tended to own lunch boxes and were invariably neat—and removed from it a thermos of coffee and his walkie-talkie.

It wasn't yet three, but he was ready for a rest from his pruning. And he needed to talk to Chalmers or Guthrie. He suspected that the men in the white overalls, whatever the sign on their van may have said, were not carpet cleaners.

Any more than he was a gardener.

The phone call from Volkhov put Serafin in a quandary. What Volkhov had told him was that *they*—meaning Kasparov and Serafin— should drive out in the van and assist the two teams sent to pick up Becker. There was nothing unusual in this—it was standard procedure in this kind of situation to send a backup and to operate in pairs—but what Volkhov had not known was that Kasparov, though technically on duty and therefore confined until needed to the apartment, was out at the supermarket, buying lemons. Serafin had thought it best not to share this information. Volkhov, being something of a gourmet himself, would no doubt have agreed that the oiliness of lox (which, with cream cheese and bagels, was what Serafin and Kasparov had on the menu for lunch) cried out for the astringency of a squeeze of lemon. But he wouldn't have seen this as excusing dereliction of duty. Serafin's quandary was therefore this: He could leave immediately and hope to keep Kasparov's absence a secret, or he could wait for Kasparov and hope that they wouldn't be late.

He decided to wait ten minutes; if Kasparov were not back by then, he would leave without him. This compromise, intended to maximize his chances of escaping censure, achieved instead everything he had hoped to avoid. He was half an hour late (fifteen minutes of waiting for Kasparov plus another fifteen spent changing a flat on the Beltway). He was forced to operate solo. And both these facts came to Volkhov's attention. The lateness, as it turned out, was lucky. The absence of Kasparov, on the other hand, was not.

The call came through on the unlisted phone in the basement. Becker answered, handed the receiver to Vladek.

"For you. Someone called Guthrie."

Vladek took the phone, listened for about a minute, asked Guthrie to ring back in five minutes for further instructions, and hung up. He turned to Becker.

"That was one of my people outside. It seems two men from a carpet-cleaning service were here asking for someone called Wanamaker. Tried the front door and the back and looked in the downstairs windows. Told my guy in the garden they had an appointment. When he told them they had the wrong house, they went away. But not *far* away. Guthrie says their van is parked a couple of blocks up the street. Guthrie also says that a van of the same make just now pulled over and parked a block or so *down* the street." Vladek paused. "I would guess your friends are back."

Becker nodded. "And not just for surveillance, or they wouldn't have come knocking on the door. I think this settles our question about Stoneman. They questioned him and he talked. I think they came to invite me to a beheading."

Pause.

"I think so, too," Vladek said. "What will you do?"

Becker shrugged. "I think this settles *all* our questions. I don't see it leaves me very much choice." He paused and smiled. "My father was right. To get to heaven, you have to be dead."

Vladek nodded. "And meanwhile you have to spend time in limbo. A week, maybe more. These things take time to arrange."

"Limbo . . ." Becker made a face. "Are there books and booze?"

"Back numbers of the *National Geographic*. A couple of cases of Red Ripple." Vladek grinned. "Don't worry. Provisions will be made for your comfort." He paused. "What about the girl? . . . I mean," Becker's look made him correct himself, "what about Arlen? Should I send a message to cancel?"

Becker shook his head. "I've got to talk to her."

"Talk to her?" Vladek looked doubtful. "It's an added risk. Is it necessary?"

Becker thought about this. Logically, he supposed, Vladek might be right. The danger to Arlen, if any, had always been that the KGB might try to use her to find out about him. But since the KGB (if Stoneman's death and this latest development meant what he thought they *must* mean) already *knew* about him, they had no rational motive for continued interest in her. For the sake of her safety—and his—he should probably ignore her message. But the trouble with this conclusion was the word "probably." The reasoning made assumptions that *might* be mistaken. In a situation where much was obscure, the fact that he couldn't think of a rational motive for KGB interest in Arlen didn't mean there wasn't one. And KGB motives were (to put it mildly) not necessarily rational. It would help, he thought, if he knew exactly what had happened to Arlen and when, but the crucial part of her message . . . "The people you warned me about have been back in touch" . . . had left these issues vague.

It was possible, of course, that the message was a fake, designed to lure him into the open, but he didn't think so. For one thing, this latest KGB approach suggested that they saw no need for luring but intended simply to come and get him. This reasoning, of course, and the ancillary conclusion that she was still at liberty to send him messages, suggested in turn that, whatever the KGB's interest in her had been originally, they now saw her as irrelevant to the situation.

But if the message were genuine, she was scared. Her note had said *that,* though it hadn't needed to. The mere fact of her contacting him, given the tone and circumstances of their parting, was enough to indicate how scared she was. He couldn't just leave her to deal with that by herself, to think that he hadn't cared enough to help. He couldn't leave her dangling. He owed her.

But what to tell her? . . . To get out of the country? To put as much distance as possible between her and this mess and stay till it was safe to come back? But would she be safe anywhere, necessarily? Mightn't they follow her? Mightn't they construe the very fact of her flight as indicating that she knew more than she should? . . . He didn't really know what to tell her. The problem—it went back to the irritating vagueness of her note—was that he didn't know the extent of the problem. Or even if there was one.

He needed to talk to her. And since it couldn't be on the phone (though this basement phone seemed secure, you had to assume hers was bugged), and since you couldn't conduct a conversation by messenger service (the bopping back and forth between his office and her apartment would invite the attention he wished to avoid), it would have to be face to face. This would be risky, of course; they might be doing exactly what the KGB wanted them to do. But he could see no alternative.

And besides, he wanted to see her. He might not get another chance.

"I owe her." He regarded Vladek steadily. "You don't get to heaven if you don't pay your debts."

"Well . . ." Vladek shrugged. "It's your funeral."

"I hope not." Becker gave a wry smile.

Vladek shrugged. "I guess we're about to find out."

CHAPTER FORTY-ONE

THE RED PORSCHE HAD TINTED WINDOWS. IT HAD BEEN HARD, AS THE men in the vans explained later to Volkhov, to see who was driving. And the problem had been compounded by two facts: a) that the Porsche, given their conviction that Becker was not at home, had made its unexpected appearance from a wholly unlooked-for direction, and b) that by the time it came level with the van it had been doing at least eighty miles an hour. In the subsequent chase, in which both vans of necessity took part, they'd been hampered by their relative lack of speed, and, of course, by the absence of the backup team (those gourmandizing clowns, Kasparov and Serafin). Nevertheless, they'd done well, keeping the Porsche in sight—the beeper had helped a lot there, as had the traffic on the Beltway—until it reached Georgetown. At that point it had parked in an open-air lot, and its driver, emerging from the cockpit and strolling carelessly to a nearby bar as if unaware of being the focus of so much attention, had revealed himself to be, not Becker, but someone else entirely.

By the time they'd returned to the house on River Road, of course, Becker was already gone.

The VW belonging to Garland did not have tinted windows. Thus Serafin, who encountered it, moving quite slowly, near Becker's house

217

about fifteen minutes after the Porsche's departure, had no problem recognizing Becker as the driver. The other vans were nowhere to be seen and failed to respond to his efforts to make radio contact.

He had no choice, he figured, but to operate solo.

CHAPTER FORTY-TWO

THE KNOCK AT HIS DOOR HAD BECKER INSTANTLY SUSPICIOUS. THOUGH his watch informed him it was close to four-thirty, the time he'd instructed Arlen to meet him, he'd also made a point of asking her to call from the desk before coming to the room. She could have forgotten, of course, not appreciating, perhaps, the need for such precautions, but on the other hand . . .

On the other hand there was the question of the grey van.

It was true that when he had made a left to turn in at the motel, the grey van had not followed. It had gone on, in fact, to the next corner and then turned *right*, away from the motel. It was also true that the grey van was of a different make and color than the ones that had followed Vladek; and it had been occupied, unlike them, by only one person. In town, moreover, during rush hour, when the traffic moved in a solid wedge at a speed determined by the general will (which was, in fact, nobody's will), it was next to impossible to distinguish vehicles that were deliberately following you from those that just happened to be travelling in the same direction. The grey van, however, had been behind him for at least fifteen minutes (ten blocks, he figured, given the rate of crawl of the traffic), and it had sported the kind of radio antenna (long, sturdy, and mounted on a spring) that one associated with owner-ship of a CB radio. And one associated *that,* he thought, with a need, while driving, to talk to one's confederates. The vans that had followed Vladek had been equipped with CB radios.

219

The knock at his door was repeated.

"Who is it?"

"Housekeeping." The voice that answered was clear and reassuringly female, the accent somewhat Hispanic. "You need towels and soap."

He crossed to the window, edged back the curtain, peered out.

A woman in an apron stood next to a cart, presumably loaded with towels and soap. He was tempted to tell her he *didn't* need towels or soap, but that, though true, offended his instinct not to draw attention to himself. What normal motel guest, after all, declined an offer of towels and soap, admitted up front to not washing? He could tell her to come back later perhaps. . . .

Paranoia. He was tired of it, tired of premeditating even the most trivial of his actions. After Vladek had left in the Porsche, after all, his people—hadn't they?—had swept the neighborhood and found nothing suspicious, no trace of a backup for the vans that had followed Vladek. So why force this woman, obviously a motel employee and no doubt with plenty to do already, to make another pointless journey? Why not just take the damn towels and soap and send her on her way?

He took off the chain and opened the door.

She was well inside the room before Serafin stepped out from behind the doorpost. As he did so, he took a gun from his pocket and pointed it at Becker.

"So . . ." Becker watched him enter and close the door behind him. He was amazed to find himself, in the face of what was plainly disaster, calm almost to the point of indifference. It was as if he welcomed, in some part of him, the deliverance—any deliverance—from the limbo of uncertainty his life had fallen into. "To get to heaven, you have to be dead." One way or another, he thought, he soon would be. "An emissary, I presume, from the powers that be, bearing an invitation I shan't be able to refuse."

The woman, who'd been headed for the bathroom, turned. When she saw Serafin's gun, her hand flew to her mouth. She gave a gasp of terror.

"Shut up," Serafin snapped. "Don't move and you won't get hurt."

"But you told me . . ." She started to protest, then turned to Becker, her eyes imploring his belief. "He said he wanted to surprise you. He told me he was your friend."

"So I lied about being a friend." Serafin shrugged, thought for a moment. "Go into the bathroom and take off your clothes."

She stared at him.

"Do it," he said. "Nobody's going to touch you. Just do what I say and nothing will happen. Take your clothes off—all of them—and toss them out here. Then, if you want, you can lock the door. . . . While you're at it," he added, "give me back my twenty dollars."

She stared at him for a moment then, reaching into her pocket, took out a crumpled bill and tossed it at his feet. "Cheapshit." She glanced over at Becker, the fear in her face giving way to contempt. "Not only a bandit but also cheap."

"Let her keep it," Becker said. "It's not your money."

"It's public money." Keeping the gun very steady on Becker, Serafin knelt down to retrieve the bill. "Not to be thrown away. I have to account for every last penny." He paused. "You too, Comrade, have some accounting to do."

He turned back to the woman. "Go into the bathroom. Throw your clothes out here. Then shut the door and wait ten minutes. When you come out, we won't be here. Your clothes will be in the cart at the end of the corridor."

"How am I going to get them?" She still didn't move. Her fear, Becker noted, had been supplanted by anger, and anger was making her obstinate. He began to see a glimmer of hope. If she kept it up, she might distract this thug's attention long enough for him to try something. "You want me to run around naked?"

Serafin grinned and shrugged. "Why not? You might make somebody's day."

"Pervert."

His response was to slap her. He did it with his free hand, backhanded and without taking his eyes off Becker, the blow powerful enough to whip her head back and so rapid that it was over almost before Becker could register what had happened.

"Stupid," Serafin said. "I'm trying to do this without hurting you. But if I have to hurt you, believe me I will."

"Do what he says." Becker gave up hope for her creating a diversion. Now that he'd gotten back most of his wits, he was thinking of Arlen. She could arrive any minute and blunder in. Two people, maybe three, might be casualties here. One was enough. "Give us time to get clear. And don't bother with calling the cops. It won't do any good."

She inspected him, her interest mixed with sympathy. "What's this about, anyway? Drugs?"

He shook his head. "Politics."

"Politics." She made a face. "In my country we know about them. Pigmen with guns kidnapping people, torturing people, making them disappear, telling them it's all for their own good." She turned back to the other man. "OK, Pigman, you've got the pistol. I'm going into the bathroom now to take my clothes off for the good of the people."

She disappeared into the bathroom. A shoe flew out and landed on the floor. It was followed by another. Then a skirt and a blouse, then stockings, each item accompanied by the same chanted comment, a kind of litany, it struck Becker, of contempt: "Shoes for the good of the people . . . Skirt for the good of the people . . . Blouse for the good of the people . . ."

The man with the gun watched without expression until she was finished. Then he crossed over to the phone by the bed and yanked the cord out of the wall.

"Phone for the good of the people . . ." He grinned nastily at Becker and nodded at the pile of her clothes on the floor. "Bundle those up and bring them over here."

Becker did so.

"Put them on the bed."

Becker turned to obey. Something, something unbelievably hard and heavy, thudded into the base of his skull. Light exploded behind his eyes. . . . Then nothing.

Serafin put the pistol back in his pocket and bent down to examine Becker. He was breathing, which was good, and unconscious, which of course had been the object of hitting him, but how long would he stay unconscious? Not necessarily long enough to assure his still being here when Serafin returned with the van, or to assure his good behavior on the journey to the safe house. He would need to be tied and gagged.

The gag was easy. Checking to see that Becker could breathe through his nose (one didn't want him to die, or at any rate not yet) he took a piece of the woman's underwear (panties for the good of the people?) and stuffed them in Becker's mouth. Then, dragging Becker onto the bed, he looked round for some substitute for rope.

The telephone extension cord, luckily, was a long one. He cut it into lengths with a penknife, tied Becker's hands behind his back, and then tied his feet.

Now for the van.

It was around the corner (parking it outside the room might have alerted Becker). He would have to leave him here while he got it, and that would be risky. The woman was still in the bathroom, with only her modesty, if any, to keep her there. If she heard him leave, she might start yelling. But he could scarcely haul Becker, bound and gagged, across the motel parking lot in plain daylight. There was nothing for it. He would have to trust his luck.

He turned on the TV to cover the noise of his departure, then eased the door open and peered around it.

No one was around.

He tiptoed out, leaving the door just slightly ajar. He did this to avoid making noise, but when he was halfway to the van, he realized with a stab of panic that, since he hadn't thought to take the room keys with him, only luck had stopped him locking himself out. He toyed with the notion of going back for the keys, but decided not to. It would waste time. The longer he stuck around here, the more chance something would go wrong. His luck had held so far; it would hold, he decided, a little farther.

He just wished he hadn't sent Kasparov out for those lemons.

He wished it more fervently when he returned with the van. Though Becker was still gagged and bound on the bed, and the woman he'd left naked in the bathroom was still, so he presumed, in that condition, the situation had somehow acquired in his absence a new and disturbing element, one that revealed itself by emerging from behind the door only when he was too far inside the room for retreat to be an option.

A woman, but not the woman he'd left in the bathroom . . .

Becker's girlfriend.

He recognized her instantly from their previous encounters. And she, quite obviously, recognized him. Why otherwise, he asked himself, would she be aiming at him what he also recognized as a nine millimeter Luger?

CHAPTER FORTY-THREE

THE SHOCK MADE HIM STUPID, BUT ONLY FOR A MOMENT. ALMOST at once, the reflexes of his training took over. The will took command of the nerves, the mind subjected this new development to orderly, dispassionate appraisal. The gun, he began by noting, was properly cocked; the hand that held it reasonably steady. His captor, on the other hand, was young and female, manifestly nervous, almost certainly unused to handling firearms. One could safely take it for granted that she had never shot anyone, or even *at* anyone. It was also quite likely, though he couldn't be sure from this angle, that she had the safety on. He remembered an incident told him by a weapons instructor at Kiev: how a police marksman, facing a man gone berserk, had drawn his pistol and, at a range of less than three paces, had fired five times and hit the target once. If he jumped her, he told himself, the chances were better than even that she'd fail to pull the trigger or would miss him if she did. On the other hand . . .

On the other hand, there was no need to rush into anything.

"Whatever you're thinking of doing, don't." Her words seemed confident, but her voice struck him as shaky. One could detect in it, perhaps, the tremor of panic held barely in check. "Sit on the floor and put your hands on your head."

"You won't shoot." He spoke calmly, made no move to obey. "We both of us know that, I think."

She shook her head. "Don't bet on it. You're a foreign agent,

225

abducting a U.S. citizen. If I shoot you they'll probably give me a medal. . . . Sit on the floor and put your hands behind your head.''

But her look, he thought, was anxious, the self-doubt in her voice more apparent. What was phrased as an order came out sounding like a plea. He saw on the TV a table lamp with a fairly long cord. If he could somehow edge over to it, he could hurl it as he went for her gun. The distraction would give him an added margin of safety.

He shifted his weight to his right, edged his left foot, casually, towards the TV.

"Don't move! . . . . If you move, I swear I'll shoot."

A different command, he noted, or rather, a new and unconvincing threat. Conceivably she might shoot if she felt threatened, but not—he was sure of it—just because he didn't follow orders. If he kept her talking, moreover, her indecision would grow.

"And *have* you shot anyone, ever?'' His enquiry was almost conversational, as if the discussion were of hunting partridge. "It's very messy. Especially with that nine millimeter cannon you've got there. Hit me in the head with one of those slugs, you'll shatter it like a light bulb. There'll be blood all over the place. . . . Bone fragments . . . Brains.''

He took another half-step to the left.

"Don't move . . . !''

She was right on the edge now. The muzzle of the Luger wavered, moved abruptly from his head to his midriff. Though improving her chances of hitting him if she fired, the shift confirmed, he thought, that his grasp of her psychology was sure. Another step and he could reach the lamp. He'd duck low and to his right, at the same time sweeping the lamp off the TV at her. Almost certainly, she'd react too late. The picture he'd just forced her to imagine would make her hesitate. If she fired, she would will herself to miss. . . . But if she fired, he thought, someone would hear the shot. His options would be reduced to one: get out of here, fast. But what he wanted, needed, was to capture the sleeper and deliver him to Volkhov. There must be no shooting.

And besides, if she fired she might hit him by mistake.

He needed something more certain. He needed it now.

"But while that's true, of course . . .'' As he talked, an idea came to him. It was an old trick—no professional would fall for it—but he was dealing with a novice. "While that's true, of course, it's not how I know you're not going to shoot." He paused. "The reason I know you're not going to shoot is this . . . You can't pull the trigger with the safety on."

It was an old trick, but it worked. For a moment her eyes flicked from him to the gun. The muzzle wandered. But as it did, as he started for the lamp, he heard a noise behind him and realized, with the absolute, frozen clarity that occurs sometimes when events pass from human control and enter the realm of the inevitable, that he, too, had made an error; that in his preoccupation with this new element in the situation he had completely forgotten an old one.

The woman in the bathroom.

It occurred to Arlen to wonder if someone had fed her acid. In the past few minutes, starting from the moment she had spotted Serafin in the parking lot, life had turned surreal and altogether too vivid. It was as if blinders had been ripped from her eyes to reveal a world that lay normally outside her vision. It was violent and frightening, strange to the point of insanity, a place in which she was just a spectator, even— and this was what horrified her most—as she went through the motions of playing a part. It reminded her of those dreams where you wandered on stage in the middle of a play and the other characters all knew their lines and you knew nothing, not even the plot. . . . She'd discovered Becker, bound and gagged, presumably in the throes of being kid-napped. She'd found herself mounting a rescue, drawing the pistol, cocking it, pointing it at a man. She'd heard him describe in technicolor language what would happen to his head at the impact of her bullet, and she'd known that at any moment she might have to pull the trigger. What she'd *not* known—she'd not had the faintest idea—was what, when it came right down to it, she would do.

But none of this, weird as it all was, had prepared her what had ultimately happened: the sudden irruption, from the bathroom, of a stark naked woman, who, just when she, Arlen, was discovering she couldn't pull the trigger, had removed the need by striking down the kidnapper with what looked like a length of metal pipe.

Under the circumstances, she consoled herself later, she could hardly be blamed if her first words verged on irrelevance.

"What's that you hit him with?"

"The towel rail . . . Pow!" The woman waved it, grinned triumphantly.

It occurred to Arlen to wonder what this amazon had been *doing* in the bathroom. Taking a bath? . . . And *why* taking a bath? . . . There was an obvious answer to that. But it was nonsense, wasn't it? Not even Becker, surely, would arrange a rendezvous to coincide with a love tryst.

"What happened to your clothes?"

"Pigman took them." The woman prodded his inert form with the towel rail. She seemed unembarrassed by her nakedness; and indeed, Arlen thought, had nothing much to be embarrassed about, since her figure, though muscular, was close to perfect. "My name is Maria Dolores Vargas. . . . This one"—gesturing with her weapon at the man she had felled—"gives me twenty dollars, tells me he is friends with that one"—nodding at the bed on which Becker lay, lost to the world—"tricks me into letting him in here. Then he pulls a gun, forces me into the bathroom. . . ."

She broke off, her attention recaptured by the Luger, which Arlen, absently, was holding at her side.

"But *you* have a gun. . . . Are you part of it too?"

"Part of what?"

"This . . ." The contemptuous shrug struck Arlen as quintessentially Latin, seemed to include not just this bizarre scene, but also the world that gave rise to such scenes. "What they were fighting about. He said it was politics."

Arlen found herself wanting to be rid of the Luger. She uncocked it, placed it on the dresser beside her. "I'm nothing to do with it, really."

"Then what are you doing with the gun?" Maria Dolores, pondering the question a moment, came up with what evidently struck her as an acceptable reason. "That one on the bed, he's your boyfriend?"

"Not exactly . . ." Arlen hesitated. "It's complicated. Too complicated to explain."

"But you like him." Maria Dolores smiled. "I like him too. When the Pigman wanted his money back, he told him to let me keep it . . . *Simpatico*." She pronounced judgement. *"Hombre simpatico y guapo."*

Arlen didn't reply. Though she agreed, perhaps, in the matter of

Becker's looks, her feelings about the rest were at this stage decidedly mixed. She pointed to Serafin. "What shall we do with *him?*"

Maria Dolores considered. "You don't want to call the police?"

Arlen thought back to her last encounter with Becker. Whatever he was caught up in here, he'd seemed to feel the police were better excluded. She shook her head.

"OK. We tie him up. Untie your friend. Use the same cord on Pigman. Tie him tight. While you tie, I'll guard. If he wakes up . . ." She brandished the towel rail. "Pow!"

CHAPTER FORTY-FOUR

IT WAS BECKER'S IMPRESSION THAT FOR HOURS HE'D BEEN DRIFTING in and out of a dream. Memories and images swirled in his head, some pleasant, some not, none of them making a great deal of sense. He seemed to recall being tied up, then released. He seemed to recall seeing women, several of whom were Arlen, and at least one of whom was naked. He seemed to recall a motel room, and a man, not himself, lying trussed up, minus trousers, on a bed. He seemed to recall being helped into a car and then later out of it. But in all this haze of recollection, there was no discernible sequence, and there were many, too many, blanks.

All he could really be sure of, when consciousness returned, was that he was lying on a couch in a place he didn't recognize, that next to him, seated on an ottoman, was Arlen (now reassuringly singular), and that his head was threatening to blow apart.

"Where am I?" he asked.

She subjected him to what struck him as an overly clinical inspection.

"Your color's better," she informed him. "Your pupils are both the same size. . . . Do you know who you are?"

The question, it seemed to him, invited a variety of answers. He chose the simplest. "I'm Becker."

"Do you know who *I* am?"

He smiled at her weakly. "I think you must be my guardian angel."

230

"You have a concussion." She ignored his attempt at levity. "I should send for a doctor."

"No." He tried to sit up, winced, and gave up the attempt. "Where are we?"

"In a beach house I own on the Chesapeake Bay. We should be safe," she paused, "till your friends catch up with us again."

Her tone, he noted, was unfriendly.

"They're not my friends."

She shrugged. "I'd gathered."

"What happened back there at the motel?"

"I arrived to find you being kidnapped. With the help of maid service, I rescued you." She paused. "What I'm wondering now . . ."

"What you're wondering now," he anticipated, "is why you bothered."

"That too," she agreed. "But what I'm mostly wondering is what I did to deserve getting mixed up with you in the first place."

"Just lucky, I guess." He paused, but there was no response to this. "You want to know what's going on?"

She nodded. "That'd be nice."

"I can tell you this much," he said. "I probably owe you my life."

"You owe your life to Maria Dolores. She's the maid service I mentioned, and one very gutsy lady." Arlen paused. "What you owe me is an explanation. Who are you? Who was that thug back there? What makes you so hazardous to people's health?"

He hesitated. "It's complicated."

"Isn't it always?" She rolled her eyes. "Let's skip the complications. Just tell me this . . . Are you one of the good guys?"

He shook his head. "I wouldn't say good guys, exactly."

She thought about this. "What *would* you say, exactly? Are you at least one of the *relatively* good guys?"

"I wouldn't say that, either." He paused. Evasions suggested themselves, but he ignored them. There wasn't much point now in evasions. "What I am is a Russian spy. Or to be precise, a Russian ex-spy. I'm trying to take early retirement."

"A Russian ex-spy?" She didn't, he noted, seem very surprised. "Then the man I rescued you from is one of the good guys?" She smiled without noticeable humor. "You're saying I've been helping the wrong side?"

"That man you rescued me from is a KGB thug. They don't want me to take early retirement. You could think of it this way," Becker said. "There are fairly bad guys and really bad guys. *Relatively* you've been helping the right side."

"Some consolation." She frowned. "I do wonder why I bothered. Maybe I should have let him have you."

"Maybe you should." Becker paused. "I really do owe you my life. I don't know what I can do to repay you."

"To start with you might think about getting us out of this mess."

"Us?" he queried.

"Me, mostly," she amended. "But we're in it together, as I understand."

"Not necessarily. They'll be temporarily interested in you, but only as a means of getting to me. That was why I broke things off before, if you remember."

"Oh, indeed," she said drily. "I remember vividly."

It was not a digression he saw profit in pursuing.

"I can get you out of it quite easily," he said. "In a couple of days you *will* be out of it. Meanwhile, you just need to lie low."

She thought for a moment.

"And what about you? Can you get yourself out of it?"

"Maybe." Becker shrugged. "In any case, would you care?"

"Would I care what happened to a KGB spy, who claims to be taking early retirement?" She thought about it. "Depends a lot on the spy. I'd have to know more about him. Did he ever kill anyone? How many people did he hurt? How much damage did he do? Details like that." She paused, fixed him with a penetrating stare. "But seriously, Mister ex-KGB man, how am I going to get any answers?"

"You could ask," Becker said.

"I'm sure I could," she said. "And I'm sure you'd tell me something. And I'm sure it would sound plausible, because you guys make a habit of sounding plausible. But how would I know it was the truth?"

Becker shrugged. "I guess you'd have to go with your instinct."

"My instinct?" She made a face. "My instinct is to get on the phone to the Russian Embassy or the CIA, tell them where they can find their ex-spy."

Silence. Exchange of chilly stares.

"Then do it." Becker was bored with the subject. For the moment, at least, he didn't care what she thought. He was tired; his head hurt; he needed to sleep. "The way I feel now, I probably couldn't stop you. And who knows?" he shrugged. "Maybe I wouldn't try. So if that's your instinct, why not follow it?"

More silence. Their eyes met, held for a moment, then her gaze wandered up and beyond him, seemed to find something to interest it on the ceiling.

"Trouble is," she said finally, "that's only one of my instincts."

CHAPTER FORTY-FIVE

THE RADIO FORECAST SAID THE NIGHT OF NOVEMBER EIGHTEENTH WOULD be the coldest of the year so far. For Elton Thompson, thirty-six, male, Caucasian, with no regular occupation or fixed address, this was just one more piece of bad news. That morning, on the grounds of his habitual overindulgence in alcohol (it was the noise, they'd told him, more than the liquor), he'd been finally and without hope of reprieve expelled from the Amazing Grace Shelter for the Homeless. Since the Amazing Grace was the only institution of its kind in the D.C. area still willing to extend its hospitality to him, the prospects seemed better than average that he would spend the night on the streets, with nothing but some layers of newspaper and a couple of pints of Red Ripple to protect him against temperatures expected to descend, so the radio said, into low single figures.

At ten P.M., he was thrown out of the last of the series of neighborhood bars and coffee shops in which he'd sought temporary refuge. By that time, thanks more to his intake of Red Ripple than to any protection offered by the layers of newspaper, he wasn't particularly feeling the cold. He wasn't, indeed, feeling anything much but a thirst for more Red Ripple and a generalized desire to keep moving. By ten-thirty, his wanderings had brought him to a residential neighborhood, whose inhabitants, mainly black, were animated mostly by the desire to mind their own business and steer clear of the law. Both his bottles were empty, and the desire to keep moving had been overtaken by liquor and fatigue. He lay down on the sidewalk and lapsed into a stupor that blurred the boundary between sleep and coma.

At ten-fifty-three, a phone call, naturally anonymous, sent Otis Skinner and Marvin Handleman to the scene. Some drunk, their dispatcher informed them, had reportedly passed out in the street. This was not an unusual occurrence in the neighborhood, but neither were false alarms. This explained, perhaps, the scepticism expressed by the dispatcher's use of the word "reportedly" and the relative lack of haste displayed by the two ambulance men, who took time to finish their coffee before answering the call. It was close to eleven-fifteen when they got to Elton Thompson, whom they found on the sidewalk, his head in the gutter, apparently drowned in his own vomit.

Otis and Marvin were trained paramedics. What they should have employed, before getting their patient to the warmth of the ambulance, were mouth-to-mouth resuscitation and CPR. It seemed probable, however, that hypothermia and some lungfuls of vomit had placed Elton Thompson beyond reach of their efforts. In any case, though the body was moved to the ambulance, the efforts were never made. Giving Elton Thompson the kiss of life was not an appetizing prospect. It was easier, more palatable, to get rid of him somehow and report it to the dispatcher as another false alarm. As Marvin expressed it to Vladek in the course of negotiations that relieved the paramedics of the burden of their negligence and gained them each five hundred dollars:

"Shit, man, we'd just ate."

CHAPTER FORTY-SIX

THERE WERE DAYS, SERAFIN THOUGHT, THAT IN ANY PROPERLY OR-
ganized calendar would be known as the "Let's all dump on Serafin"
days, days that started badly, got steadily worse, and ended in such a
crescendo of misfortune as to make one feel that the concentrated wrath
of heaven was aimed at one's unprotected head. Such days, if one only
knew about them in advance (and in the screwed-up nature of things of
course one couldn't), one would greet by bolting the bedroom door and
slitting one's wrists with a razor. Today had been a day like that, he
thought, and to judge from the look on the Resident's face, they were
about to arrive at the crescendo.

"If I may summarize the farrago of apology and self-justification
which in your view seems to constitute a report . . ." The Resident's
voice had an edge like a scalpel. "To gratify your overdeveloped taste
for bourgeois delicacies, you ignored your orders and sent your associ-
ate to buy lemons. As a result of which action, you not only failed to
apprehend the sleeper but got yourself arrested on a charge of public
indecency." She paused. "Would that be accurate?"

Not entirely, Serafin thought. Indeed, not even partially. While perhaps it was true that had Kasparov been with him at the motel, things
would not have turned out as they did, it was surely unreasonable to
blame on him alone a failure in which others—notably those fools
who'd gone chasing after the Porsche—could claim at least equal shares.
As for the indecency charge, they owed that to the vindictive spirit and

236

doubtful sense of humor of that bitch, the motel housekeeper. To leave him a note misinforming him that his trousers could be found in a trash can at the end of the passageway, then to lock him out when he went in search of them, had been, he thought bitterly, to pile insult on injury.

"In fairness, Colonel," Volkhov, surprisingly, came to his rescue, "I should perhaps point out that it was due to Lieutenant Serafin's lateness that he even had a chance of apprehending the sleeper. Otherwise he, too, would no doubt have gone after the Porsche. I should also point out that the sleeper, quite clearly, was anticipating our action." He paused before adding, with an emphasis that struck Serafin as verging on insubordinate, "And not because of Lieutenant Serafin's mistakes."

"Irrelevant," she snapped. "Being lucky, if he was lucky, does not excuse dereliction of duty. As soon as his replacement can be arranged, Lieutenant Serafin will be returning to Moscow. He will not," she added darkly, "be returning to Moscow alone."

There was a long silence. Almost imperceptibly, Volkhov shrugged.

"Meanwhile," she went on, "the sleeper is still at liberty. Perhaps you would tell me what you plan to do about that."

More silence.

"The sleeper and the girl have gone to ground," Volkhov said. "The driver of the Porsche, however, has been traced and identified as the man to whom most of the sleeper's recent phone calls were made. Though the sleeper addresses him as 'Vladek,' his apartment is rented under the name of Thomas Hannigan."

He paused. She made a gesture of impatience. "So? . . ."

"Tracking devices have been placed in the Porsche and in this Vladek's car. Since he's evidently been helping the sleeper, I think we can expect that at some point he will contact him. With the help of the tracking devices, we can hope to follow him to his rendezvous with the sleeper."

She thought about this for a moment, then nodded.

"But Major." She caught his gaze. "Please understand that *hoping* will not be enough. Only success will be tolerated. I want the sleeper found and captured. Or, if capture is not possible, killed."

Hoping will not be enough. . . . But it had been more than a bureaucratic instinct for caution, he thought later, that had prompted him to express his intentions as hopes. Though he'd not wished to share his reservations with the Resident—one could take nay-saying, after all, only so far—there were aspects of the situation that made him uneasy. The sleeper, it appeared, had read the circumstances of Stoneman's death correctly. He'd anticipated, at least, the attempt to pick him up. Presumably, he'd expect another attempt and would recognize also that his point of vulnerability was this Vladek, who had aided his escape last time. He was, moreover, a KGB agent, trained in the techniques of countersurveillance, alert to the possibilities offered by tracking devices. And this Vladek, who appeared to run some sort of detective agency, himself had experience with surveillance work and presumably commanded an experienced staff.

Then why, Volkhov wondered, had it been so easy to put beepers in the cars?

CHAPTER FORTY-SEVEN

IT WAS NOT FULLY LIGHT WHEN BECKER AWOKE. FOR A MOMENT HE didn't know where he was. Then he saw, silhouetted against the silvery rectangle of a window, a woman, whom memory returning, informed him was Arlen.

"I've been lying awake feeling lonely," she said. "I thought I'd find how you were feeling."

"Actually, I was asleep," Becker said.

"I know," she said. "But now that you're not, how are you feeling?"

"Better," Becker said.

"You did have a headache." She came over, sat on the bed. She was wearing a man's shirt, he saw. Unbuttoned except at the waist, it covered her less than strict modesty might have demanded. "Do you still have a headache?"

He reached up and touched her face. His fingertips traced the line of her jaw and, descending, brushed her neck. They drifted along her collarbone, then, encountering no resistance, slipped inside the shirt and gently circled a breast. The nipple hardened to his touch.

"No headache," he said.

She pulled back the covers and slid into bed beside him. For a while they lay there, side by side, not touching.

"Does this mean," he asked, "that you've made up your mind which instinct to follow?"

Her answer was to turn and pull him towards her.

"I'm not sure what it means," she said. "Perhaps all it means is that Russian ex-spies make me horny."

CHAPTER FORTY-EIGHT

THE GROCERY STORE WAS A MA AND PA OPERATION (WIZENED PROprietor, withered old stick of a wife) whose busy time, if it *had* a busy time, would be the tourist season, June, July, and August. In November, Garland guessed, paying customers would be few and far between, and the store probably stayed open, not in the expectation of attracting any business, but to provide Ma and Pa with a reason for getting out of bed. To judge from the tone of his reception, and it was typical of the town, when they'd gotten out of bed this morning it had been on the wrong side.

Ain't seen 'im.'' Pa handed the photograph back to Garland, gestured vaguely at his better half. "She ain't seen 'im either."

"Since "she" had not yet been granted a chance to look for herself, the second statement struck Garland as essentially speculative. He offered the photograph, an eight-by-ten glossy, to Ma. She did flick a glance at it, but almost immediately her stare, bright and incurious as a bird's, returned to Garland.

"Ain't seen 'im." She paused. "Nice-lookin feller."

"Take another look," Garland urged. "It would have been sometime in the last few days."

"If she sez she ain't seen 'im, she ain't seen 'im." This from Pa. He paused, gazed censoriously at Garland. "Did you say you was some kind of private eye?"

Garland nodded.

"Do you maybe have some ID? . . . Papers, or something you could show us?"

Garland inspected him for a moment. . . . Make an impression, Hannigan had said, leave them with something to talk about later.

"I've got ID," he said. "I *could* show it to you. . . . The thing is,"—he turned and started for the door—"I don't have to."

Garland was puzzled. As he left the grocery store, where he had once more succeeded in raising more questions than would ever be provided with answers, he found himself reflecting again on the strangeness of this latest assignment. Last time had been bad enough (though he thanked his stars it hadn't, in the end, involved weeding), but at least *there,* he thought, he'd had some grasp of what was going on. The charade of gardening had served as cover for a serious purpose. Here, on the other hand, in this one-horse town (if you could call it a town) on the eastern shore of the Chesapeake Bay, where the natives were taciturn and, when not taciturn, hostile, what he was doing, it struck him, was charade, pure and simple.

It involved, for one thing, dressing up. He hated suits; they offended his instincts for anonymity and comfort. (Hannigan, he thought bitterly, should try traipsing around on a mild November day throttled by collar and tie, entombed, so to speak, in grey flannel.) But worse than suits were hats. Nobody wore hats. Even in the relatively inoffensive fedora Hannigan had specified, he felt foolish, conspicuous. But conspicuous, he thought, seemed part of the point. Indeed, perhaps it was *all* of the point. It explained, at least, the odd lack of subtlety in the operating procedure Hannigan had suggested. (Store-hopping down Main Street with an eight-by-ten glossy, which you shoved in people's faces while asking a bunch of peremptory questions, wasn't Garland's idea of how to conduct a missing persons search.) It also explained the black Ford sedan Hannigan had insisted on his using. It even explained, at a pinch, Hannigan's enigmatic parting instruction: "Say you're a private investigator, but don't show ID. Act like a cop."

What it didn't explain was why he was conducting a missing persons search for a person who, to the best of his knowledge, wasn't missing.

Some minutes after Garland's abrupt departure, the proprietor of the grocery store came out of his thoughtful trance. He crossed over to the doorway and peered down the street to where Garland's black Ford was parked outside the hardware store. He looked back at his wife.

"That feller weren't no private eye."

"He weren't? . . . Why not?"

"Grey suit," the proprietor said. "Silly little hat. Drives a big black limo with Virginia plates and wears sunglasses when the sun ain't shone in days. . . . Private eye my ass." He paused to give a snort of mirthless laughter. "That feller's a spook."

"You could call him a friend of a friend," Vladek said. "He's male, Caucasian, aged about forty. Color of hair, such as there is of it, brown. Color of eyes, blue. Height, five eleven. Weight, about one sixty."

"Couldn't you have gotten someone younger?" Becker asked.

Vladek shrugged. "Beggars can't be choosers. He's close enough to a fit."

"I think this is gruesome," Arlen said.

Becker and Vladek exchanged glances.

"To get to heaven, you have to be dead," Becker said.

"I also think it's crazy."

"I think it's inspired," Becker said. "Russian ex-spy becomes late Russian ex-spy. It's the natural progression."

"It's not the destination I dispute," Arlen said, "just the route. I don't see the need for this little piece of theater."

"This little piece of theater is exactly the point," Becker said. "Seeing's believing. A picture is worth a thousand words."

"You don't bolster your case by mouthing clichés." Arlen turned to Vladek. "This was your idea originally. For Christ's sake, *you* tell him."

Vladek shrugged. "She's right in one way. When you complicate things, you add to your chances of screwing up. Do it my way and something goes wrong, at least it won't be fatal. Mess up under their noses and you're dead."

Becker shrugged. "We're not going to mess up."

"There's many a slip . . ." Arlen said.

"You don't bolster your case by mouthing clichés," Becker said. "Look. There's nothing very complicated about this. They've put beepers in the Porsche and in Vladek's car, so its clear they expect him to lead them to me. We'll be waiting for them. We'll let them get close, but not too close." He paused. "I don't see what there is to mess up."

Vladek shrugged. "It's *your* funeral."

"I wish you wouldn't keep saying that." Becker grinned.

Arlen exploded. "Goddammit, would you two stop joking about this!" She turned to Becker. "Things *can* go wrong. You can get killed. If those boys get hold of you, you can get worse than killed. So do what you want—you will anyway—but for Christ's sake let's not have any more of this Central European machismo." She paused and added quietly, "Becker, you bastard, I worry about you."

"Don't." He took her hand and squeezed it. "Get yourself to Geneva. Vladek will see you're not followed. You can expect me in about a week. In the meantime, don't believe what you read in the papers."

CHAPTER FORTY-NINE

IT WAS ALMOST A WEEK BEFORE VOLKHOV'S WATCHERS WERE RE-warded. Till then, though forty-three of Vladek's phone calls were recorded and analyzed, and his movements were under constant electronic surveillance, the listeners overhead nothing of interest and the watchers saw nothing but normal coming and going. Apart from his evident preference for driving Becker's Porsche instead of his own battered and elderly Saab, nothing in Vladek's behavior suggested that Becker was in any way on his mind. On the sixth day, however, towards two P.M., the watchers reported to Volkhov "a possibly significant divergence from the normal pattern of movement." Vladek, driving the Porsche on what had looked like a routine run between his office and his apartment, had turned east off the Beltway onto Highway 301 and was headed towards Annapolis and the Chesapeake Bay.

"Maybe he's just going away for the weekend," Serafin said.

Volkhov said nothing. Since the Porsche's apparent destination was an area devoted to rest and recreation, and the departure had occurred at an hour that might easily have been chosen to avoid weekend traffic, Serafin might well be right. Instinct, however, told him otherwise. Instinct told him the Porsche was about to be reunited with its owner.

This wasn't the only thing instinct told him.

He looked at the map again. Some ten miles beyond the Bay Bridge,

245

the Porsche had turned off 301 towards the Eastern Shore, taking a minor road, which it followed for about three miles before turning onto an even more minor road heading south down a narrow peninsula that stuck out into the Bay. Halfway down the peninsula, as his glance at the map confirmed, the road passed through a small town or village, after which it continued for approximately a mile, then dead-ended abruptly. Which meant that, unless they had a boat, Becker and/or the driver of the Porsche were boxed in.

Or that he, Volkhov, was about to be.

Unless they had a boat . . . What you had to do here, he told himself, was see the situation from their point of view. If they planned to make their getaway in a boat, it implied that they expected to be followed. But if they expected to be followed, then making a getaway in a boat, or for that matter in anything else, didn't make much sense. It achieved for them, perhaps, the fleeting satisfaction of thumbing their noses at the enemy, but it resolved nothing; at the end they would all be back where they had started. And while he could see Becker deriving considerable enjoyment from thumbing his nose at the enemy, he couldn't see him contenting himself with that. So either they weren't expecting to be followed, or . . .

Or they had something other than escape on their minds.

This made more sense. The abortive attempt to pick Becker up had amounted, Volkhov thought, to a clear declaration of war. Becker would know his survival was at stake, that there was nothing to be achieved by playing games. He would be desperate, and therefore dangerous. Very dangerous, Volkhov thought, because, in addition to being desperate, he was intelligent.

And he had help.

And he was armed.

You had to see the situation from their point of view. . . . This included conceding them the ability to reason. Becker, after all, was a computer wizard; reasoning might be said to be his forte. What conclusions, then, might his reasoning have led him to? . . . First, that the Porsche and his friend Vladek (or Hannigan) having helped him foil the KGB once, would thereafter become objects of KGB interest. Second, that the Porsche, being utterly conspicuous and, in view of its interest to the KGB, quite possibly fitted with electronic transmitting devices, should be the *last* vehicle to be taken to a rendezvous.

Unless he *wanted* it to be followed.

And if he wanted it to be followed, that must mean, by virtue of previous deductions, that he had something other than escape in mind.

Volkhov let Serafin drive through the village. About half a mile beyond it, he made him pull over to the side of the road. The other van, which contained the monitoring equipment, plus Kasparov and two of his colleagues, pulled in behind. There were no other cars on the road. They had met none in the last several miles. It was mid afternoon, but the sky was overcast, and already the air was chilly. The peninsula, Volkhov saw, was mostly duneland. It was low and flat, desolate, imbued, it struck him, with the spirit of winter and the death of the year. Overhead, the occasional seagull assailed the silence with thin, despondent cries. With binoculars, he scanned the waters of the bay. They looked cold and uninviting. In the main channel were what he took to be fishing boats; inshore no boats of any kind. . . . They were not planning their escape, he thought. Somewhere out on the point they were waiting for him, waiting for him on carefully chosen terrain. This was a box. Someone was going to be trapped in it.

It wasn't, he resolved, going to be him.

"Make a reconnaissance," he told Kasparov. "Take the binoculars. Walk down to the point. Try not to be seen. Or if you have to be seen," he cast a dubious glance at Kasparov's sportcoat and thin-soled Italian loafers, "try to look like a bird watcher."

It was close to two hours before Kasparov returned. He was sweaty, covered with mud, considerably disgruntled. His trousers were wet to the knees, and his loafers, Volkhov noted with satisfaction, were ruined. To establish his cover as a bird watcher—he made the claim with a reproachful look at Volkhov—he had left the road and cut along the shore. At the end of the road marked on the map, he reported, was another, not marked, that served the two or three houses located on the point. These were vacation homes, and all but one seemed unoccupied. The exception had some kind of car in its garage—Kasparov had not gotten close enough to determine which kind—and, parked outside in the driveway, a red Porsche.

"So we know where they are," he concluded. "Now we go in and take them."

Volkhov shook his head.

"We know where they are, so now we wait."

CHAPTER FIFTY

VLADEK WAS UNEASY: IN BODY BECAUSE HE HAD FINISHED THE THERMOS of coffee and was cramped for three hours of lying in a foxhole with the chill of late November invading his bones to the marrow, and because he needed to pee; in spirit because nothing had happened and it was getting dark. More than three hours had passed since he'd parked the Porsche in front of the house for all the world to see, and the Russians, though they had to be out there somewhere, had still not made their move.

They had to be out there somewhere. Unless they'd been planning to track him back to Becker, why bother to put a beeper in the Porsche? They had to be out there somewhere, and the fact that they'd not shown themselves yet was therefore fraught with sinister implications. It meant—he could think of no other explanation—that they must be suspecting some kind of trap. And if they suspected some kind of trap, no doubt they were planning some trap of their own. In another few minutes it would be totally dark, and in his foxhole on this sand dune that by daylight commanded all the landward approaches to the house, he would be blind.

They would be too, of course. Blinder than he, in fact, on this night whose blackness the blanket of low cloud would pretty soon render absolute—because he only had to stay put and watch, whereas they had to move. And moving, whether among these sand dunes or along the rocky shoreline or even on the rutted cart track that served as driveway to the house, was not a thing to be contemplated sightless. They would need to use flashlights, and it would give them away. This, at least, had been Becker's theory when Vladek had raised the issue earlier. People with lawful intentions, Becker said, did not creep up on houses at night with flashlights. So Vladek should keep watching the landward approaches. If he saw anything that looked like a flashlight, he should warn Becker with three evenly spaced beeps on the transmitter. In the meantime, for safety, he should check in (five evenly spaced beeps on the transmitter) every half hour.

That at least was the theory. And Vladek, to be honest, hadn't been able to point to a flaw. Not on a rational level. He couldn't help feeling, however, at a level that fell somewhere between instinct and superstition, that somehow Becker had overlooked something, that what Arlen called "this little piece of theater" was way too clever for its own good. It tempted fate, and that, Vladek thought, was never smart to do. It was something, at any rate, that made him very uneasy. That, he thought, and the darkness, and his cramped and chilly position, and the waiting, which was getting on his nerves.

And the fact that he badly needed to pee.

He wished now that he'd backed Arlen more strongly, that he could talk to Becker, persuade him to accept a change of plan. Or even a change of timing. This thing didn't *have* to happen—did it?—absolutely under their noses. At the very least, he thought, since the Russians would focus their attentions on the house, he wished he could warn Becker to get his ass out of there.

But it was too late now for second thoughts, which in any case Becker would reject. (He was watching from an upstairs room, he would say, because that was the best place, the *logical* place, to watch from.) And besides, he, Vladek, *couldn't* go talk to Becker, not only because he needed to keep watching, but because, by moving, he might very well give himself away. If there was a flaw in Becker's plan, it was too late to do anything about it.

They would have to live with it.

Or do the other thing.

He looked at his watch. It was five forty-two. Three minutes and he should signal, check in again with Becker. In the meantime . . .

In the meantime, he simply *had* to pee.

*   *   *

Serafin wished he could use his flashlight. These infra-red scanners, which worked, in so far as they worked at all, by registering variations in temperature, in theory enabled you to see in the dark without, at the same time, being seen. The trouble was that, apart from being bulky and awkward to use, they didn't, at least in the present conditions, allow you to see very much. They weren't a lot of help, at any rate, in alerting you to minor unevenness in the terrain. Which was why, he thought bitterly, his progress through these sand dunes had been slow, laborious, and occasionally painful.

He knew why Volkhov had picked him for this assignment. For the same reason Kasparov had been sent on the two-hour hike that had muddied his clothes and ruined his loafers. Now it was his, Serafin's, turn to be punished. The tall sand dune that was his immediate objective was, since it commanded an all around view of the area, the obvious place to post a lookout. It would also be difficult to get to, and the lookout would probably be armed. Volkhov had expressed the wish that Serafin not crown his labors by getting himself shot, but if somebody had to be—the suggestion had not been particularly subtle—Serafin was the number one choice.

But Serafin was not, he promised himself, going to get himself shot. Through excessive zeal on a previous occasion, he'd gotten himself sentenced to return to Moscow. Excesses here would be on the side of caution. He would not, though the impulse to do it was strong, risk using his flashlight to check his position. And, before attacking the twenty or so feet that would bring him to the crest of the dune, he would take the time to catch his breath and think.

In the last few minutes a wind had picked up. It was in his face, and for this he was grateful. It would cover the sound of his movements and the noisier rasp of his breath, and at the same time make it easier for him to hear noise up ahead. He knelt in the sand and surveyed the crest with the scanner. The darkness was now total, but the crest, having cooled less quickly than the surrounding air, stood out quite clearly in silhouette in the viewer. But it wasn't the same as really seeing, he thought, because you couldn't relate what you saw to yourself or to your whereabouts, spatially. It was therefore disorienting, like looking through a periscope at a moonscape—a green-and-black moonscape, at that, the normal tonal values all backwards. All in all, he preferred to use his ears.

He lowered the scanner. Instead of going *over* the crest, thus taking the risk of blundering into a lookout, he should work his way round it in a flanking movement, then use the scanner to detect the lookout, if any, and at that point figure out how to proceed.

He was halfway round when he thought he heard something. Movement, perhaps, from the far side of the crest. He froze, held his breath, strained his ears to filter out the wind, to detect, beneath its fitful swish and sigh, any noise not equally natural. Presently he seemed to hear something—a couple of muted thuds—that could have been someone stamping his feet in the sand, followed by a click, as of metal striking metal. He aimed the scanner where he guessed the sound had come from. Above the outline of the crest, sharply, almost shockingly visible in the scanner, was a rough half-dome of green, surrounded with an aura like a halo.

Something very much warmer than its surroundings.

Like the top of a head.

It moved, vanished below the crest. He stayed quite still, the scanner trained on where the head had disappeared. His body went briefly haywire, made all the normal responses to the adrenalin that now flooded his system. But part of him—it was something he'd come to expect and be grateful for—stayed calm, detached even from the questions (Which way had the head been turned? Was it *looking* at him? Had it *heard* something? Had it seen him? What should he *do?*) that crowded his mind and demanded answers. For in his situation, as training had drilled into him so often as to make his response automatic, there was only one thing to do, one answer to all questions:

Wait.

So he waited and was presently rewarded by a further series of sounds: A kind of ripping noise. A pause. Then, startling but also reassuring, a sound so familiar as to be quite beyond mistaking.

The hiss and splatter of water onto sand.

Somebody peeing.

Vladek's problem had been the wind. It was at his back, blowing quite briskly up the peninsula and towards the crest of the sand dune.

And his foxhole was just below the crest on a fairly sharp slope, so that while he was shielded from the sight of anyone coming down the peninsula, anyone passing to either side (as anyone would have to who wanted to get to the house) would necessarily come (assuming it was daylight and one could actually *see*) within his range of vision. Which in terms of military strategy was just fine, but in terms of creature comforts could cause problems. For while the slope barred standing in the foxhole peeing *towards* the crest, the wind precluded standing in the foxhole peeing *away* from the crest. What the situation had demanded, therefore, was a compromise: kneeling on the edge of the foxhole, facing outwards, peeing at right angles to both the wind and the slope.

It had meant—though Vladek never knew this until later, never knew anything, in fact, till he was summoned back to consciousness by the roar of the blast—peeing with his back to Serafin.

CHAPTER FIFTY-ONE

WHEN VLADEK FAILED TO MAKE THE FIVE FORTY-FIVE CHECK-IN, Becker was not, at first, worried. Probably Vladek was daydreaming, had forgotten to look at his watch. His sense of time, in any case, had never been very exact. None of his previous check-ins, though Becker had stressed the need for precision, had been on the dot. Five forty-five, to Vladek, seemed to mean anywhere between five-forty and ten of six. The trouble was, of course, that because the noise of any radio reception could give Vladek's existence and position away, Vladek was set up to make transmissions only and could therefore not be raised. Becker decided to give him five minutes. *Then* he would worry.

He already was worried a little, of course, by the fact, that the KGB had not yet made a move. This was not unexpected, in fact the reverse was true. It could be attributed to routine caution, the natural desire of the would-be kidnapper to cover his actions with a cloak of darkness. But it could mean the KGB suspected a trap. If so, they'd expect him to post a lookout. And if they expected that . . .

This line of thought was not new, of course. He'd been over it with Vladek half a dozen times. Whether they came by day or night, and whether or not they suspected a trap, it was much more probable Vladek would spot them than vice versa. And in any case, all he needed from Vladek was a couple of minutes warning. . . . But thinking which in daylight seemed clear and flawless tended, at night, to develop shad-

254

ows. If by five forty-eight he was still not very worried, by five fifty-two he was feeling shivers of premonition.

What if they had somehow got to Vladek?

If so, he was in the wrong place. Because the front upstairs bedroom, though perfect for scanning the seaward approaches to the house, was more or less blind on the landward side. And if they *had* somehow got to Vladek, the landward side was where they'd be coming from. And the front upstairs bedroom, with only one door and a fifteen-foot drop from the window onto flagstones below, was a less than ideal place to hide out—or, worse, to be bottled up in. If there *was* an ideal place— he'd thought about it when at Vladek's insistence they'd done some worst-case planning—it was behind the garage in the dumpster, which the builders had used for their garbage and had still not taken away. He needed to get himself out of the bedroom and into the dumpster.

He needed to do it now.

He was down the stairs and in the front hall on his way to the kitchen when a noise from outside, in the front, perhaps the scrunch of a footfall on gravel, made him freeze. He quit breathing, shut his eyes, willed his heart to quit pounding, channeled all his energy and awareness into one focussed effort to hear. For a moment there was nothing. Then, from the back, a low whistle.

He tried to tell himself it had been made by a bird, but he knew it hadn't. Maybe on Dzerzinskii Street there were birds that sounded like that; in Maryland, to his best recollection, there weren't. Someone at the back of the house was signalling to someone in front.

Which meant he wouldn't make it to the dumpster.

So he should use the gizmo now.

But when he went to act on this decision, the reasoning behind it was instantly undermined by new and dismaying information: that what his right hand was holding was not what he'd thought it was when he snatched it up from the window ledge in the bedroom. It was not, in fact, the gizmo, but instead, the walkie-talkie.

Volkhov knew that action was about to be joined when, at the same instant, every light in the house went out. Till then he thought he'd achieved surprise. The lights going out informed him otherwise. If *one* light went out, it need mean no more than that someone, moving from room to room, had flipped a switch. When they all went out together, on the other hand, it had to mean that someone had jerked the master fuse. And that must mean that Igor was inside, that he knew that they were outside, and—since you didn't deprive yourself of light if you planned any serious shooting—that he was hoping to escape.

That was fine, Volkhov thought, because, as Kasparov's inept bird-call from the back had informed him, the house was now surrounded. And while Igor had an edge, perhaps, in knowing the terrain, they— some of them—could see in the dark and he, almost certainly, couldn't. It was also now clear he had no support other than the solitary lookout Serafin had dealt with. There was no point in hanging back giving him time to think. He was trapped, outnumbered. When the enemy was in his condition, your strategy was obvious.

Immediate assault on all fronts.

From the moment he realized he'd left the gizmo upstairs, Becker knew he was out of options. The gizmo was essential to his plan; he had to go back and get it. But by going back he would confirm what they might not yet be sure of: that he was somewhere in the house. And if he used the gizmo when they knew he was in the house, he might win himself temporary safety perhaps, but the real point of using it would be lost; his whole plan would go up in smoke. Killing the lights was his only hope of collecting the gizmo *and* getting out of the house, but it would also immediately tell them where he was, inevitably bring them in after him. So the choice was dead simple, to his mind no choice at all . . .

Risk big or lose.

Topography was the key. The master fuse was in a box beneath the stairs. On the first floor landing was a glass-fronted dresser he could use to barricade the stairs and slow pursuit a little. On the landing there was also a window that gave onto the flat roof, which left only a drop of perhaps ten feet to the flagstones outside the kitchen. The obvious procedure was: (1) jerk the fuse; (2) race upstairs and wrestle the dresser into position; (3) dash to the bedroom, collect the gizmo, climb out through the window onto the flat roof; (4) drop to the flagstones outside the kitchen, sprint round past the garage, and take cover in the dumpster; (5) while attempting each of the preceding steps, pray.

Killing the lights, as he'd hoped, gave them temporary pause. He was on the landing and had the dresser in place before they burst through the front door and, simultaneously, the back. By the time he'd retrieved the gizmo, however, they were on the stairs. A voice in the hallway, speaking Russian, calmly issued orders. Flashlights flicked on, probed the darkness for him. Unless he could cause confusion, gain more time, he was lost.

He almost used the gizmo, but he was able to stop himself in time.

Keep calm, he commanded himself. Don't blow everything.

Think.

The wardrobe . . . As it toppled, a voice in the hallway yelled a warning, but it crashed down on top of them, their cries of alarm engulfed by a sudden crash of shattering wood and glass. By then he was out of the window and onto the flat roof. But as he steadied himself for the leap to the flagstones below, he heard, through the uproar behind, the same commanding voice, more urgent now, sending someone back through the kitchen to intercept.

CHAPTER FIFTY-TWO

SERAFIN COULDN'T RUN *AND* AIM THE FLASHLIGHT. IN ANY CASE, THERE was no time. When he hit the back door he was fifteen or twenty paces behind; his quarry was around the corner of the house, footsteps already sounding on the gravel. If the sleeper made it past the garage to the sand dunes he might get away again. And once more he, Serafin, would be blamed. This was no time to be messing with flashlights.

He took off at a dead run after the footsteps.

At the garage, the footsteps halted. He checked up for a moment, slowed to a jog, and was rewarded by hearing the click of a latch, the rattle of doors rolling back . . . The car. Instead of trying for the sand dunes, where at least he might have had a chance, the stupid bastard was going for the car.

He wouldn't make it, didn't have enough of a lead. By the time he'd reached the car, had the key in the ignition, Serafin would be up to him with flashlight and automatic, ready to stop him with a couple of slugs through the windshield.

But coming round the side of the garage, at the same time drawing and cocking the automatic, he sensed that this scenario was wrong. There was no sound coming from within. His impulse was to explore with the flashlight, but he rejected it at once. No point giving Igor an easy target. No point, either, standing in the doorway. He wasn't going to fall for any traps. Igor, presumably, was in the garage. Somehow or other he would have to come out. Serafin, therefore, had the advantage

and saw no need in taking pointless risks. He would do what instinct
and training prescribed for moments of uncertainty.

He would wait.

A rush of movement from the far side of the garage, ending in a crash
from the vicinity of the dumpster, informed him that instinct and
training had been right. But the satisfaction this gave him was brief. At
the exact moment he started for the dumpster, the garage blew apart.
The blast scattered parts of it hundreds of feet and was audible, some
instants later, in Annapolis.

But Serafin himself never heard it.

CHAPTER FIFTY-THREE

POLICE INVESTIGATIONS TOOK UP THE WEEKEND. BY MONDAY, WHEN Volkhov reported to the Resident, the facts had become at least partially clear.

"Someone planted a bomb in his car?"

"In a car he rented, actually," Volkhov said. "It was quite a large bomb. It destroyed the garage, blew out most of the windows of the house, and hurled a section of garage wall into Grigori Serafin, killing him instantly. And according to the newspapers at least, it more or less vaporized the rental car and its driver."

The Resident frowned. "According to the newspapers? You weren't able to investigate yourselves?"

"If the Colonel will take a moment to visualize the situation . . ." Volkhov restrained a sigh. "Six Soviet citizens, including four accredited members of the Embassy in Washington, were where they had absolutely no business to be, on private property in a remote region of Maryland, doing what they had absolutely no business to be doing, attempting to kidnap a U.S. citizen. When, in the midst of all this, something that seemed like a small atomic bomb exploded with a blast heard for twenty-five miles, my judgement was that, rather than wait and render ourselves liable for explanations that could only be embarrassing, our best course was to leave at once, taking our casualties with us." He paused, added silkily, "I'm sure the Ambassador, if our part in the incident were to come to his attention, would concur in this judgement."

260

She considered for a moment, weighing his reasoning. She seemed to find it compelling. Especially, he thought, the part about the Ambassador.

"Casualties? . . . You mean there was more than one?"

"Two of our men were injured, one quite badly, when Igor overturned a large glass-fronted cabinet on them as they pursued him up some stairs. I myself," he fingered a cut on his cheek, "suffered scratches."

"Very regrettable." Her tone, deliberately he felt, made ambiguous what it was she found so regrettable, his wounds or their superficial nature. "And you think the Americans planted the bomb?"

"It seems the only plausible conclusion. I know *we* didn't. One presumes he didn't do it himself." Volkhov shrugged. "There are also some positive indications. . . . A few days before the explosion, according to the newspaper reports, a man in a black limousine, who claimed to be a private detective but would produce no evidence to support that claim, made enquiries in the village about Igor. He wore a grey suit and a hat. Also sunglasses." Volkhov paused. "Since he wasn't one of ours, who was he?"

She thought about this.

"But why would the Americans have wanted to kill him?"

"He was a double agent, a role always somewhat precarious. We wanted to kill him because we thought he'd betrayed us." Volkhov shrugged. "Maybe the Americans had the same idea."

"Which, of course, is your usual speculation."

"Which is why I said 'maybe.' In the absence of facts, one is sometimes forced to speculate." He paused. "Let me tell you what isn't speculation. . . . I asked the Tass Agency to send someone to investigate the explosion. Since it happened quite close to our telecommunications center on the Eastern Shore, it seemed to me that some mild interest from the Soviet press would not be out of place. The reporter observed that among those asking questions was a young man, not with the police, whose presence the police quite clearly resented."

He handed the Resident a photograph. She examined it briefly.

"CIA?" she asked.

"His name is Sherwood," Volkhov nodded. "We believe he works in counterintelligence, as an errand boy for Hollister."

"In other words, you think the sleeper is dead. That the CIA, for reasons unknown, was responsible."

Volkhov considered. Actually, he wasn't sure what to think. Though the reasoning he'd expounded was clear and plausible, aspects of the situation continued to bother him. . . . If Igor had always been as vigilant as he'd been on the night of the explosion, how had the CIA put a bomb in his car undetected? And why had the explosion been so large? If you wanted to kill someone with a car bomb (and the CIA, presumably, had experience killing people with car bombs), why use so much plastic that your victim got smeared all over the landscape? The obvious answer—that you wished to conceal his identity—made no sense here, where so much circumstantial evidence (the wallet, the brief case, the rental car documentation, Igor's books and other belongings in the beach house) had been left behind. Unless, of course, what you wanted was not to conceal the victim's identity, but to mislead people about it. Volkhov cast his mind over the night's fiasco. *That* made more sense. It explained the otherwise inexplicable: why Igor, for instance, as was proved by the existence of a lookout, had expected, perhaps even invited, their pursuit. Perhaps he *had* invited them, as an audience to the staging of his death. Perhaps *he* had blown up the car. Put a body inside it, used so much plastic that physical identification of the body was all but impossible, and arranged the circumstantial evidence to suggest that the body was his own. And if so, Volkhov thought, the beauty of it was that nobody would have reason to question the circumstantial evidence (or to look too closely at what was left of the body). Each side would assume that the other was to blame.

But then what had happened to Igor? When the bomb had gone off, Serafin, hot on his heels, had died at once. How had Igor escaped? . . . Volkhov tried to recall the scene as it had revealed itself in those first stunned moments after the blast . . . The air thick with dust, opaque to the beams of their flashlights, heavy with the reek of burned oil and scorched rubber. The garage was almost demolished, just a corner and part of one wall still drunkenly standing. The landscape was like a garbage dump hit by a tornado, littered with wreckage: glass, masonry, pieces of twisted metal, and here and there strips of what looked like organic matter, whose exact nature one hadn't known and hadn't cared to investigate. But there was something missing from this picture, something in some way appropriate to the scene, and after a moment he remembered what it was . . . the dumpster. In his mind's eye he could see it now quite clearly—behind what was left of the garage, the dark, squat shape of the dumpster, which the blast had caught amidships and hurled on its side, and which, being steel, had survived the shock intact . . . like a bomb shelter.

"You seem to have left me, Major." The Resident's voice cut into these cogitations. "I asked, if you recall, a question."

A question? . . . There was very much a question, Volkhov thought, as to what had really happened. But what good would be done by raising it? Serafin was dead. So was Stoneman. And Daisy. Marigold had vanished, one presumed, for good. Assets carefully accrued had been wasted by this fool of a Resident. And the CIA's new computer system, even the issue of whether it existed, remained as much of a mystery as ever.

And Igor?

Igor had wanted out. Whatever else might be obscure, that much was not. Volkhov thought about his one-time agent: the mask without eyes he'd presented to the world, the ironic intelligence that lurked behind it. This woman, using words to Volkhov that were almost without meaning, had called him a traitor, demanded his punishment. But punishment, if it was anything, was a public matter, a ceremony of state. Pursued secretly, it achieved nothing. It was foolishness, another neurosis in a world that, in Volkhov's opinion, had far too many already. The sleeper, Igor, had declared his independence. Alive or dead, he was not going to spy for anyone. He had sought the oblivion of some kind of sleep. Why not leave him to sleep in peace?

What purpose would be served by one more death?

He looked at her steadily. "I think we must assume, Colonel, that the sleeper has passed beyond our reach."

CHAPTER FIFTY-FOUR

"I DON'T KNOW, BECKER," ARLEN LOOKED DUBIOUS. "I MEAN, ONE of these days I was planning to go back to school. I've got courses to finish, a dissertation to write."

It was eleven A.M., ten days after the explosion at the beach house. Four days ago, the Chief Medical Examiner for the State of Maryland, who in fact had seen no reason to do more than glance at the collection of human remains the police had assembled for his inspection, had announced himself officially satisfied that the human remains in question belonged to one Klaus Becker and pronounced him dead by murder at the hands of a person, or persons, unknown. The deceased and Arlen were in Zermatt, in one of the larger suites of the Hotel Mont Cervin, surrounded by the wreckage of breakfast (strawberries, cream, croissants, sweet butter, black cherry jam), in bed.

"You could transfer to another school." Becker paused. "You've got to stop calling me Becker. Becker is dead. Becker no longer exists. My name is Black."

"That's exactly my point," Arlen said,. "I don't even know you. I'm in bed with a perfect stranger, and that's bad enough. Why compound the mistake by committing marriage?" She paused. "Who would you ask to be witness, Vladek?"

Becker nodded. "He's willing."

"Some marriage." Arlen rolled her eyes. "The bridegroom under an assumed name, the witness under an assumed name, the bride, poor

264

sucker, *assuming* an assumed name." She paused. "What nationality of man would I be marrying?"

"I'm not sure," Becker said. "I'll have to look at my passport. Maybe Bolivian."

"Jesus . . ." She groaned. "Look, Becker. The only reason I can think of for having a husband is to take him home to mother, to convince her you haven't been left on the shelf. My mother's not around to convince. And if she were, I couldn't take you home to show her." She paused. "Persuade me. Give me three good reasons for marrying you."

"Reason Number One is, I love you," Becker said. "Reason Number Two is, I love you. Ditto for Reason Number Three."

Silence. He leaned over and kissed her.

"I do love you," he said. "And I may not have a real name, but after fifteen years of make-believe bullshit, I'm about to be a real person. I'm going to have a real life. I want it to be with you."

More silence. She took his hand, and held it for a moment. Then she smiled.

"That's quite a persuasive reason. And I shall certainly think about it," she said. "In the meantime you could bolster your case by offering some more tangible proof of your affections."

He took her in his arms.

"Why don't I do that now?" he said.

EPILOGUE

VOLKHOV STARED DOWN AT THE WORDS HE HAD SCRAWLED ON THE
paper in front of him. Then, with a brisk stroke of the pen, he put a line
through them. They were, he thought, lacking in inspiration. Though
now, for the first time in weeks, he had leisure to devote to his poem,
the Resident having relieved him of all but the most trivial of his duties,
the desire to write had left him. His imagination remained stubbornly
earthbound. He reread, for the umpteenth time, the line he had, for the
umpteenth time, redrafted and scratched out: "Swift-footed minions of
grim-visaged dawn . . ."

"Swift-footed"? . . . He wrinkled his face in disgust. "*Club*-footed"
would be more to the point.

Marigold was dead. The announcement had appeared two days ago in
The Washington Post. A brief column at the foot of page four. Richard
de Freitas, fifty-two, a senior officer with the CIA, had shot himself in a
hotel room in Vancouver, apparently to spare himself the rigors of
terminal cancer. So to this extent the Resident had been right: Marigold
had quit because he was dying. It was a fact that, had they known it at
the time, would have made them all do many things differently. Something stirred in Volkhov's memory. A line, imperfectly recalled, from a
poem in English (or some barbaric variant thereof), seemed somehow
relevant. It was something about "best laid plans . . ."

Marigold was dead. And Major Volkhov's career was effectively
over. His replacement was already on the way. He himself remained in

266

Washington only for reasons of timing: if the diplomatic cover of the new Third Secretary (Economic) was to be any more effective than the Emperor's new clothes, it was necessary that his arrival not coincide too closely with the departure of an assistant cultural attaché whose own diplomatic cover had long since been worn threadbare. Not that diplomatic cover was ever effective for much longer than three months, Volkhov thought. It only lasted *that* long because the first three months in a post were spent learning the ropes; one was far too new to *do* anything. Besides, he thought, every Soviet diplomat was viewed by the Americans as essentially a spy. And quite rightly, too. Sometimes he wondered why they bothered with cover.

In Moscow he would face the Fitness Board. And though, in view of his past service (he had, after all, recruited and for five years controlled the highest placed traitor in the CIA's recent history), he would probably manage to duck the charge of disloyalty, some of the mud that the bitch had flung at him would stick. He lacked "drive." She had called him in, made him stand on the carpet in front of her desk, had read him her report before sending it to Moscow. He lacked "ideological commitment." He relied too much on out-of-date methods and displayed "an arrogant disregard for contrary opinion and a misplaced confidence in his own hunches." He'd developed "bourgeois habits of thought and a taste for bourgeois comforts that impair his efficiency as a Soviet intelligence officer." Above all, he had failed. The CIA's new computer system was unpenetrated, his agent Marigold had jumped ship, the sleeper, Igor, under his control, had defected. That none of this was his fault, that none of the other charges were true, would, even if he succeeded in proving it, make little difference. That the charges had been made was enough. His next posting, if there was a next posting, would be Zaire.

He told himself to think about something else. He'd be here for weeks, perhaps months; he mustn't give in to depression. With an effort, he forced his attention to the line of poetry in front of him. The words still struck him as empty, lame. They strained too much for effect. "Grim-visaged," for instance, though intended to sound Homeric, succeeded only in sounding pretentious. Perhaps . . .

The buzzer sounded.

"Yes, Colonel."

"Kasparov tells me someone has sent us some kind of anonymous package. It's probably a bomb. Deal with it, would you, Major?"

"With pleasure, Colonel."

And this was it, he thought. Rock bottom. The ultimate insult. Mailboy.

"It's not a bomb," Kasparov said. "Not that kind of bomb, anyway. It's actually a movie." He paused. "I think you should take a look."

They watched it in the Embassy's AV room, with an interest that became, as the odd little drama unfolded, embarrassment, and finally, stupefaction.

"The man," Volkhov whispered in an awed voice to Kasparov. "It's Hollister, isn't it?"

Kasparov nodded. "I told you it was worth a look."

"What did you tell the Resident?"

"I told her there was this package. She said she'd get you to deal with it. . . . What do you want me to tell her?"

Volkhov considered. This little movie was manna from heaven. It could change the world. Or at least *his* world, which was all of the world that concerned him right now. What would Hollister do, he wondered, if confronted with this little gem?

Properly handled, almost anything.

He turned to Kasparov, regarded him quizzically. "Tell me, Lieutenant. Would you like your career to take a marked turn for the better?"

"I should like that very much, Major." Kasparov's tone was carefully neutral. "As I imagine you, yourself, would."

"Then tell her it was nothing," Volkhov said. "Tell her it was hate mail. Dog turds, or something like that. . . . Tell her Major Volkhov disposed of it."

Tell her Major Volkhov is back in business.